Submission to an Alpha

The Rayne Pack Series

Book 2

E. Bowser

CONTENTS

GLOSSARY

Hunter- a human that has been given unique gifts and a mission to keep the peace of all species on earth. A Hunter's primary mission is to hunt demons and send them back to Hell. Five Family Houses lead and train Hunters: Cross, Ryder, Okar, Diya, and Wellsley.

True Alpha- a wolf from the bloodline of the firstborn wolf shifter. They have abilities far past any wolf shifter. The True Alpha is over all wolves and is the leader of all Packs across the world. The True Alpha must protect and guide the wolf shifters according to the laws set by their Deity at the beginning. The True Alpha has Alpha beneath him/her to help accomplish the task and help him/her lead the wolf shifter nation so they may prosper.

Alpha/Luna- the leader. He/She is the main one in control and sets the laws of his/her Pack. They are not required to hunt with the Pack, but most typically do. They demand respect and are in the position to exile, banish, or even kill those who do not show it. This position can be challenged, and if the challenger wins the fight, the challenger, being the new Alpha, can do what he/she pleases with the previous leaders. This rarely happens because it would result in a considerable change within the Pack.

Beta- the second-in-command who enforces the law when the current Alpha is not present. If both Alphas die, the Beta(s) take the Alpha position and lead the Pack unless the Alpha has said otherwise. This position cannot be challenged without the Alpha's approval.

Sentinel- There are four sentinels, two mated pairs, in the Pack. The Alphas and Betas specially choose each pair. The Alphas and Betas train the sentinels to take their places if anything should happen to them. Since becoming one can start as early as one year, the sentinels rarely have authority over the Pack unless the Alpha or Beta have publicly given it to them. They are respected, though. Messing with a sentinel is messing with the Alphas and Betas themselves. This rank cannot be challenged whatsoever.

Assassin- the most fitting name for this rank because it is self-explanatory. They are also spies for the Pack. There can be a total of only three assassins in each Pack.

Lead Warrior/Enforcer- takes his/her orders directly from the Alpha and sometimes the Beta. They are the main leader, general, or captain of the warriors in the Pack. They are appointed by the Alpha and are the best of the best of warriors.

Pups/Cubs- I'm pretty sure that this is self-explanatory. They are the children of the Packs.

Gamma- Those holding this position are usually, if not always, the oldest and wisest of the Pack. They pass on their stories and phrases to the others within the Pack as their pearls of wisdom. They delight in telling stories to pups, though sometimes what they tell is just legend. Still, each story usually has some moral to it. They may have been the Alpha at one time, and usually, that is true. However, the current Alphas may put other Gamma's here if it seems right. Those who hold this position are much respected and loved by the rest of the Pack.

Delta- the messengers of the Pack, the go-between among the allies, and sometimes even the axis. They risk their own lives by doing so, but it is their duty to make sure that those who need to know are told. Those seeking this position must be agile, patient, and even-tempered while speaking with other packs.

Zeta- the war general of the Pack that takes direct orders from the Alpha in case of a war. The Alpha may be the one to declare war, but the Zeta leads the army and comes up with the war plans. They also train recruits for a position as an Enforcer and train younger wolves for this position to take their place in the future. Typically, there is only a single Zeta, but there can be as many as three, if the populace is high or the Alpha declares it.

Gammazeta- A Gammazeta is a cross between a Zeta and Gamma. They must be born of the two wolves who carry those titles and the True Alpha bloodline. These wolves are very rare, and if you have one in your Pack, you have a wolf full of knowledge of Pack lore and the strength of an Alpha.

Kannuck- Kannuck is the Deity and creator of wolf shifters. He is also the moon god and chooses if you will be an Alpha/Luna and grants each Alpha/Luna some of his powers.

Rogue- werewolves that have either been kicked out of their Pack or left of their own free will. Rogues are usually the wolves who have gone against Pack laws and the True Alpha.

Lone Wolf- acts independently or generally lives or spends time alone instead of with a Pack. Usually, wolves that have left their Pack are described as lone wolves who operate as individuals, acts independently, and prefer to do things on their own. They primarily prefer solitude or work alone. They are still part of the Pack and will return when their Alpha calls.

Cadejo/Black dog- will cause disease, destruction, confusion, chaos, and death. It may appear as a dog but do not mistake it for what it truly is, a possessed shifter. Once it has possessed a shifter, it can now walk like a human. It will no longer need to hide in the shadows of night to whisper poison from afar. It will now have a voice and a willing soul that will feed it the power of life.

Shade- described as a supernatural entity of the underworld and various shadowy creatures. They are also called demons, but are more once they find their Queen/King to serve. They could become good or bad, depending on whether they follow evil or what is right.

Necromancer- someone that uses the practice of magic or black magic involving communication with the dead– either by summoning their spirits as apparitions or visions or raising them bodily – for divination, imparting the means to foretell future events and discover hidden knowledge. They can bring someone back from the dead to use the dead as a weapon. A Necromancer's magic is sometimes referred to as "Death Magic."

Livyatan- a soul of whatever water species you can transform into in the realm of Hyquadra. Livyatan is what they are as a species, but can transform into sharks, whales, squids, snakes, dolphins, etc.

R'lyehan- s race of demon whose goal is to move from realm to realm and conquer its people.

Aeternum- the Hyquadra people word for forever, eternally, soulmate.

Rehema "Remi" Zhavia

Hyquadra (Water Realm)

I could feel my heart slamming in my chest as I ran for the nearest gate that would lead to another realm. It was another world where we had another Kingdom. I looked back with wide eyes as more and more black ooze dripped down the walls, covering everything I loved. I knew there was nothing I could do alone against the invaders in my world. The opening at the end of the hall showed the endless sightline of the waters that covered my world. I felt my anger grow even more as the once beautiful multi-jeweled-colored sky was slowly consumed by the darkness of betrayal.

"Princess Rehema, there is nowhere for you to run. Accept defeat and do your people a favor and submit!"

The rumbling of his voice only fueled my anger. I reached the edge, looked down at the swirling waters, and saw the gate closing. The deep blues, purples, and reds burned brightly from the magic used to open the last chance I had to help my people. I spun around at the edge because I did not fucking submit to anyone! These... these *Beings* believed they could come to our world and take it as theirs. They were insane. None of us would back down, but I knew we could not stop them alone.

"You know nothing of MY people! You may have won the battle, but this shit is far from over!" I could feel my *Livyatan* pushing to be released.

"This realm is ours now, just like the others before yours. I am offering you a chance to save what little people are left. I am doing this for you, Rehema. You have a chance to save your people from extinction, but you run like a scared child," Idhan chuckled.

I gritted my teeth as I heard the screams and roars of my people all around me. They would fight and die to protect this world and this Kingdom. My mind raced at his words because, what if he was right, and I could stop all of this if I just gave them what they wanted? I didn't know where my parents were or if they were still alive. I felt for their tether, but it was like a wall of darkness blocked me. I knew it was *HIS* doing.

The cries of my people filled my mind as they screamed the royal name while they tried to fight off the enemy.

"Zhavia! Zhavia!"

I knew I should do whatever it took to get it done if I could save them. If that meant handing my mind, body, and soul over to protect them, then it was my duty to do it. It would just be for now, because there was no way I would ever stop fighting to free all my people from this horror. I saw what they would do if they didn't kill you outright. The thick liquid blackness that wrapped around their bodies infected their target. The tentacles dug into their body and turned them into nothing more than puppets that now fought on their side.

I saw mothers attack their children and husbands attack their wives. I clenched my fists and took one step away from the edge as Idhan stepped into view. I held my eyes to the color of parts of the water in this world. His burning cyan eyes looked me up and down, anticipating what was to come. Idhan's lips curved into a smirk, pulling the intricate tattoo covering the right side of his face up. His outer appearance was beautiful, but I knew the ugliness inside him. Idhan stepped in my direction as the same mark covering his face began covering his obsidian green skin. It moved over his muscular frame as if it were its own living thing, but I didn't give a shit. My home was slowly being covered in this black ooze while the skies grew just as dark.

I had to do what I could to stop the death around me and find my family. Their plan had been in the works for far too long. Then to find out that some of our own turned against us and used what weakened us to help this attack happen had me reeling. I could feel the draining effect of the poison pushing my other half down, but that shit would not last for long. The problem is, will I regain my full power fast enough to make a difference, or would it be too late? I had to do something, and fast.

"If I am to do this, I want my parents freed," I gritted. Idhan walked toward me. His smirk grew into a smile that showed his sharp white teeth.

"No."

"No?!" My blood was pumping, and I clenched my fists, fighting the urge to shift.

"I think you should really watch who you are talking to right now, Princess. I hold the lives of your mother and father. One word and their heads will roll. So, calm the fuck down," he grunted. I leaned back, taking in his six-foot-four frame, and watched as the black tattoos along his obsidian green skin squirmed.

"Let. Them. Go," I said, shaking.

I was at the point where I was about to say fuck it when I heard the scream. I knew exactly who it was, and my heart stopped. Idhan held up a hand, and another R'lyehan came to a stop, pushing a child down in front of Idhan. The girl fell to the ground hard, and I darted toward her to pick her up. I wanted to throw her to the waters below because I knew she had a better chance in the deep. Idhan moved, scooping the girl up before I could get to her, pulling me back. I knew my teal eyes were burning because of the glow covering the terrified child's face.

"Rehema! Remi, help!"

"It's alright. Everything will be alright, Meera," I whispered.

My eyes were on Idhan and the bastard that brought Meera into this fucked up situation. Meera was scared out of her mind, making her begin to shift. The light brown of her skin turned a baby blue as her face stretched and sharp teeth emerged. Her nose stretched into something that looked like a hammer. I had to stop this, and right now.

"See, Rehema. I hold another in my hands, and all you need to do is submit it to me. I will let her live if you kneel."

I could feel my teeth bunching together as the strength of my Livyatan pushed itself forward.

"Remi!" Meera cried. I felt my power building up, but everyone I loved would die if I made one wrong move.

I gritted my teeth, trying to control my emotions. I could feel him probing at the barriers of my mind to look for the doorway to where the rest of my people were, but I was not about to let that shit happen. They would be safe, at least for now.

"It's okay, Meera," I soothed as I decided.

Idhan must have seen the decision in my eyes from his smile. I swallowed and clutched at my mesh dress just as he moved. Idhan tossed Meera aside like she was nothing and was in front of me with his claw-tipped fingers around my throat. He used his other hand to form a liquid black wall to the side of us. He leaned down, placed his nose in the crook of my neck, and breathed.

"Mmmm, you will do just fine, Rehema. The power you have inside of you will be delicious each time I taste it. Now look," Idhan growled. He forced my head to the side, causing his claws to draw blood. I felt a long, hot, wet, and smooth tongue lick the side of my neck as things in the portal became clear. My mother and father faced me, but I knew that they could not see me.

"Mother! Father! What the fuck is this shit?" I screamed. He tightened his grip before pulling back and looking at the portal.

"Your mother will die today, but I will spare your father as long as you kneel. I will even cease this war if you tell me how to get to the others."

"No," I whispered. I felt the tears burning the backs of my eyes. I could hear Meera whimpering somewhere close.

"Never say I didn't give you a choice," Idhan growled. He waved his hand, and I knew when my parents noticed me.

"Remi!"

"Remi, you know…"

"Take her head!" Idhan roared.

Everything inside of me broke as my mother's head rolled to the floor and her body hit the ground.

"No, no, no, no!" I screamed, and everything in me snapped. I broke his hold over me as I dropped low, kicking him in the chest. He grunted, but I was already moving toward him. I jumped and went over his body, using my fist to strike out, hitting him in the back of the head. I landed behind him and spun in place. My hand shifted into a hardened fin, and I struck out, taking the head of the one who'd captured Meera. I scooped her up just as I was hit in the back. I stumbled, but I didn't go down. Idhan laughed as he reached out for me, but I ducked under his grasp, holding Meera close to my chest. I made my way toward the window, hoping the gateway was still open. I felt a sharp stabbing pain in my side just as I was yanked back. I pushed Meera toward the window and screamed, "Run, Meera! Get away from this place." I saw Meera leap out of the window, and I prayed she missed the swirling opening of the gate. It should ignore her because it was keyed to me and anyone else unless they went with me. I felt Idhan's claws dig into my skin as he turned me to face him. I smiled at the blood covering his face from my nails.

"Fuck you!" I growled.

"You will do more than just that," he growled. "I still have your father!"

I heard the hissing sound a split second before he did, and it was all the time needed.

"Remi, go!" Oceayn hissed. I felt a cold barrier force its way between us, pushing me so hard I was a foot away from Idhan. I saw Oceayn for just a second as she placed herself between us.

"Oceayn! What the..."

"Go!" Oceayn screamed as she put out a hand, and that cold feeling pushed me so hard that I flew out of the window. I looked up at the jeweled sky once more before angling myself down. The waters swirled, but it wasn't as big as before. I hit the water and was swallowed by the turbulent waves as I was pulled down to depths I had never been to before. My mother was dead, and possibly my father as well. I knew the only way to save the rest of my people and realm would be to find help in the realm my brother called home.

Thomas Rayne

The Rayne Pack Land

I could feel something coming, but I wasn't sure what it could be or when. The feeling was almost foreboding, but I couldn't separate it from the bombardment of emotions consuming my every thought and feeling. I stared at the ceiling, trying to figure out how I would tell my family that I was leaving for a while. After getting six boys, my mother just had a baby girl, something she always wanted. None of us could deny that even this child was unique and an Alpha. We were now a family of Alphas that was not of a royal house. From what Dax told me, nothing like that had happened in over five hundred or more years. Even my father fell to his knees praying to our creator, *Kannuck*, when Hayley was born and he felt her power and purpose. That was a gift that hadn't been passed down to his children.

An Alpha knows his Pack members, but not in the way my father knew a wolf's one true purpose in life. I would rather sense someone's purpose than their fucking feelings. All I could hear was Dax's baritone voice in my head. *"You are still young. Your gift will grow, and you will learn to master it."* I needed space to be alone, so I didn't have to feel everything from everyone. I had to leave to accomplish what Dax said I should be able to do. I gritted my teeth as every member of the Pack's emotions struck me at every turn. It didn't matter if it was happiness, sadness, frustration, or elation, I felt all of it and it was so overwhelming I had to go. I had to get it under control if I would be of any use to my family or a Pack of my own someday. I shook my head, thinking about how stupid I was for trusting something evil. I only knew I would give just about anything to stop the madness, if only for a while.

I began doing things that I shouldn't. I knew messing with spells or rituals was definitely the wrong way, but nothing else worked. Nothing quieted the voices and emotions quite like the magic of a Necromancer. I knew it was dark magic, something forbidden. Dimitri taught us never to mess with anything that had to do with dark magic at a young age. But, when I found the book of spells and rituals in Dimitri's library, I thought I had found an answer to everything.

At ninety years of age and an Alpha, I knew I was powerful enough that if the Necromancer was on some bullshit I could handle it. *I should never have made that deal.* I hadn't expected the Necromancer to be female and for her to only want a night with me. She only asked for my essence and to have a night with an Alpha, not something that could harm me or anyone else. It wasn't like a blood oath or bond connecting me to her, or giving her access to my mind and body. A blood oath was something I would never do, no matter what it promised.

I closed my eyes and fought back the tide of emotions and the dark urges in my thoughts. I had to fight it and gain a hold of my own gifts. I knew that I would have to leave to accomplish any of this. I just hoped everyone would understand. I got up, trying to figure out where I could go so that no one would come looking for me. Somewhere I wouldn't need to hear or feel anyone else. I knew of one place I could go and get help. I reached for my cell and dialed a number I had never thought to use. I frequented the underground club *Sinful Secrets* most nights to release...release the pent-up emotions I was stuck with. Dominating someone where I could have them on the edge of pleasure and pain seemed to satisfy the cravings inside. At least for a few days. I let out a breath as I thought about my first meeting with the club owner, Shannara Cane, a Succubus that seemed to sense what I needed at the time. It felt like her laser blue eyes saw into my soul, and I wouldn't put it past her if she could. She may have been sex walking, but she was deadly. She took me to a room and whispered in my ear.

"I have seen you watching my sessions. I can feel your soul, Thomas, and it is in turmoil. I like your family, so let me help you. Let me teach you how to separate from your mind and only focus on the pleasure and pain you can give. Doing this will bring some peace, but it is like a drug. Can you feel this room, and how all you can feel are those two

emotions? You need to be careful how long you spend in a place like this. It will be hard to break away, but it will teach you to be able to control how you feel emotions, because you will learn to be in control."

I should've taken the offer at that time. I had no clue if she would ever offer something like that again without a price. There was always a price to be paid and no one fucked over Shannara. I heard the phone click and then a brief silence.

"Speak."

"Jasper, may I speak with your Queen?" I knew, dealing with Shannara's Shades, that you had to be respectful and be very careful not to disrespect her in their presence. I was powerful and an Alpha, but I was nowhere near his or Shannara's level or age. Not yet. They were ancient compared to my brothers or me.

"Oh, is this the little pup? I didn't expect you to call, but my Queen already knew the time would come. Has it come, Thomas?"

I swallowed hard, knowing what I would need to do, but I refused to let that place gain a hold of me, as she said. I would fight it and come out on the other side, able to control what, when, and how I felt all emotions.

"I wasn't expecting to call, either. Being in a part of *Hell* itself doesn't seem like the thing to do, but—"

"But you've decided to anyway," he grunted. "The offer to help you was on the fact that my Queen likes your family, Thomas. But don't get it twisted, young wolf, this will not be an easy ride and requires you to give a piece of your soul willingly."

"Wait, what now? Why the hell would I do something like that?"

"It's for your own good. You want someone with the power to pull your ass out of the Hell dimension, which is the price. You are lucky that it is only a piece of your soul.

OTHERS HAVE PAID MORE," HE CHUCKLED. "THIS IS THE COST OF WHAT YOU SEEK. WILL YOU PAY IT?"

I didn't know if I could trust a Succubus or this Shade, that was a form of demon. I closed my eyes, thinking about my choices and what would help me become who I was meant to be. I thought back to my first meeting with Shannara and examined the emotions and feelings I got from her at that time. Once I focused on it, I felt her concern, pity, and resolve. I could feel her respect for my entire family, but specifically my parents. She held high regard for them, and it felt like a close friendship. But when and how? I opened my eyes, coming to my decision.

"YES."

"SAY NO MORE," Jasper growled.

The line went silent, but I felt something shift in the air, making me look around. It was almost as if all the air was sucked away and it grew hot. I felt an enormous power that seemed to burn my skin as a black opening appeared across from me. I hit the end button as a tall, dark-skinned man stepped through, followed by a woman with long locs braided to the side. Shannara was beautiful, and she could make any male fall to their knees if she wanted. I fought against the pull of her power. A slow smile covered her face as she studied me.

"Good. You have the *Will* to keep standing. That will serve you well, Thomas."

Her voice was like honey and sin that wrapped around you.

"I wouldn't be the Alpha I am if I didn't have the *Will* to stand up to anyone," I said, raising my head. Jasper smirked while looking around.

"He's just like his brothers. Strong and meant for greater things," Shannara smiled.

"Well, let's go. Just you and nothing else," Jasper said. Shannara moved and stood in front of me with blazing blue eyes.

"It is time, Thomas. Will you pay the price to become who you are meant to be by controlling what has been gifted to you before you were a thought in your parents' minds?"

My eyes widened. All I could do was stare into those eyes as everything else fell away, and the only thing I could think of was what my answer would be.

"Yes."

Everything began to turn the shade of her eyes. My room began to disappear as everything got warmer and faded to black. I could hear Shannara whispering words I couldn't understand as the thoughts that plagued my mind faded as well. Those thoughts were clear in my mind for a split second before they faded away as well. I swear the voice sounded like the Necromancer but I was unsure at this point. Before I could focus more on it, everything ceased to exist, and it was the first time I felt nothing.

THOMAS

I wanted to know why I couldn't handle this new Pack alone. I didn't need anyone else with me unless it was one of my brothers. Why it had to be Remi, of all shifters, I didn't know. But after this meeting, I was going to speak to Quinn alone. If Hayley could handle these shifters, then there was no reason why I couldn't deal with them myself. My agitation was getting worse lately, and I had no clue why. But who would disagree with the True Alpha? It's like almost since I first met her, something about her would just set me off. I was the quietest out of all my brothers, but I couldn't stop the smart-ass remarks whenever she was around. Just like right now, we were waiting for her to start this meeting, which was bullshit.

"What's up with all that shaking and shit? Can't wait to see your sugar mama?" Malic smirked. I side-eyed him for a quick minute, debating if I should say something. I was ready to get this shit over with and find out what else I had to do for Dax since he would be on the "good Samaritan mission" with the Hunters. I wasn't too fond of it, nor were the rest of the brothers. But, whatever the True Alpha ordered, it was done without complaint.

"I'm good. What's up with you sneaking off during your perimeter walks?"

"What the fuck are you trying to say, little brother? I don't fuck around on my duties," Malic snapped. I turned around to look at him this time because, why was he taking me seriously? That wasn't like Malic, and as I let his emotions through my barrier, I could tell he was off. This shit was getting serious, and we needed to figure out what exactly was happening with him.

"Now I am serious. Since I will be in charge and Alpha, I think you should at least talk to me about what's up," I said, raising an eyebrow. Malic sucked his teeth and leaned back as he tapped on the oak table.

"Y'all bitches don't believe me, so what the hell is the point," Malic grunted.

"Is this about the owl you keep saying you're seeing?"

"I am seeing it, Thomas!"

I leaned away as Malic's outburst caught everyone's attention, including Dax. I looked at Max, Jarod, Alex, and then at Dax, and we all had the exact same expression on our faces. We really needed to have this sit-down with Malic sooner rather than later. Dax stood up, catching all of our attention as he crossed his arms over his massive chest.

"Malic, listen to us—"

The doors to the office opened, and Remi stepped through with a smile. I threw up my arms and shook my head.

"It would be you coming in late. When Dax leaves, I don't do tardiness," I grunted.

More prominent than most supernaturals, Remi's teal eyes shifted toward me. It didn't matter how much I didn't trust her, when she entered a room, my body went on alert. I tried to play it off like she was a threat, but nothing I said could remove the knowledge of how hard I got by just her scent. Remi's smooth, dark mahogany skin seemed to glow a faint blue at times, but felt as soft as silk whenever we came into contact. But what messed with my mind was that I saw the savage way she fought and the defiant look in her eyes. It was the exact look she was giving me now. Her smile fell, and it was replaced with a bland look before she turned to Dax.

"I find it funny how children act when they get a little responsibility in class," Remi said as she pushed the door open wider. That's when I realized the expressions on my brothers' faces and when the scent hit me.

"Thank you, Remi, for speaking to Hayley first. Come in here, baby wolf," Dax boomed.

I should have scented Hayley long before now, but I would need to examine that shit later. I stood up to give my little sister some love, but caught Remi's eyes first. Her scent was like the crashing of waves that engulfed you, taking you under while embracing you simultaneously. Her lips curved up into a smile, and I narrowed my eyes. She got that one for now.

I noticed that Malic pulled Hayley into a tight hug before slipping out. I felt that he didn't want to hear what we all had to say, and honestly, I didn't want to tell him. The pain he felt that night still woke me up at times. It was just that I knew that now was the time, and we couldn't keep this shit from him any longer. I looked at Max, who watched the door his twin closed firmly in his face. I could feel his indecision on staying or going after Malic. We both knew that shit would turn into a beat-down before any talking was accomplished if he did. It would be best if it were all of us.

"Max," I said, grabbing his shoulder. I sent waves of calm through our bond and took in what he felt. I felt him relax slightly before he looked at me.

"We need to tell him," Max said, releasing his breath.

"You are voicing my thoughts, brother," I said.

We both turned toward the large table as the phone rang. Dax looked at us and nodded. I knew he heard and felt exactly what we were thinking, but now it was time to handle business for the True Alpha. We had time to talk to Malic when this meeting was done. The situation with Malic would be something I spoke up about, and I would stand with Max this time, because Malic needed the truth.

We all moved to take our seats just as Dax hit the speaker button so we all could hear the orders directly from the mouth of our True Alpha. I pulled the seat back and sat down, trying not to notice that Remi had taken Malic's chair beside me.

"Quinn, we are all here and listening. Tell us what you need to be done," Dax stated. He sat down and looked at the empty chair his Luna usually occupied. Devana was in her own meeting with her family and the other Hunters.

"Good. Hayley, you will need to fill in Thomas about the Jamison Pack and what you accomplished with the shifters. Also, Thomas, before we even jump into all of that, I will need you to head down to Florida. After thinking on this for a few nights, I think it would be best for this Pack to stay on their lands. They need to work hard and build it back to what it once was, instead of moving to something that is finished," Quinn said.

I sat back in the chair, nodding as if he could see me. I didn't particularly like talking, but I knew it was necessary, which meant I could travel. He never mentioned Remi, so things may be lookin up for me on that note. I had to distance myself from her and maybe hit up Sinful Secrets before flying out. I could feel the rage and darkness in my body, threatening to boil over.

"Thomas!" Dax snapped. I looked up into violet eyes, telling me to open my damn mouth.

"Yeah, yeah, that sounds good, Alpha. I have no problems with all that," I said.

"Good, good. Remi, you will accompany Thomas as his Beta and have his back on everything. I do not need to tell you anything could happen, especially now. You all know the prophecies and what is coming at us. Be on your guard, but Hayley has told me you both should be good since she and Camron have taken out the most significant threat down there."

"That's my baby sister! That's how a Rayne gets down," Max smiled.

"Thank you, Max. I learned from the best," Hayley laughed.

"I know. I taught you well."

"Ahh, no. You meant Dimitri and Alex taught me well? You let me jump off a cliff when I was six!"

"That is neither here nor there," Max said, cutting his hand through the air.

"Quiet. We can talk about how you let your little sister damn near fall to her death when you were in charge after we finish here," Dax snapped.

He was still mad as hell at Max for that one, and I couldn't blame him for it. We all knew that Dax looked at Hayley as if she was his child. She damn near was since she was the only one who never knew our parents. She was just a few months old the night of the attack. A night I would not forget and the night that changed me forever. I felt a hand cover my thigh and realized that I was gripping the chair's leather arms so tight that it was coming apart at the seams.

I relaxed slightly at her touch, but she moved her hand away before I could think more about it. I glanced over at her but kept my mouth shut. I knew for a fact that she didn't like to be touched, but the reasons weren't clear. She was the one *Being* whose emotions I could not sense. It was as if a barrier was up that I couldn't break through when I tried. I didn't even think she knew why or how it was happening. Dax wanted to help her regain her memories. But honestly, how did we know if we could even trust her when we knew nothing about her or where she came from? Quinn is now including her in the Pack business as if she were truly one of us.

"You should pay attention instead of watching me."

I raised a brow at the mental thought sent my way. The ease of Remi's mind connecting with mine was surprising because of her barriers and my own. I leaned back in the chair, rubbing my hands on the smooth leather.

"Someone has to watch you." I side-eyed her and caught the pink tip of her tongue, licking her full lips. I wanted to taste them, but I knew that

would be a conflict of interest. She crossed her legs, and the motion made me turn to face her fully. She raised a perfect brow and narrowed her eyes.

"Well, you do a good job at it. Things will go smoothly if you pay as much attention to our mission as you do me."

Things would definitely go smoother if I tied her to the Saw-Horse bench. Remi flashed sharp teeth as she bit her lip, and I wondered if she could hear my private thoughts. She crossed her arms over her chest, but I saw her nipples harden before she could hide them from my sight. I smirked at her knowing I would need to get rid of this sexual frustration if I had to go anywhere with her alone.

"Oh, believe me, you won't need to worry about my mission and responsibility. There is no need for you even to go. But since I know you will not sit back on this, just make sure you follow YOUR Alpha's lead."

Remi sucked her teeth and screwed her face up but said nothing else. I focused on the conversation as Hayley explained what was up with these wolves.

"They are so set in their old ways, but I know they have potential. Yes, some are still holding out for the older ways to come back because that's all they know. They have done nothing worth bringing them in front of the Pack for justice," Hayley stated. She leaned back in her chair and placed a hand on her stomach. A flash of something crossed her face before she schooled her expression. Something was up, and I knew I would need to corner her before she left today.

"Well, if they can't get it together soon, they will be brought in front of me," Quinn stated. I sat forward, placing my forearms on the table.

"If I can't get a handle on them, Alpha, I will bring them to you myself for justice. I will be able to tell where their allegiance lies and go from that point," I said. I saw Dax nod his agreement with my statement.

"Some will try to challenge you regardless of how peaceful you come to them," Hayley sighed. She looked drained and exhausted, which shouldn't be the case for a pregnant shifter. Her case could be different because her Mate was a Vampire. I would have to read her baby to make sure things were good.

"As Alpha–"

"As Thomas's Beta, I will deal with any challenges thrown his way. That way, he can focus on the other problems within the Pack."

I couldn't help cutting my eyes at Remi, who didn't turn to look at me. Her teal eyes held satisfaction at cutting me off. I would deal with that slick mouth later. As the conversation continued, I shook my head as if this was normal. Remi did not belong here or a part of this meeting, let alone being my Beta. There was something more surrounding her that I did not like at all. The emotions, energy, and foreboding feelings that followed her told me that she would bring trouble. Those feelings were usually enough to say something to Dax about the potential problem, but I couldn't. I had to figure it out for myself before I went to anyone on a serious note. This was my responsibility because, since the first time she stepped foot on this land, I knew our world would change, and maybe not for the better. This trip would allow me to discover what Remi was really up to and why she was here.

"Exactly the right idea, Remi. I am not worried about the challenges but the fact that there are many pups there, and we know that our children are being targeted. We need to make sure this Pack is healed and has a strong Alpha. I do not want what happened there to happen again," Quinn gritted.

"As I said before, I have had no problem like what happened here. But, if a demon-possessed wolf had hit that Pack, they would not have survived. Either they would have been dead or become a part of that Pack. Now, they could put up a fight, but they still need our guidance," Hayley stated.

"Thomas and Remi, I want you to get with Hayley. Figure out where to start and who are the problems of the Pack. I think you both should leave as soon as tomorrow. I don't particularly like that they are there without an Alpha present. Dax, I would like to speak with just you for a moment," Quinn ordered. Dax reached out and picked the phone up, taking it off the speaker. He looked at us all, and we knew it was time for us to leave. Remi stood before I did and moved quickly toward the door, pulling it open and slipping out without a word.

We all filed out, and I knew Max would look for Malic. He gave me a look, and I shook my head. Max knew the best way to go about Malic would be for all of us to be there. If I had to leave by tomorrow, we would have to deal with Malic and this owl tonight. I turned around to find Hayley leaning against the wall, looking at her phone.

"Everything good with you, little sister?" Before speaking to her, I waited for everyone to move along and get to their duties. I knew Hayley as I knew myself. Something was wrong, and it had nothing to do with the Jamison Pack in Florida. Alex came out last and stopped before me, shaking his head.

"From what little I heard, we might have to deal with this Malic situation once you come back. I think you and Remi will be leaving tonight. I will probably follow you in a few days, but I think Malic will be in charge. Maybe that will keep him occupied while we handle this shit," Alex said.

"Damn, Quinn just said tomorrow. What happened that quick to change his mind?"

"Not sure. Dax didn't say anything and just watched us until I walked out. It sounded like Quinn got some info about some shit going on down there right now."

"Malic? I hope he's sure this is a good idea."

"I think so. This will be a good distraction for him until we can figure out what the hell is going on," Alex growled. "But, you need to focus on dealing with whatever this Pack has going on."

"I was hoping this would be a quick fix and bounce situation. Whatever the case, I will handle it," I grunted. Alex smiled and chuckled as he backed away.

"You mean you and Remi will handle the situation," he laughed before turning away. He walked by Hayley and kissed the top of her head before making his way around the corner. Everyone had jokes, but no one would laugh when I found her secrets. Something was not right with the older shifter, and I would figure it out. I turned to Hayley just as she looked up from her phone.

She looked up with brows raised and smiled. She looked exactly like our mother with our father's complexion. I ground my teeth together, thinking about how she never got the chance to know them like any of us did. I still didn't know all there was about our parents, which was my fault.

"Yes, Thomas. I'm just a little tired. It's nothing to worry about," she brushed my hands away. Hayley looked up at me with her hands on her hips.

"At least let me check it out. You just seem very, ahh."

"Thomas! Boy bye! My Mate is a Vampire for one, and he is a healer. He has found nothing wrong with me or the babies, so chill," she laughed. She ran her hands through long, thick, jet-black hair and breathed.

"Fine, but if you feel something is wrong, you must bring your ass home. Do you understand?" I stared down at her and looked into her glowing gray eyes. I saw the silver creeping in and the power that was still growing.

I could feel her Alpha wolf straining against the order, but being her older brother won out.

"If it makes you feel better. Now, enough about me and being tired. We need to plan so you know what's up when you get there," she said. I wrapped an arm around her shoulder and walked toward the stairs to go outside. If Alex was right, I should get all the information I could on these wolves before heading out. I dampened my emotions when I touched her because I knew her gift worked slightly differently from my own. Close enough, but still different.

"Well, I can feel a sense of something either coming or there already. Ever since you all had that battle here, other wolf shifters and different shifters started showing up on Pack lands every other day. You know how we do and that we have no problem with other shifters, but it's...some are things I have never seen before," she murmured.

We made it outside, and I saw Remi standing with Meesha in her arms. No matter what I thought about her, the mask she wore faded away whenever she was with that child. I even felt small doses of energy come from her, but it was chaotic. I looked down and caught Hayley watching me. I knew she was reading my emotions, and I quickly pulled away.

"There are many shifters out there, Hayley, but you did the right thing. We, as Rayne's, do not turn others away. If they follow Pack law, then we're all good, but why do I feel there is something else?"

"Because there is something else."

"Why didn't you say it in the meeting?"

"Because this will be your responsibility. If you want to share it with everyone, you can. But I can't without knowing if this shit is real. A woman came to ask for sanctuary, and I swear she held the same energy as Remi. I know that Remi is something ancient. We all know this, but when you see this woman, you might think not ancient but something not from this world," Hayley speculated. I looked up and watched as Remi spoke to

Meesha about God only knows and felt that the answers I was looking for might be in Florida.

"Did you touch her?"

"Yes, and all I could feel was death."

I spoke to Hayley a bit more, but she had nothing more except that the female didn't seem to cause all the death and didn't seem like the problem. It was just that the problem may have followed her here, which would place the Pack in danger. *Same energy as Remi gave off.* That meant we did need to get out of here soon because the longer an Alpha was away, the more vulnerable the Pack was to attack.

"I got this, little sis. Whatever it is, it can't be as bad as a demon-possessed wolf with delusions of being a True Alpha. I will handle it while you take it easy and stop stressing. It will all be good," I promised. I could see her visibly relax before she hugged me around my waist.

"Thanks. Just take this piece of advice from your sister and try, please, try not to cut anyone's heads off." We burst out laughing, but I could tell she was serious.

"I won't do it unless it's needed," I said. "Now go on home to Camron and let him know to make sure you are resting. I will fill Remi in on the information you just gave me," I stated as she pulled away.

"Yeah, make sure you do. Oh, and be on the lookout for Talika. She will be a great Alpha one day. We just need to make sure she has the chance."

"I got you."

"And, don't be an ass with Remi. She's good peoples. You just need to get to know her a little more," Hayley smiled.

"I will check this girl out for you, and yeah, as for Remi, it's always best to know your enemy," I grunted as Hayley chuckled.

I looked back to Remi just to stare into those teal eyes. It was almost like swimming in the deepest parts of the ocean just to be dragged down in the depths by something so large you couldn't tell where it ended. She raised her head as if she looked down on me, but I watched as her eyes traveled down and then back. I saw something swim in her gaze, which made my wolf perk up. I felt a pull at my emotions like I was supposed to know something or feel something other than the danger I sensed. I shook my head because I would figure it out. I made my way toward the two when I heard a squeal from Meesha. I watched as she wiggled out of Remi's arms to run toward me with her arms wide open.

Remi

I swallowed hard as I watched Meesha running toward Thomas. He could be so nonchalant and dismissive at times. Then at other times, the way he watched me made me feel like a hand was near my throat. Almost like he wanted me pinned down, but no way I would go down without a fight. A word whispered at the back of my mind, but I couldn't quite get it. It was important and also something from my past. It only happened when I was anywhere near Thomas or when he brushed up against me. I wanted to reach out and pull him toward me to taste and claim him.

Every time that thought crossed my mind, I was smacked back to reality when he would say something aggravating. I knew that was why I loved to watch him with Meesha because when I saw him with her, it always amazed me how he treated the little girl. He treated the other children as wonderful just as well, but everyone could see their bond when they were together. Meesha reminded me of someone I knew, but it disappeared anytime I tried to put deep thought into it. I closed my eyes, trying to remember what had happened to me. I squeezed my eyes tight, trying to look back into my earliest memory, but all I could see was the day I washed up out of the

Chesapeake Bay on the shores of Maryland. I had no clue where the hell I was or how I got here and just so happened to find this place.

"Remi! Why do you guys have to leave? I don't want you to leave," Meesha cried.

I opened my eyes and saw Thomas carrying Meesha upside down as they made their way back to where I was standing. He was watching me with deep brown eyes, but if you looked carefully and long enough, you could see the glowing ring around his pupils. At first look, it was the same violet as his brothers, but when you truly paid attention, you knew it was different. They were not violet but more an indigo shade. They always seemed to burn the brightest when he watched me. Thomas was always so quiet, so I could never figure out why he had so much to say when it came to me. I knew he didn't trust me and that he watched me like I would hurt anyone here. Luckily he was not the Alpha of this Pack, so I could care less what he thought. I just needed a little longer to figure out who the fuck I was and where I truly belonged.

"Oh baby, I don't want to leave, but we have to soon. We will come back as soon as we can," I smiled. I could feel the heat of Thomas's gaze as his eyes traced every inch of my skin. His power pressed along my senses, trying to find a way inside to read me like he did everyone else.

That was not happening.

He flipped Meesha back up into his arms while she giggled hysterically. His eyes narrowed on mine before he looked at Meesha, who rubbed his face with both hands.

"Thomas, just stay here. Who will make sure nuffing is under my bed?"

"Meesha, our Alpha needs me to follow orders. If you ask Remi really nice, maybe she will stay with you until I get back."

I folded my arms across my chest and chuckled while shaking my head. He really believed he was going to get me to stay here. He had another thing coming, because I was not about to do that. The first mention of Florida almost had me pleading not to go so I could get a few days away from him. When I actually researched this place, something deep inside my gut, my soul, screamed for me to be there. It felt like something was pulling me to go, like I would miss out on something if I didn't. I smiled at Meesha when she looked at me, but I kept my eyes on Thomas. When I first saw Thomas, I knew his sexy ass would be a problem. I couldn't fault him because I didn't know if I was running from something or to something. I could be putting these shifters in danger just by being here. I needed more information, and I knew for sure I was going to find it in Florida.

"Thomas knows I have to go with him to watch his back. Don't you want me to make sure Thomas is taken care of? You have Dimitri, Max, and Malic all right here with you. I will call every day," I smiled.

"I don't want you to go. If you and Thomas go, I wanna go too!"

I moved close to them and plucked Meesha from his arms. I could feel his Alpha energy trying to press down on me and his power trying to influence my emotions, but I squashed it. I raised a brow at him as Meesha squeezed her tiny arms around my neck. The indigo ring in his eyes sparked, and a low growl escaped his lips. I knew I was challenging the wolf inside him, but I didn't care. I had to go, and just because he had a problem with me wouldn't stop me from doing what was asked of me.

"This is a bad idea," Thomas growled.

I opened my mouth to tell him that playing with my emotions would get him and his wolf down. I was stopped by the front doors opening, and Dax and Devana walking out. I could tell by Dax's expression that shit just got real. The energy in the air changed, making Thomas spin around as they approached us.

"Thomas, the plan has changed. You and Remi will need to leave tonight. Quinn wants you with the Pack as soon as possible. He got a call, and something has happened," Dax announced.

I could feel the other Pack members coming closer to listen. I saw Max with Malic coming from around the side of the house with the Enforcers. Jamel and Ezra were laughing at first until they got closer and felt what we all were feeling. Something significant had happened in just a short amount of time, and it seemed we needed to get going. I looked past Dax to see if Journee was behind them, because I figured a portal would be the fastest way if we were leaving ASAP. I didn't see her, but I saw Maeze and Jarod coming out together. I could only make out some of what they were arguing about, but my eavesdropping was cut short.

"What happened? Can I get a rundown on why we need to leave early?" Thomas asked.

My gaze shifted to Meesha because she was so quiet. I saw the panic in her eyes as she began trembling as if something was scaring her, but nothing was happening. Devana stepped forward with hands on her hips, looking as if shit was about to go down, and nothing could be done about it.

"Meesha, what's wrong?" I whispered in her ear. Meesha's tiny arms got tighter as she laid her head on my shoulder.

"I have to go with you. I have to," she whispered.

Her voice was so low that I didn't think anyone else heard her, but I saw Thomas's eyes flicked toward us. His usually calm demeanor did a quick shift into protective mode. I watched as his smooth golden-brown skin ripped slightly as if he were about to shift. He took one step, which brought him closer to us. Thomas was so close that I could feel the heat of his skin and the pressure of his power surrounding the both of us.

"Let me listen to the Alphas baby, and then we will figure something out," I whispered in her ear and saw the slight nod from Thomas agreeing with me.

"Well, as both of you know, I have visions, and I had one a few minutes ago, which has made things shift all of our timelines. Not only has Quinn received a call from the Miami Pack, but my added vision did not help matters at all," Devana stated.

If she had a vision, that could only mean one of two things. Either a Hunter was in trouble, or we were about to have some demon problems. Thomas sucked in a breath, causing me to side-eye him, and that's when

I saw the other side of his nature. The one I saw when we were fighting to save the lives of the pups and cubs. I knew he was thinking about that demon-possessed rogue wolf and how he'd almost destroyed this Pack. That night, Thomas was entirely different, and I wasn't about to front like it didn't scare me a little. I didn't want to admit that I liked it to anyone, especially myself. Watching him bring someone to their knees just by his sheer dominance had me slick between my thighs.

"So, what is it? Tell me so I can go handle it since it has something to do with my Pack," Thomas asked.

I switched Meesha to the other side and let my other hand fall to my side. I reached out to touch Thomas because I could tell his wolf was peeking out. His Alpha energy was rising, but something else peeked through when that happened, and right now, we didn't need that. I looked back at Dax and Devana, and I could tell Dax saw it. He stepped forward but stopped to look around.

"We need to do this right! Pack meeting in ten minutes. I want everyone at the Pit in ten! Pups and cubs as well," Dax stated. He looked at the shifters standing around us and nodded before reaching for Devana's hand. They both turned and walked away, heading towards the Pit. I looked back to Thomas, who stared at his brother's back, but I could tell when they were speaking mind-to-mind.

"So? What did he say?" I asked. Thomas looked down at me and then at the hand that rested on his forearm.

"More than three children have gone missing in Florida. That was the information he got from Quinn when he asked us to leave, but he said everything else would be discussed in the Pit. Devana's vision saw something rise out of the water, claiming to be a *God*. She got a name out of it before it noticed her watching. *ZAMMIUNTAU* is what she told Dax, but what the name translated to is fucked up," he growled. I looked at Meesha, and she was staring at Thomas as if she knew the name.

"This is why I have to go. I have to protect you, Thomas. He will hurt all the children or come here to get me if I don't go. He told me he is the eater of souls and devours kids like me," Meesha cried.

I felt my skin go cold and stretch tight. I gritted my teeth together as I tried to hold back my shift. I knew my eyes glowed brightly when I looked back at Thomas. He was just as on edge as I was as he stared at a crying Meesha. His dark brown eyes flicked to me, and the indigo ring seemed to grow brighter.

"Devana said its name translates to *Devourer of Children, eater of souls.*"

I hugged Meesha tighter and fought the urge just to take her and run.

Neither Thomas nor I said a word when walking into the Pit. My mind was reeling from what Meesha had said. Thomas stayed close to us as we sat down in the front. We managed to get Meesha to sit down next to us, because nothing we did or said would make her sit with the other pups and cubs her age. I didn't want to take a child into danger. But was it true if she stayed, the demon would come for her here? I shook my head, trying to calm my racing thoughts, when I felt a large hand settle on my thigh. I sucked in a sharp breath as if I had forgotten how to breathe on land. The thought of water and Thomas's warm hand seemed to calm everything around me. I closed my eyes as flashes of memories crashed into my mind like a tidal wave. I was underwater and could see flashing lights as I was sucked deep into the ocean's depths. I wasn't shifted as I tried to swim for the surface. I couldn't breathe like I usually would have been able to as I fought the current of the water, trying to swallow me whole. I heard screaming around me or coming from inside me, from someone who thought to claim me.

"You can not run from me! You will belong to me. Submit, or everything you love, touch, and desire will DIE! I will find you REHE–,"

I felt another presence also surround me, but my eyes snapped open when I felt pressure on my legs. I looked down where I felt the pressure to see Thomas squeezing my thigh so tight his veins popped out. He noticed me looking down, and he moved his hand away quickly. Thomas crossed his arms over his chest with a frown covering his usually impassive face. I looked back to where Dax and Devana stood in the middle of the dirt Pit, deciding not to believe that Thomas saw the flashback I just had. All I could think of was, what if whatever was after me would come for the people here if I stayed any longer?

But I would not run. I refused to run.

Now with this Meesha situation, we had to figure this thing out. What did she have to do with any of this? Why would a demon want her in the first place?

"We called you all here because my Mate and I will leave earlier than we believed. Things are escalating with other shifter communities in my new area. Because of this, we will need the help of Hunters. Your Luna and I will be at the front of this, and while I am gone, Malic will be the Alpha in charge of this Pack."

"Alpha?" I looked over to see Leodora standing up, rubbing her arms. She was seated next to Malic, who looked stunned. He quickly wiped the look of shock off his face and stood up as well.

"Yes, Leodora?"

"Is this the work of another demon? Will we be attacked once again?" Leodora asked. Mummers and nods to her question filtered throughout the space, and Dax raised his hands to quiet them.

"I know we have been through our fair share of being attacked, but we need to remember all that is happening in this world. Once we, as supernatural people, stopped hiding, all that meant was that evil could as well. Will a demon attack us again? I can't tell you no, but I can tell you that you have the best of the best here if and when something goes down. Nowhere is safe anymore, and I expect all of us to do our part in keeping evil in check," Dax stated.

I could feel the weight of his Alpha power pressing down on all of us. I looked around and saw frightened faces but also determined ones. This Pack was strong, and being a Pack with more than one Alpha, we were better equipped for what was coming. I just prayed that whatever I was running from wouldn't find its way here. I would rather deal with whatever I felt that was coming to me on my terms. It was time to stop hiding and force myself to remember, or at the very least figure out why exactly I was here in the first place. Leodora sat down as the other Pack members began to nod at Dax's words. They understood that we all had greater responsibility in this world. We could see the evil far more clearly than humans could see it. Devana stepped forward, and I could feel the sudden change in the open space from the Pack. Immediately, the Pack began to calm down as she pushed her energy outward. I respected the Hunter, but it didn't affect me like everyone else. My gaze flicked to Thoams, and I could tell it didn't affect him, either. Humm—

"I know we have gone through our fair share of demon mess, but we must stand strong for others. There have been reports from other Packs across the states about missing children and missing adult Pack members. This isn't just happening to us, but to everyone, and not just wolves," Devana said, meeting the Pack members' eyes. "Quinn has tasked two of our Pack members to get started in Florida since two more children have gone missing since this morning. So, right now, at least six kids are missing. Dax and I have also been tasked to meet with other Alphas, leaders, and Hunters to figure out how to stop this and find the missing," Devana stated.

"Yes, and we will be leaving tonight. Our Pack is strong, and I know you will fight to protect our pups, cubs, and land. Again, Malic will be Alpha while we are away. Just know that we are safe, but if we have to fight, this Pack will do what is necessary to ensure we are victorious. You will listen to my brothers as if the orders came from your Luna or me. Thomas, the Jamison Pack, now belongs to you until the time you pass it along to its rightful Alpha. You and your Beta Remi will leave tonight and show this Pack what it is to function as a Pack should," Dax demanded.

"NO! The demon will come for me! They can't leave! Alpha, please don't make them go!" Meesha screamed, causing every eye to fall on her as she cried. Dax looked from Meesha to Thomas and me. Dax looked at everyone else as the mummers began to grow once more.

"Meesha, you will be safe here. Thomas and Remi won't be gone long. We will all protect—"

"No, Alpha! He wants to eat me. He's coming for me, and he won't stop! If he comes, he might eat all of us!" Meesha cried. It pissed me off to hear the fear in Meesha's voice. Thomas stood before I could stand to tell everyone to shut the hell up. The whispers and gasps from the Pack members were loud. I could hear some saying that maybe Meesha shouldn't be with the other children, or she could be another that was possessed. I felt my anger building as my teeth sharpened, signaling my shift's start.

"Quiet!" His ordinarily calm tone sounded like a clap of thunder this time.

The sudden silence was eerie because even the birds and insects didn't make a noise. I picked up Meesha and moved to leave to calm her down, but before I could, I felt Thoams's hand grab my arm. He pulled us closer to him and slightly behind his body.

"This Pack has always protected each other and others of different species. Since when have we turned our backs on those that need help? Especially our pups and cubs. Understandably, you all would be afraid for your children and family, but we are one, and we fight like one," Thomas growled.

I noticed that every Pack member leaned away from us because of the aggression Thomas was throwing off. I placed my palm on his back and felt the anger and tension inside his muscles. I could tell Dax and Devana were moving, and before I knew it, they stood in front of us, blocking the Pack from Thomas's rage. I understood precisely how he felt because I was already on my way there with him.

"My brother is correct. If you can not protect all who belong to this Pack, then there is no need for you to be here. I understand the concerns, but it is being handled. No one in this Pack suffers alone, and no one in this Pack turns their backs on the other. Do you understand?" Dax's voice boomed through the Pit, and the power behind his words had every shifter except a few bowing their heads. I heard some whining from the children and a few adult shifters until he reigned in his Alpha energy. "Good. Dismissed," Dax growled. Everyone scattered from the two pissed-off Alphas except the inner circle. Dax turned toward us as the last of the Pack exited the Pit.

"I can't leave her here," Thomas gritted. I could feel Meesha's tears on my neck, causing me to hold her closer. I looked at Thomas sharply because, what the hell was he thinking? We were going into an unsafe situation with little to no backup, but he wanted to bring a child.

"Thomas, Meesha will be safe here. Malic, Max, Maeze, Jarod, and the others will be here to protect Meesha. She can not go—"

"Dax! I made a promise to her parents. I know the risks, but I cannot handle what I need to handle if I am distracted. If she is with us, then I can focus," Thomas said as he gestured to me. Dax looked at me, but I bit down on my tongue. I did not think this would be as easy as Thomas made it out to be or a good idea. But, for some reason, I trusted him. I trusted his decision on this because I knew he would always do what was best for Meesha.

"Thomas is right. We've got this," I stated. I met Thomas's eyes, and I made sure he knew we would be discussing this shit later.

I made my way to the house Meesha, and the other orphan children lived in. I pushed open the door and caught two wolf shifter women speaking. "How do we protect the others if she is here? I don't want to end up being killed in my sleep by a possessed—"

"Who the hell said anything about her being possessed?" I snapped. I leaned down and put Meesha on her feet. "Baby, I want you to go to your room, and I will be there to help you in a second," I said softly. Meesha stared up at me with large brown eyes as she wiped the tears from her face.

"Yes, Remi," she mumbled before running up the stairs. I stood up to my full height and took in the two wolves who stood with crossed arms.

"I don't think you understand how much we have on our plates," Lena sniffed. "You don't know what it is like caring for all of these children." I looked into the kitchen on the right, but it was empty. I went further inside the living area, where the two wolves stood side-by-side.

"Lena, I don't know you that well, but what I do know is if I go upstairs and that little girl is crying, I will show you what possessed really looks like," I said under my breath. I felt my teeth sharpen and my skin thicken as I got closer to them. I looked at Jessica, who looked away from the glowing teal of my eyes. "Do you feel as she does, Jessica? You have grown up here, so you should know better! We take care of Pack!"

"Remi, I...I know that. It's just, with everything that has happened, we need to know if she will endanger the other children," Jessica explained.

"Why are you even explaining anything? They aren't true Pack! They are not even wolves! This is a fucking—"

Jessica screamed as I darted forward and had Lena by the throat. I pressed her against the wall and squeezed. Her light brown skin began to turn red while I began to shift. My face began to elongate as my mouth stretched wider. I didn't think anyone would miss one wolf.

"Remi!"

Thomas's voice cut through the haze of hate and anger at this shifter. How many children knew her true feelings toward them? How was she treating them when no one was around?

"Drop her, Remi. I will handle it. Get Meesha so we can go." The command in Thomas's voice hit something deep inside of me. I wanted to rebel, slap the shit out of him and bite these hoes' heads off, but the sniff behind me had me dropping the wolf shifter to the ground. I turned away and saw Meesha at the top of the stairs. I moved quickly to her as I let my shift go so I could get her away from these people. I looked back as Lena pulled herself to her feet. I could feel the hatred coming off her in waves, making me smile.

"Next time, Alpha Thomas will not be around to protect you, and I will swallow you whole."

THOMAS

I listened for the door to shut before I said a word. I could feel the hate, fear, and malice coming from where the other children were sitting when we were in the Pit. My eyes narrowed on Lena and Jessica. I watched as Lena, new to this Pack, tried to stand tall with her head held high. Lena was one of the women who came to this Pack after the fight with the demon-possessed wolf. She hadn't come out and said where she came from or what Pack she belonged to, but she was not the only one with that problem. I thought maybe her hate and fear that spilled into the Pit came from her being kidnapped by that fake Alpha. I had sensed no hatred or disdain for different species until today. *What have we missed?*

"That bitch does not belong here! She nearly killed me," Lena shouted. I could see Jessica putting distance between her and the other shifter. Jessica had grown up in this house, and I knew damn well that she loved each of the children that found themselves here.

"Lena, if Remi wanted you dead, you would be a bloody spot on the floor," I said, stepping closer. I saw the slight trimmer, but she raised her head and crossed her arms.

"This is not how Pack law works. We do not go around killing each other. It is not her place—"

"You know who I am and what I can do, correct?"

"Ye— yes," she gritted. She brushed her pinkish-colored hair, that closely matched the coral shade of her eyes, over her shoulders.

"Then you know I can feel every emotion you have. You also know that I am also an Alpha in this Pack, and when my brother is not around, responsibilities fall to whatever Alpha is around at the time. What I know is that you started those whispers about Meesha earlier, and you continued when you left the Pit. What I know is that you do not need to be around any pup, cub, or any child. Get your shit and get out of this house. I will let Alpha Malic figure out what should be done with you since I am too fucking close to the situation," I growled. I didn't realize how close I was to her until I finished speaking. Lena was backed up to the wall as I towered over her 5'8" slim frame. I saw her jaw clench tight as she gave me a sharp nod.

"Yes, Alpha," she mumbled. I stared at her as she kept her back pressed firmly against the wall while she slid to the side. Something about her wasn't right, but I had no time to figure it out. I would need to let Malic know about this so he could handle it. Maybe that would keep his mind off this Owl situation.

"Th— Thomas I, I don't have a problem with the children. I love all—"

"Jessica, I know," I said, holding up a hand. "I will speak to Dimitri about finding a replacement for Lena. You need to learn how to speak up if you are going to be taking care of the young."

"I know, I know it's just...just something about her just...I'm not sure. I will not fail to speak up again," Jessica sighed. I turned to the stairs as tiny feet flew down the stairs, followed by slower, steadier ones.

"Thomas! Are we leaving now?" Meesha smiled. I could see the fear in her eyes as she clutched a stuffed wolf to her chest.

"Yes. We need to go see Malic first, then meet Tree and Journee behind the house," I said. I reached how the small duffle bag and took it from Remi. Her teal eyes still glowed, but she forced a smile for Meesha.

"Meesha, is Lena and Jessica nice to you and the other kids?" I asked.

"Jessica is always nice even when she is mad. Lena used to be nice, but...I don't know. I'll find Malic!" Meesha screamed and ran out of the door.

"Did you see her face, and how scared was she looking? I'm going to..."

"Remi!" I growled. I needed her to focus before she got mad and went after Lena. I don't know if I would stop her. She cut her eyes at me before looking away.

"I thought we were flying?"

"Things change. Let's go, or will you try to bite my head off?"

We left Jessica and followed Meesha out of the door. Remi was walking fast as Meesha screamed for Malic to come outside.

"So? Will we be transported directly onto their Pack lands or what?" Remi asked. Usually, I couldn't feel anything coming off of her except quick flashes of emotions. But it seemed I was picking up on something ever since that little connection happened in the Pit. I could feel the rage and terror rolling off of her in waves. It felt as if we stood in the middle of a storm while in the sea. I reached out for her just as Malic came out of the door.

"You need to chill. Whatever is happening, you need to rein that all in because everyone will pick up on it, and I will not have Meesha afraid again," I gritted. I felt like I was drowning in her scent as she stared at me. I could see the otherness in those teal eyes and the secrets I just couldn't figure out.

"What has she done or said to Meesha when no one was around? Hell, what has she said to any of the children?"

"It will be taken care of, Remi," I said calmly. I pushed calming waves to her and throughout the Pack. Remi snatched her arm out of my hand and took a step back.

"Don't try to control my emotions! Let me feel how the hell I feel, Thomas. I don't have anything else that is mine, so let me have this at least," she snapped. "I don't need calm. I need...I need—"

I raised a brow and took two steps forward. It was fast, and I knew I had caught Remi off-guard. I was so close that it caused Remi to lean back slightly so she could look up. I may not trust her entirely, but the attraction and need that filled me when I was around her was becoming harder to control. I needed that control, and I would have it.

"What? What do you need, Remi?"

"At this moment, I need you to back the fuck up or—"

"You want to fight? Is that what you need to work through your emotions? You need someone who can go toe-to-toe with you and make you submit. Is that what you need?"

"What I do know is I will never submit to anyone, but I will take you up on that fight if you think you can handle it."

"If I can knock you on your ass in one minute, then you agree to let me help you with all this aggression," I growled. My wolf was close to the surface, I could feel it clawing to get out. I took a deep breath, and all I could smell, taste, and feel was Remi.

"And if I win, tell me where you go when your anger takes control. I want to know what you do to relieve all that anger you are hiding," she whispered.

I narrowed my eyes as a growl escaped my lips because no one should have known when I left this property except Dax. What was this woman? What would she think about the places I went when the violence in my soul got too overwhelming? Could she handle the knowledge of what I needed to do to release it?

"Fine," I grunted.

I took a step back, and she readied herself for a fight. I knew we weren't alone, but it felt like we were in our own private bubble. The angrier she got, the more her mind began to open for me. Remi came at me blindingly fast, but I could track her movement. I stepped to the side, but she moved with me and raised her leg. I leaned back, just missing the kick by inches. Before she could get her foot back on the ground, I moved. I was on her before that right foot could touch the dirt. I pushed up on her and encircled her neck with my hand. They were already transformed into claws, and I felt them pierce her skin. It was shallow, but it was enough to make her pause. I stepped into her and lifted her so we could see eye-to-eye. I moved before she could break my hold and stepped behind a large tree that blocked us from prying eyes for a moment. I pushed her up against the tree's trunk and pressed my body along hers as her scent became overwhelming.

"If you think you will win this, puppy, you have lost your mind," she gritted. I wanted to know what else was going on inside of her mind. It wasn't just the situation with Lena, but it was more. Hayley's words filtered through my thoughts, and maybe she was right, and Remi wasn't the danger, but she was running from the evil I sensed.

"I'll let you pet me anytime you want, but that is only for good girls that follow my instructions," I smirked. She bucked, and I pressed her harder against the tree, using my body to hold her in place. I could feel my teeth sharpen as I leaned forward and nipped her soft neck.

"I don't play with children!"

I laughed, "What do you think you're doing right now?"

Remi growled as she took that moment to push me hard, making me back up. I backed away just as she brought up a knee, but I blocked it, grabbed her around the waist, and spun her around to face me. I wrapped her up again, pulling her close so I could feel her body against mine. I wanted to do things to her just to kill that look in her teal eyes. She liked this rough play, but at the same time, it pissed her off. I could see the pleasure, pain, and irritation in her gaze. It set something off inside me, screaming to tie her body down until she cried out. I knew that playing any game with

Remi, either she would need a safe word or I would. I couldn't help the growl that left my lips at the way she stared at me.

"You like a little pain, don't you, Remi?"

I squeezed tighter, leaned forward, and licked her lips. Remi's eyes filled with something other than rage, making my wolf press harder against my skin. I knew my eyes were glowing as well, and the indigo had become more prominent. I used my other hand to push her teal-tipped hair so I could whisper in her ear.

"If you are going to be my Beta, then you need to learn to use control. But don't worry, because I get to teach you how."

I let go without warning, and she fell to her feet, but her eyes never left mine. Her lips were parted, and her tongue snaked out to lick them. Her eyes glowed brighter, and the teal turned into the different colors of the sea. I reached out and placed my hand on her chest, close to her neck, and her breathing picked up. I couldn't help the smile that crept across my face as I pushed her backward.

"I won."

I left Remi sitting there and turned to inform Malic about the bullshit going down at the children's house. My skin itched to feel her again just to see how she would respond to my touch when I gave her those lessons. I shook my head and focused on my brother, who eyed me with a raised brow.

"What, are y'all role-playing or something? What was that? Teacher versus student? Sugar mama fighting with her little pup? If you start walking around with a collar on, I will never let that shit go, because whatever shit you do at Sinful Secrets just might be done to you messing with that old lady."

"I don't have time for all your shit, Mal," I sighed. Remi was messing with my mind because the thought of her taking control had me ready to turn around. What the fuck?

I looked down at Meesha, who held Malic's hand as she stared past me. She looked almost as if she wasn't truly here.

"Your thoughts were wide open when you were playing tag over there. I will take care of it," Malic said. "But Journee is ready for y'all. Make sure you bring your little ass back in one piece, and don't cut anyone's heads off, please. That came from Dax, because I don't care if they deserve it," Malic shrugged. I felt the crashing sea against my senses and knew Remi was behind me. I carefully locked down my thoughts and put up my shields. I looked down again, but Meesha still stared into the distance.

"Meesha! Meesha," I shouted. She blinked quickly and then looked up at me.

"Is it time to go?" she giggled. I frowned and felt Remi's earlier emotions fade as concern took over.

"Yes. Yes, it is. Let's go, little bear," I said, picking Meesha up.

I made my way to the powerful energy that began to pick up. Remi was at my side, but she said nothing. I reached out emotionally and mentally. There it was, just like it never left. I could still feel the danger, but this time, it was closer than ever. I couldn't tell if it was because of Remi or coming from the portal.

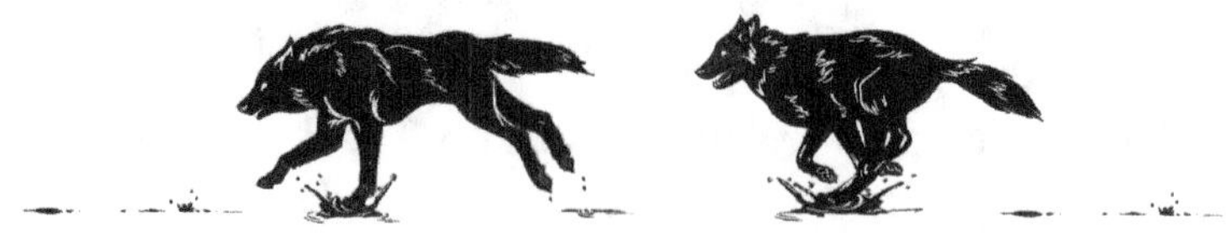

We all stepped through, and I could feel the temperature difference immediately. We all thought it would be best if we didn't come out onto the Pack lands. I wanted to drive the rest of the way to get a feel of the land and what could be giving me such a sense of pure evil.

"Thomas, it feels icky here," Meesha said. I looked down, and her face was scrunched up as she stared at the sun. Remi stepped forward, shading her eyes as everything around us came into focus. We were in a small town, and it almost looked like we had stepped back into the 1950s.

"You're right, MeMe, it does feel icky, but we aren't staying here," Remi smiled. She took Meesha's hand, grabbed her bag, and started walking. We stood at a sign that said, "Welcome to Sunset Port" and the feeling I got was definitely off. The further we got into the town, the more I realized that this place was full of shifters. Wolf shifters, to be exact, and I knew damn well that this little city was not on the list. I saw Remi's back stiffen, and I knew she noticed all the stares we were getting from people on the street and the closed houses.

"Thomas? What is this place? Are you sure this isn't where we are supposed to be because these are—"

"I know. Let's just get to the rental spot, then I will ask who the Alpha is here," I said.

I let my wall down and felt for the emotions and thoughts of this town. I stopped walking and closed my eyes for a moment, then frowned. I could feel warmth at my side and knew it was Meesha pressing into me. Remi stood close, and I could tell she was watching my back. I snapped my eyes open and turned toward a large white building where four male shifters stood.

"The hell Thomas? Why is everyone suddenly coming outside?" Remi mumbled.

"We are about to find out. There is a problem here, and the True Alpha must be told about this place. I will do the talking," I said. As I started walking, I felt that teal gaze on my back and knew she wouldn't keep that mouth closed. That was another thing that would need to be taught. It felt like she did things just to get a reaction out of me.

"What do you need here? I hope you are just passing through our humble town," a large man said, standing. He was tall, maybe an inch or two over me, and he probably was used to thinking his larger frame was enough. He wasn't the Alpha or the Beta of these wolves, but no one contested his words. His gaze traveled to Remi and then down to Meesha, who stared at him with a snarl curling her lips. "We don't do those kinds around here or any..." He let his tawny eyes move from Meesha to Remi, then landed on me. He looked me over with disgust. "We also don't associate with your kind, either."

I looked around with a raised brow because these assholes had to be trippin' on something. If Malic or Max were here, we probably would have already been throwing hands. But they weren't. None of my brothers were with me, and I had to trust that if some shit went down, Remi would have my back for real. I sucked in a breath as I came to the understanding that I couldn't feel nor hear a damn thing coming from these people. Their emotions and minds were closed off from me more than how Remi's was, and that didn't sit right with me.

"If you think I give a shit about who you don't associate with, you're mistaken. We are not staying, but I want to speak with your Alpha before leaving. Your blatant disrespect for the True Alpha's laws is fucking disgusting."

I used my words deliberately to get a reaction from these wolves. I didn't miss the widening of Remi's eyes like she couldn't believe I wasn't trying to calm the masses. Maybe I would have tried it if I wasn't so sure that it wouldn't work and if I had made it to Sinful Secrets for a session. The rage was building inside of me, looking for release.

"Who the hell do you think you are speaking—" The man was cut off when he took one step in my direction. I cocked my head to the side, appreciating Remi's curves and strength as she held the shifter in the air by the front of his shirt.

"My Alpha asked to speak with your Alpha, *DOG*." Remi spat the dog at him as her teeth begin to sharpen into points. "If you do anything other than get who is running this piece of shit town, you will see exactly what my kind is, but you won't live to tell about it." Remi's words were low, but I knew everyone gathered here heard the threat loud and clear. I felt myself harden just from her display of strength and dominance, but what made my length throb was when she said *my Alpha*. I wanted her to repeat those words while I made her beg to cum for me.

I pushed those thoughts from my mind when Remi dropped the idiot to the ground and stepped back.

"Garvin! Just get Edwin before things get out of hand. We just want to get these people moving along." I looked past Garvin as a short round woman stepped out of the white building that Garvin was sitting in front of a moment ago. The woman came closer as she wiped her hands with a linen towel before holding her hand out to shake. "My name is Darlena. Don't mind my brother. He has no manners, and we don't get many strangers here in the Port," Darlena grimaced. While Remi was fighting not to beat that fool, I pulled out my phone, texted Quinn, and requested a ride through the rideshare app. I was not about to drive anything these people had in this town. It was just wrong here like a heavy presence was settled into the ground this town was built on. I pocketed my phone and shook her offered hand. I could tell she didn't want to touch me, but touching her gave me a glimpse inside of her mind. The worst part was the emotions of intense hatred toward us all.

"Thank you, Darlena, but you know what? I think I am good at meeting with your Alpha this time," I said as my phone beeped. I saw a black SUV creeping along the street and knew it was for us.

"Tell Edwin I will see him soon about this little spot he got going on here. Since I am now the Alpha of Florida, some changes will definitely need to be made, and I expect it to be done."

I turned my back on Darlena and whoever the hell else was standing around. I leaned down and picked up Meesha. I made sure we had all of our stuff and waved down the truck. Remi was on my heels, but she was still facing the shifters of Port. I guess she did have my back after all. I knew it to be true, but I fought with myself about Remi. I wanted her in ways I shouldn't, which confused me because I did not have that Mate pull. I wanted to know what was hiding in her mind, but more importantly, I just wanted her. It all started, or I only acknowledged it, that night when we fought side-by-side. Something was connecting us, and I would find out what it was.

After jumping into the SUV, I pulled my phone back out as Remi jumped inside and slammed the door.

"Drive," she growled. The driver, Kaleem, just raised his brows and hit the gas. He looked at Remi a few times in the rearview mirror before she flashed her sharp teeth at him.

"Chill," I laughed. Kaleem caught the drift and kept his eyes forward.

"I didn't like that place, Thomas, they were icky people, and it was so smelly," Meesha whispered. She leaned against Remi and breathed in her scent, trying to wipe the smell of death from her nose.

"I know, baby. Once we are in Miami and settled, we will get cleaned up and breathe in the scent of the beach. How about that?" I asked. I messaged for Quinn to hit me up ASAP because whatever the hell was happening in that place was all the way fucked up.

"What the fuck was that, Thomas?"

"Something that should not exist. I contacted Quinn, but now I think maybe we need to hit up Hayley or Camron."

"Camron?"

"Her Mate. He was with her while she was down here, but she said nothing about a separate group. I think I might try Cam first because I don't want to bother Hayley anymore about this mess unless I need to," I stated.

"Okay, but you didn't answer me. What happened back there? Why does it—" Her gaze went to the front and then back to me as she lowered her voice. She leaned closer as her teal eyes glowed brighter than usual. The scent of her filled my nose, and she smelled decadent. "Why does it smell like there was a damn massacre that just happened? I would have thought there had been one right before we got there if it hadn't been so clean. It almost feels—" Remi trailed off, but before I could ask her anything, my phone went off. I looked down, saw Cam's name pop up, and slid the bar over to answer it.

"Yo, what's good?" Camron asked. "Who are you talking to? Let me see who are you cheating on the puppy with?" Another voice came over the line, and I rolled my eyes. We didn't have time for this bullshit right now. "Damon! Why won't you just shut the hell up sometimes? Give—"

"Hello? Who is this calling my little cousin?"

"Damon, put Cam back on the phone, please. I don't—"

"Thomas! Boy, don't try to act like you're all grown and shit. Show your honorary uncle some respect. Whatever you need to know, just ask Uncle Damon 'cause we know Cam doesn't know shit," Damon laughed. I could hear Cam growl in the background, knowing his fangs were out.

"I need more info on Florida about this place called Sunset Port. Also, about some wolves acting out of character. I don't think you would know about it unless you were down here again dropping bodies," I grunted.

"Oh, that's what we're doing? I might know more than your young ass thinks, like the fact that the Port has always been a Silent Hill type of place. If people live there again, they are beyond messed up in the head, so be careful. Also, I've killed no one in Florida lately, but I can tell you that those wolves down there are on some weird ass shit. They don't follow in the teachings of *Kunnuck,*" he said thoughtfully. "What Camron probably doesn't know, and neither would Hayley, is that the Jamison Pack was not always called the Jamison Pack, if you know what I mean," Damon grunted.

"That is interesting. Hayley didn't know any of this?"

"Give me the damn phone, Damon! Thomas, my bad," Cam said.

"Yeah, did you and Hayley know about that?"

"Naw, definitely not. But honestly, we were doing more healing of the minds and helping the economy down there. Once that was up and moving, and Hayley began to teach Pack Laws, we found out she was expecting. Then things began happening with the children, and different species of shifters started to show up. By the time we got everyone on one page and what she expected out of them, I had to put my foot down. She needs the rest, physically and mentally. You know her gift of feeling emotions through touch is strong, but it got worse the further along she got. Anyway, what set off your alarm?"

"Do you know an Alpha named Edwin?"

"Edwin? Are you sure?"

"Yeah. We arrived at a place called Sunset Port, and things are not right there," I concluded.

"If it's who I am thinking about, that crazy purest is not an Alpha. He was the Jamison's Packs Sentinel. Him and his crazy ass wife, Darlena. She's actually more insane than Edwin and probably the one in charge. Edwin is...he more-or-less likes the praise, not the work. They actually left early on once I was introduced to the Pack. They chose to become loners and stated they would leave Florida. A few others also left the Pack here and there over time as

WELL," Cam stated. I leaned back into the leather seat and flicked my gaze to Remi, who studied my face intently. I knew she could hear our convo, and I sensed her wanting to go back to Port.

"AIGHT, THANKS, CAM. I DIDN'T REALLY WANT TO HIT UP HAYLEY, SO THANK YOU FOR CALLING BACK. I WILL GET IT ALL SORTED OUT ONCE QUINN CALLS BACK. I WANT TO LET HIM KNOW WHAT'S UP."

"HE HAS BEEN IN MEETINGS ALL DAY, BUT I WILL TELL HIM TO CALL YOU AS SOON AS HE GETS A BREAK, UNLESS YOU NEED HIM SOONER."

"NAW, NAW, THAT'S GOOD WITH ME."

"CALL ME IF YOU NEED TO ASK ANYTHING ELSE."

Cam disconnected the call, but I understood the undertone of that request. He didn't want Hayley bothered as well, which only told me that she was not handling carrying this baby well at all. I looked back at Remi, but her eyes were closed this time. I studied her teal-tipped lashes that were barely noticeable. My eyes traced over her features, stopping at her plump lips, causing me to picture them wrapped around my length while I fisted her hair. I shook my head, trying to get rid it of these images. I wanted to wake her and tell her to finish what she was saying just to hear her husky tone, but I would wait. Once we made it to Miami, I would be asking her to finish that statement because it seemed like she just may have remembered something.

Meesha pulled my arm up, snuggled into my stomach, and fell back asleep. I took in a deep breath as calm flowed through my body. I had no clue why Meesha always affected me, but I'd stopped trying to figure it out after a while. I leaned back, closed my eyes, and opened myself up to the land as we traveled to the Jamison Pack. I could immediately tell that this land was saddened and its people damaged. I also felt evil other than Sunset Port or Silent Hill, as Damon called it. That's when I felt my consciousness pulled away and toward a violet light that shimmered with red, blue, yellow, green, and white. I blinked once, and the most enormous wolf I ever saw stood in front of me. I immediately got to one knee and bowed my head. I knew exactly who or what he was, and it was an honor that I did not deserve for him to appear to me.

"Thomas, the sixth son of the seven children born, all Alphas, you may stand," Kannuck said.

I stood up but still kept my head down to show respect to the first of our kind. The creator of wolf shifters around this earth all belonged to this being standing before me. The power that pressed along my senses and body had me feeling like I would break apart. But this was the first time since my birth that I felt absolutely nothing but peace.

"Is there something I need to know about where I am going?"

"There are many things you need to know, but I can tell you that you must look beyond the normal. Your enemies are not of this world, and you will need a great power beside you to win this fight."

"My brother will join me here as well. Will we need another to fight what is coming?"

"Your brother is of this world. You are all of me, so, therefore, you will need someone, not of this world, but you must fight as one. No boundaries, no mistrust, but most importantly, the love of another, the love of your Mate."

I opened my mouth to ask another question, but I felt my consciousness being pushed away as I slammed back into my body. My eyes snapped open just as the vehicle slowed to a stop. I looked out the window and knew we were in the right place. I watched the wolves as they came out of houses and buildings to see who had come onto their land. The sense of knowing these people needed guidance and the feeling that something else had happened had my wolf peeking out.

"Ahh, this is your destination, correct?" Kaleem stuttered. I felt Remi shift, and I looked at her as she gripped the handle.

"Yes, and thank you for the safe ride," Remi stated before turning to look at me. "I will get out first."

I raised a brow, but before I could tell her ass all that was unnecessary, she was out of the door. Remi's features were imprinted into my mind, but the more I examined it, the more things that didn't add up. I knew water shifters, and none had invisible diamond-dusted skin. Few people noticed the indigo in my eyes until I was on the verge of shifting, and none knew what they could do. I could see what's hidden beneath or what others are hiding. So, what was Remi? I would find out. But first, I needed to find out what was taking the children and had to figure out how to show these shifters the proper Pack way of life.

Remi

I hopped out of the truck as soon as I could before Thomas began asking questions. It wasn't that I didn't want to tell him or anyone else about it, but more the fact that I still didn't know what it meant. I could feel fear, anger, disgust, and sadness while drowning, which shouldn't be possible. I had to figure it out before something huge went down, and I couldn't do a damn thing because I could not entirely shift. How could I shift if I didn't know exactly who I was or where I belonged? I shook my head and made my way around the truck. I looked through the front window of the SUV and smiled. The driver's eyes were huge, and I didn't understand why until I heard a low growl coming from behind me. I thought it was odd that I didn't sense it before I heard it, but we already knew that things were weird around here.

"This is not a tourist spot, so I think it is best that you all get from around here."

I turned toward the growl and saw another older shifter walking along with the tan-colored wolf. The wolf was large, but I had seen and been around larger living with the Rayne Pack. I raised my head to meet the slate gray eyes. His dark brown skin seemed to stretch like he was working to stay in his human form. The older wolf looked like he was in his early forties, but that only meant he was much older. He was probably more like one hundred and forty. He had a wiry frame, but that didn't mean anything when it came to wolves. I sniffed lightly and could smell the ocean and taste the salt on my tongue. "Did you hear me? Get back in the truck or—" I raised my brow and crossed my arms over my chest.

"And who are you to think you can tell me what I should do? You are not an Alpha nor the Alpha of this Pack," I said. I heard the door open, and I knew when Thomas stepped out. His calming presence seems to have simmered down most watching, but not all. And the two in front of me differently were not feeling the effects of his gift.

Interesting.

"You aren't Pack," the man spat.

"Oh, but see, David, that is where you are wrong. She is Pack. Remi is a part of my Pack, which means she belongs to this Pack since I am the new Alpha," Thomas stated. He moved quickly toward the man and the wolf. He stood toe-to-toe with David and didn't even glance at the wolf.

"Our so-called Alpha ran off with her Vampire. She was nothing but a blood whore who did not deserve the title of Alpha. Not the way—"

I felt the moment when Thomas went from the cool, calm, and collected Alpha to the one chopping heads in the basement for information the night of the battle. I saw when he moved, but I don't think anyone else saw it until they saw David slam into the side of the building. The crash was loud, and I heard bones snap as David slammed into the brick. The wolf was next because he used that time to attack Thomas, but he was caught by the throat and thrown hard to the pavement. Thomas leaned over as his hand covered the muzzle of the wolf.

"Stay down. You should be happy my sister asked me not to cut anyone's head off. Show disrespect again, wolf, and your life is forfeit," he growled.

I could feel the two small hands pressed firmly against my legs, so I knew Meesha was safe. The wolf whined as Thomas stood back up and looked around at the shocked faces. Thomas took two precise steps back until he was beside me with Mesha between us. I opened my mouth to say anything to start all this over when David peeled himself from the ground and roared. If his wolf was close before, now it was damn near ripping its way out of his body.

"We are no longer accepting Alphas, not of this Pack. My nephew was the Alpha of this land, the state of Florida. If anything, this Pack now belongs to me! I challenge you!" David growled as spit flew from his lips, and his once slate-gray eyes changed to a color I could swear I had seen before. They glittered as the light hit them, making a sudden urge to tear them out of his face strong. Thomas moved as a mask of indifference slid over his features. I didn't want his first meeting with these wolves to be him killing their Pack member, but they did need to see we would not stand for disrespect. They had to see us as a power structure and to be able to trust him to know when to handle things.

"No need for our Alpha to fight a wolf so beneath him when he has better things that he should be doing, such as speaking with is his new Pack members," I said. That got everyone's attention, including Thomas, whose hands had already turned into claws. He paused at my words but didn't turn to look back at me.

"You are no wolf! You have no say in this! Who are you?" David growled.

"I am the one who accepts your bullshit challenge on behalf of my Alpha as his Beta. Now, since this is an Alpha Challenge, you can't back out," I said, walking forward. Meesha moved along with me, and when I reached Thomas, he said nothing.

"A non-wolf as a Beta! This has to be a joke! Whatever the case, when I am finished with whatever she is, then it will be me and you," David pointed.

In that small amount of time, I noticed how Thomas was able to gain back his composure. His hands returned to normal, and the murderous energy he was pushing out seemed to roll back inside of him. He turned slightly, leaned down, and picked up Meesha.

"So be it," he grunted.

That dismissal from Thomas had David up in his feelings, making him sloppy. I darted after Thomas but moved before he could even take two steps. My foot blurred and landed in his stomach. I heard a grunt, but I knew it wouldn't be that easy. He wasn't weak, but he was not an Alpha, either. He also was not me. The massive hand grabbed my foot and twisted, making me flip to the side, but he gave me time to use my other foot to smack him across the face with it. I landed in a crouch and felt a smile on my lips as blood seeped from the corners of David's mouth. I was finding it weird that everyone else who felt Thomas's energy had coward back, except these two. I found it even more strange at the absolute rage David was exhibiting at this moment. He came at me again but shifted into a large gray and tan wolf this time. His leap was larger, and his large body landed on top of mine. We rolled, but I fought to keep his massive jaws away from me as I managed to get wrestle the wolf to the ground. I pulled my hand back and punched him hard repeatedly with my fist. My skin was more rigid than others. At times, it felt more like steel, hard and cold. I felt claws dig into my legs, which I did take into account. At this moment, it seemed only my hands were tougher. I rolled off the wolf and cracked my neck as he got to his feet.

"Remi, we do not have all day. Finish this so we can get to what is essential," Thomas shouted. But in my mind was an entirely different reason. *"You don't need to fight to handle your aggression. Don't forget that I will be the one to teach you how to handle that."*

His presence and the feeling it evoked in me had me slipping. David leaped at me, knocking me to the ground. At least it snapped me out of the thoughts. His smooth, deep voice had me spiraling into thinking. I slammed to the ground, but I managed to get my arm between us, and my hand gripped the wolf by the throat. I was done with this, and Thomas would answer for that. I needed this little fight. I had to clear my mind to at least try to get the thought back that flashed through my mind in the truck. All I knew is it provoked so much anger that I needed to release it.

"Sorry, David, but you should have been taken out with your nephew," I gritted.

I felt my teeth begin to bunch together and lengthen. My mouth began to stretch, and my head grew more extensive along with the width of my mouth. Things became sharper. The call of the ocean became unbearable. I opened my mouth and tore the head off the wolf who dared challenge me. I shook my head as I threw the body away from me. No, that wasn't right. He did not challenge me...he...it wasn't me who... my head snapped to the siren call of the water. I turned in that direction as something called me closer to it.

"Remi! Remi, where are you going? You said you wouldn't leave," a small voice shouted. Was that Meer...Mee... wait, who is that? I...turned back and felt something grip my heart so tightly that I lost all the desire and fight inside of me. I blinked a few times and looked down at Meesha, who smiled at me. "You weren't going to leave, right?"

My mouth worked, but nothing came out. "Right?" Meesha asked again. Her large brown eyes began to moisten the longer I took to answer. A large towel entered my vision, along with a bottle of water.

"Meesha, let Remi clean up the mess she made," Thomas said as he took her hand in his.

"But, but she was gonna leave, Thomas."

"She was not going to leave you, baby. Even if she tried, I would have hunted her down and dragged her back to us...to you," Thomas said as he walked away. Thomas looked over his shoulder, and his eyes roamed over me before turning away.

"You should be happy I won if all that aggression makes you bite off heads. But that will have to wait because we have bigger problems than a wolf with authority issues."

I wanted to ask what had happened in that short amount of time, but I stayed quiet. I was more interested in how he was now so easily speaking into my mind. I noticed it before we left because it came with such ease. But this time, it felt...it felt almost natural.

"Let's get this done."

I followed a young female wolf shifter to a huge white house that definitely held the scents of Hayley and her Mate. Out of the Rayne family, Hayley was the most open and willing to help me when I didn't understand things.

"Thank you. What is your name?" I asked the wolf. She turned to me after opening the large doors and a slight smile. She had soft brown eyes, and her brown hair was done up in boxer braids with side controls that matched the gold undertones of her skin.

"I'm Harmoni, and I just want you to know that I don't think anyone will miss David," she laughed. I smiled as she pushed open the door, and we stepped inside. The home was huge but also cozy, and I could tell Hayley created this space to remind her of home.

"Well, I guess that is a good thing, but regardless if anyone did have a problem, they need to go back and reread the Pack law. Once a challenge has been accepted, it is to the death. Or forfeit and be exiled from the Pack," I stated. I entered the living room and dropped my bag next to a large tan sectional with giant cream pillows. There were no pictures or anything to say that Hayley and Camron stayed here except their scents and residual energy.

"I don't think that is right, but maybe we...we have more to learn," Harmoni said. I turned to face her once again and cocked my head to the side.

"What does your law say Harmoni?"

Harmoni looked out the bay windows at the growing crowd of shifters that walked with Thomas. She turned back to me and looked down.

"There is no forfeit. Either you win, or you die. When the shifter that challenged the Alpha dies, then that shifter's family becomes the property of the Alpha," she whispered.

"Property?" I snapped. Harmoni's brown eyes snapped to mine, then looked away.

"Yes. We became—"

"Slaves," I said low. I could tell Harmoni was becoming increasingly uncomfortable talking about this, but I knew this would be something that would have to be addressed.

"Did Hayley know about any of this?"

"Hayley? You know our Alpha?"

"Yes, and she is not your Alpha any longer. Her brother is now. Thomas Rayne is your new Alpha. So, did she know about this situation?" I asked once more. Harmoni's eyes were now huge as her hand covered her mouth. "What? What is–"

"Hayley was killed in a challenge?" Harmoni's soft voice seemed too firm at the question. She stood a little taller, and I heard a low growl. I raised an eyebrow at the young shifter, but I respected that she was hurt by the thought of Hayley being challenged. It seems like she did do some good work around here.

"No. The True Alpha ordered Hayley to go on bed rest, and he pointed to Thomas as the new Alpha until someone could present themselves as worthy of being this Packs Alpha. Now, I will ask once more. I am not asking as a visitor but as the Beta of this land. Did she know?"

Harmoni was shaking her head no before my question ended.

"No, she didn't know all the details of it, but she knew we weren't there because we wanted to be. I think she would have figured it out once our lands were restored and word began to spread through the state. She had a large job, but we all knew she would be digging once she got things on track. Then the children started to go missing, and everything just...it just got out of hand," she finished. Harmoni crossed her arms over her chest and looked out of the window. "If that's all, I would like to get a little rest before it's time for my shift."

"Shift?"

"Yes, we all go out and look for the children that don't mysteriously show back up in town. This afternoon two pups came walking back into town. We have four missing at the moment, so I am glad you both arrived when you did," Harmoni said as she moved to the doors.

I waved her out so she could rest, but what I really wanted to do was change and get back to Thomas. Four are still missing, but two just happen to come back. How was that possible, and why? We needed to speak to these children soon, but I had to get myself under control. I had a rage and anger building inside of me that seemed to now be at a tipping point. I felt like an alarm was going off inside, screaming at me to hurry. I was letting my emotions and aggression control me. I had to get it under control. I knew for a fact I had better restraint than this, but that seemed to have gone missing, just like my memory. I could feel my age press against my bones and along my skin, but I couldn't access my true power. I knew that I had only just scraped its surface, which was not going to do. I felt like being here in this place was the right and wrong move, but I would stick it out either way. I would figure out why I was drawn to this place while helping Thomas figure out what was happening with this Pack.

I rushed up the grand staircase with barely a sound. The home had wood floors throughout, with thick rugs in each living space. I looked in the four rooms and then pushed open the two doors I guessed led to the master. The room was massive, with a bed stretched along an entire wall. I took in a breath but didn't smell a faint scent. It was almost like this place, and everything inside of it, was brand new and hadn't been lived in. But that had to be wrong. I blinked and stepped out of the room, leaving that one for the Alpha. I went to the other side, chose the bedroom with its own bathroom, and closed the door. I dropped my belongings and rushed to get cleaned up so we could start figuring out this place and its people.

I rushed through a shower and pulled on a white baby tee shirt and high-waisted ripped jeans. I made my way down the stairs, hearing raised voices as I got closer to the doors. I picked up speed because I wanted to know what was happening and fill Thomas in on the information I got from Harmoni. I opened the massive doors and stepped out to a crowd of shifters screaming at another group that clearly were not wolves. I shook my head as I jogged down the steps to see what the hell was happening, so I could squash the matter and move on to why we came here. Not only were young shifters still missing, but I still had a grip around my heart on what Meesha told us before we left Maryland.

"Hey!" I clapped and could tell I startled the shifters that stood huddled together.

I took a deep breath and caught the scent of the ocean and sun-kissed waters. I knew this small group of shifters were water shifters, but I didn't know what species. My brows furrowed as a short, thin female shifter with long gray hair and a deep claw wound across her face approached. She turned to face me and sneered at me with a digested look.

"This does not concern you. As far as I and others are concerned, you and them should not be here," she spat. The older wolf raised her head to look me in the eye, and I noticed the moment she saw her own death in my gaze. I fought down my aggravation and impatience, helping the glowing teal of my eyes to simmer down. I wanted to find Meesha and Thomas and get this sideshow started, so I could figure out why the hell I could hear voices coming from the sea.

"What is your name?" I demanded. The scowl on the woman's face deepened, but I turned my back to her and faced the shifters with the blue-tinged skin.

"Do not dare to turn your back on me. I don't know who you think you are or that boy in there thinks he is, but you all will be run out of here just like we did that bitch Hayley."

My body hardened, and I fought the urge to bite her head off but knew we couldn't just go around killing everyone to accomplish what was needed in this place. The crowd quieted down as the words of the old wolf landed like blows to my back. I smiled softly at the people staring at me as if they had seen me before. I knew before I could even begin to figure that out, I had to deal with this wolf that gave me the same vibe as the people in Sunset Port. I spun around, cocked my head to the side, and narrowed my gaze on honey brown eyes with a ring of green.

"I will ask again. What. Is. Your. Name."

"Grecia Jamison! The one who should be Alpha to my late son's Pack! You know, the son that murdering half-breed killed!"

I wanted to slap this wolf, but there was no time. I needed to be inside with Thomas making sure his back was covered. But I was not about to let this wolf speak about Hayley this way. How many others here thought the same way?

"Grecia, humm, that is good to know. We will talk about you and whoever else believes in the words you just spoke after the missing children are found. I will be sure to let YOUR Alpha know exactly what you think. As for right now, if you speak, look at, or think about your Pack members standing there, you will be the next head that rolls today," I grinned. I knew my teeth were pointed, and my mouth may have stretched a little wider, but I didn't care. I looked at the other shifters, and my face softened. "Let's go. Your Alpha is speaking," I stated as I turned my back on the glare of a shifter whose time was now limited.

Idhan

I thought back to the moment I opened my eyes to pure darkness. That wasn't unusual for a *Being* like me. My family is why darkness has been spread throughout twenty realms, so this was nothing I'm not used to. What concerned me was how much time had passed, and that vast empty space surrounded me. I was no longer on Hyquadra, and Rehema was nowhere to be found. My thoughts rushed back to the present, and I was set on tearing this world apart until I found her and that beast that helped her escape. My eyes snapped open as I floated, trying to feel what had escaped me so long ago, but one hundred years was nothing but a blink in time for me.

Princess.

After making it through the gate on the heels of Rehema, I knew that time was different. When and where she came out vastly differed from when and where I landed. My mind and body were ripped apart from trying to enter a realm that had been sealed.

How did she manage to get through?

I would have died if I did not merge with another, and unfortunately or fortunately for me, something was waiting. ***Zammiuntau.*** Now where

I was one, I am now two, at least for the time being. The thought of possession was not at the top of my list, nor was it something a R'lyehan would ever condone. This was just a means to an end, and once I received what I came here to get, I would tear this demon from my body and shove it back into the depths where it belonged.

"Such harsh thoughts, Idhan. Have I not upheld the end of my bargain? I even managed to bring her closer to you."

"Don't pretend you have done any of this for me," I growled. I could not feel her in the ocean, so what Zammiuntau had said was still the truth. She hadn't been in these waters on in this realm since I had awoken. She was in hiding somewhere on these cast lands.

"What I know is that if I help you find her, she will bring me to the vessel I need to walk this earth. You, you will do what is needed until that time occurs. Now, it is time for the sacrifices. The children are gathered in Sunset, which will bring you closer to the prize you seek," *Zammiuntau* hissed.

Whenever it speaks, I see flaming crimson eyes and a large black canine creeping at the edges of my thoughts. I would need to relay the information about these *Beings* to the Goddess once I returned to Hyquadra.

"You have been saying this for far too long! I'm sick of this, demon. I will make good on my threat and deal with its consequences. I am not one of your followers, and I am more than you will ever comprehend. Do not forget that you need me just as much as you believe I need you," I gritted.

I felt the sand beneath my feet as I returned to the beach that would take me to the town of Sunset Port. As soon as I stepped on the smooth sand, I felt a snap in my mind, and my thoughts traveled to a mind I knew belonged to me. I felt a slow smile creep across my face as the thoughts of who escaped me filled my head. It was chaotic, angry, determined, and...fascinated. My eyes narrowed as I tried to hone in on where she was until I felt it. I felt her concern, affection, and desire burning in her body, mind, and soul. Glowing indigo eyes consumed her thoughts, causing a growl to escape my lips.

"You can not run from me! You will belong to me. Submit, or everything you love, touch, and desire will DIE! I will find you REHE–"

Something pushed me firmly from her thoughts just as her location was almost revealed to me.

"Damn it! Where is she?" I roared. The hissing laughter filled our mind space as boiling crimson eyes seemed to blink slowly.

"She is coming. Everything that I have done will bring us what we both want."

"We could have gone and taken what we wanted if you knew where she was this entire time!"

"You are an amusing one, Idhan. You forget that you know nothing of this realm and what magic it holds. Try if you like, but you would not make it to her as long as the family of all Alphas protects her. One of my kind has already learned that, and I will not make that mistake. Now, it is time for the sacrifice. These sacrifices will ensure we both achieve our goals."

I pulled away into a space in my thoughts where even it could not hear. I knew this entity could not be trusted, just as I could not be trusted. My power had grown since these sacrifices, and I would store this extra power away until the right time. I breathed in the night's air and played back Rehema's thoughts. I could tell the poison was still coursing through her blood and was affecting her in a way I hadn't calculated. She seemed confused about who she was or what had happened. I noticed something else that she may not have even realized that she knew. The last outpost made by Hyquadra was here in this realm. We conquered the other outposts and the realms they resided in, but this one was hidden from us. Once I had Rehema, I would take this outpost and claim this world for the R'lyehan. I tried contacting the Goddess, but I received nothing in response. I had to get back soon.

I stepped into Sunset Port with a smile that seemed to chill these people to their core. I stopped in front of a large white building surrounded by small and large canines that called themselves wolf shifters. Some were in their wolf forms, while others stayed in their human forms. They all held the looks of fanatics as they eagerly awaited the words from that they believed to be their creator. *Pitiful.* The woman who called herself Darlena stepped forward with her head lowered, and I let my mind fall back to let Zammiuntau take my place as I watched. I would wait for the moment in the sacrifice where I could take the power I needed as it glutted itself and make this world submit.

"Here are the sacrifices you require," Darlena bowed to what she believed to be her *God.* She moved aside to reveal four children with horror written across their faces. They were horrified except for the boy that shielded the other three. He had guts. This boy would be the one out of this group that Zammiuntau would let go. I think he would be the one that would bring the vessel Zammiuntau was looking for closer than ever before.

"Good. Good," *Zammiuntau* hissed in pleasure as his eyes settled on the child with the fire in his eyes.

Oceayn

I couldn't believe any of this was happening. I came here to find Remi and to get her back home so we could save our people, but so much time had passed I didn't think it mattered anymore. I had been searching for Rehema for years since coming through the gate into this realm. I couldn't find any trace of her anywhere in these waters. Without Remi, I had no way to get back to our realm and no way to know what had happened to everyone.

What would I even be going back to at this point?

I quickly realized how different things were here. I knew nothing about this land or these waters, but I quickly noticed that I didn't look like the other species that walked this realm. This realm didn't smell of the magic of home, and the waters were not full of the kind of creatures like me. If it weren't for the fact that I was cursed with this form, I might have been able to walk among these people to gain a better understanding earlier on before now. Nakeema and her husband betrayed us all to the R'lyehan for power. The poison used on my people did not work on me, and I didn't know how it happened. How did I survive the attack? I still didn't have an answer to that question when I managed to escape just in time to help Remi. I paid a heavy price for that act alone but what sealed my fate was the fascination Nakeema's husband had with me.

Gideon.

I shook my head to clear my thoughts and focused on the now. I may have managed to escape, but I'd failed to find Rehema. I could not fail at trying to find these children of a Pack that took me in as me. Not everyone accepted me, but the few who did, my staying with them was worth it. At least worth me staying long enough so I could come up with a plan to find Remi.

"Oceayn, is that, Sam?" Talika murmured.

I turned my head toward the road and away from the water that reminded me of everything I had lost. I had found new people, people who differed from me. I came to care for many of them, especially after meeting Hayley and Lika. They had no hesitation about accepting me into their home and Pack. That gave me a reason to keep living, but I didn't know how to tell them everything that happened. The feeling I got when the words would form in my mouth always had me biting my tongue. It screamed danger, and I could not put them in harm's way. Idhan was here. I could feel it, and his presence grew stronger with each day passing.

"I believe it is him. Sam!" I screamed.

We both took off toward the bloody and weaving boy who seemed lost in the night. Sam was one of the latest children, but something was different about him. Two other children had returned to us out of nowhere without a scratch or memory of what happened to them. But this was different, because this time, Sam came back covered in blood, smelling of an evil that haunted my dreams. There were more shifters from the sea daily, and they all had that haunted look in their eyes. We took them in, and many were unhappy about it, but it had to be done. Others who aren't wolves were being blamed for what was happening now. My chest tightened because I wasn't so sure that it wasn't because of me. Evil was coming, and it was near. I just didn't know where to go or how to stop it.

"What is happening? This is like Jace all over again, or maybe worse. You weren't here for that Oceayn, but I refuse to let this shit start again," Lika growled.

I had heard bits and pieces of the story of their Pack before Hayley, but I knew this wasn't it. The scent that slammed its way into my senses told me how right I had been. He was here, and Idhan would do precisely what he did to my home to theirs. Where was Remi? How in the hell could I stop this, and would anyone believe me before it was too late?

"No. Lika, this...this is worse," I whispered as Sam fell into my arms.

THOMAS

It was already getting late, but I wanted to get down to business. There would be no time to rest until the missing children had been found. I looked at Meesha on my left and saw her staring at the other children sitting at the table across from us.

"You can sit with them if you like while I deal with all this. Since you are my mini Beta, I need you to help me with all the pups and cubs," I smiled. Meesha looked up, smiling, but I knew it was forced. I could feel her fear as if it were my own. I opened my mouth to let her know she could stay beside me, but she scooted her chair back and hopped to the floor.

"I can do that, Thomas. It's not time to protect you yet," she laughed before running to the other children who stared at her as she approached.

I closed my eyes as I projected calm throughout the room and stood to look around at all that gathered. The word was put out throughout the state that everyone, including Sunset Port, needed to report. Hayley had done a great job with the rebuilding and getting the Pack back on track financially, but I could tell there was so much more work that needed to be done. I caught sight of a female and male shifter making their way toward the front where I stood and knew them to be the couple Hayley texted me about. I looked beyond them as the door opened again, and the one who escorted Remi to the house came inside. I found myself needing to see her and know that she was okay.

"Alpha! I am Gina, and this is my husband, Howard. Our son was the one who went missing this morning, and we—"

I held up my hand for them to slow down. I knew Hayley gave me the rundown about what happened with the last Alpha and how he began using the children and other adult shifters as sacrifices because he thought he could become the True Alpha. But if Hayley defeated him, why was this happening again? That's what I need to figure out first before doing anything else. Who else here still believed in Jace's bullshit? I pushed a calming wave out and saw the parents settle slightly.

"This is why I am here so quickly and do not have time for things that happened outside. I need to know what had happened here lately before the children began to go missing?"

"Them! They are what happened!" I looked to my left and saw a female wolf standing up with anger in her eyes. She was shaking, and I saw that she was on the verge of shifting as she glared to the back of the room.

"We have nothing to do with any of this! We just need to place to figure out where—"

"Bullshit! None of this started until we started letting in these other species. I do not have a problem with others. But how do we know they can be trusted?"

"Quiet! If Hayley allowed them to join the Pack, then she had good reason. They are Pack and vulnerable, just as you are right now. They have young that it could easily have happened to," I stated. The female shifter dropped into her chair as another female wrapped her arms around her shoulders.

"You talkin' the same shit as your sister, and you see where that got us. Kids are still missing, so how do we know if it was truly Jace in the first place? This is a tactic to take what belongs to us by a True Alpha we've never seen," a male shifter growled.

I let my gaze travel over everyone until I found the one who spoke. It was the same wolf I had to throw to the ground, and I could tell he still didn't know when to shut the hell up. I didn't mind his outburst because it let me know exactly who I needed to keep my eye on while I was here. As soon as I stepped foot in this state and touched these Pack lands, I made the connection. I let the energy and power flow through me as I claimed this Pack as mine. So I knew every wolf's name, strength, and emotions.

"Louis Winters. I gave you a warning outside, didn't I?" I let down my shields enough to let my Alpha energy flow through the space. I felt my wolf looking out, and I knew my eyes bled to full indigo as whimpers filled the air. "I will say this once, so everyone understands that I mean what I say. Do not lie to your Alpha, nor my Beta, and be assured she is the Beta of this Pack. You can feel it, so I know that you can sense that I know when any of you will lie before you know the lies would slip from your lips," I growled. Suddenly, I pulled back the power and heard everyone suck in a deep breath. Louis sneered as soon as I dampened my Alpha energy, and he shook his head at the other shifters. He looked at me, barely able to hold my gaze as he bared his teeth.

"I'll listen to you, Alpha, but listen to the Beta, you must be out of your damn mind," Louis chuckled. I smiled before I moved in one motion, grabbed him by the throat, and roared as my mouth grew wider and my teeth grew sharper.

"You made me break a promise to my sister, but at least I get to say I warned you," I growled. My clawed left hand flashed, and his head fell to the ground. "I hope everyone understands that what I say, I mean. Louis seemed to have figured that out the hard way," I growled. I dropped his rapidly cooling body and turned back to the two shifters, Howard and Gina. No one else spoke a word. "I know it happened today, and I will do everything in my power to find him and the other children," I started like nothing ever happened.

I opened my senses and power, it was odd because I knew how many people should be on this land, and I could sense every wolf that was in this state. So what the fuck was going on in Sunset Port? I couldn't feel anything coming from the direction of that town, and I knew there were many wolves there. I didn't pay it too much attention initially because I hadn't claimed Florida as mine until I arrived here.

"Than—" Howard started to say when the door burst open again, and a young female shifter and a blueish-green scaled woman came rushing inside holding blood-soaked child.

"Samuel!" Gina screamed.

I looked back at the child and realized that I could not feel his wolf present. What the fuck was going on in Florida?

I jumped down from the platform I stood on and rushed over to the boy faster than his parents. They weren't far behind me, but something was wrong, and only an Alpha would sense this problem.

"Alpha, something is wrong. I don't know what it is, but they did something to him," the female shifter gritted. I snapped my head up to stare at the tall brown-skinned woman who felt familiar. I looked her over and the other shifter that held Sam and saw no wounds and smelled no blood other than the boy.

"Yes, you are right," I stated. I reached out and took the boy from the unfamiliar shifter as his parents began to cry.

"Did you find Avery?"

"What about Jonas and Kendall?"

"Where did you find him?"

"Are you sure she didn't do something to the pup?"

People begin to shout out. At that moment, I wanted all of my brothers here with me. This was not my first time in charge, but it was the first time I had been given a Pack on my own. I needed everyone to shut the hell up so

I could find out what was happening. The rage and anger were at a simmer, but now it was boiling because I hadn't had a release. The ocean scent hit me before her voice rang out through the massive hall.

"If you aren't this child's parents or a healer, close your mouths. When we know more information, you all will know more information. So until then, everyone go to your homes, stay with your children, and be ready if we call. Leave this to your Alpha. That is why he is here," Remi commanded.

Once her scent hit me, I could block out everything else, knowing that my Beta was here and could deal with the unimportant things at the moment. I could sense that child's pain and feel the empty space where his wolf's soul should be. It wasn't that it was gone, but it was almost as if it were hidden. I could feel his pain as I brought a clawed hand onto his chest.

"Oh my God," Gina gasped.

I let my nails pierce his skin to establish a connection with his wolf. I pushed my energy into him, grabbed onto his soul, and pulled. I watched as thick black fluid began to leak from the wounds I had given him as Sam began to scream. I quickly leaned my forehead to his and put him into a deep healing sleep.

"Thomas? What is happening?" Remi asked. Her body was close to mine, but I knew she faced away from me.

"We need to get him somewhere safe for now."

"Our home isn't too far from here. We can go there, Alpha, just please save him," Gina pleaded.

"No! We will take him to where we will be staying." Remi stated. I wanted to know what put the ice in her voice, and her emotions were suddenly closed to me again.

"Follow my Beta," I said, raising my head. Sam's wolf was weakened, but at least it hadn't been taken. Remi wasted no time as she pushed her way through the doors and backed out onto the street. I noticed that the hall was cleared with only me, Sam, his parents, Remi, and the two that found him left inside. We quickly entered the house when every alarm inside me went off.

"Where is Meesha?" I growled. Remi was throwing a large blanket onto the massive couch when my words stopped her breathing. Her head snapped up, and she looked around in true panic.

"I am right here, Thomas," Meesha said.

I looked at her and knew damn well that I didn't sense her presence until she spoke. She stood next to the young female shifter. She clutched her hand tightly, but I saw the girl jump in surprise. I looked at Remi, and she stared at Meesha for a second before meeting my eyes. Then she looked at the girl whose hand Meesha held, and her eyes widened. That's when all of her features filtered back into my mind from the glance I gave her earlier. She had long braids with the tips ending in a faint shade of teal, but her large eyes were what caught me off-guard. They were a deep brown, but the surrounding ring faintly glowed indigo. I shook my head as I laid Sam down, trying to focus on one thing at a time.

"Meesha, can you help Remi get some clean towels for Sam?" I asked as his parents settled next to me.

"Yes, Thomas," Meesha said. I looked at Remi, trying to figure out why she was still standing there when I followed her gaze to the other shifter in the room. A shifter I had never seen or heard of before because I did not know what she could be. It was something to do with water, but as I focused more, I zeroed in on how she stared at Remi with the same prominent eyes as hers.

"Rehema? Is...is that—" The woman brought a shaking hand to her mouth. "Rehema!" she cried and babbled in a language that I had never heard before. The language seemed to twist as it rose and fell before she must have realized Remi didn't know what she was saying.

"Who? Why are you calling me by that name?"

"Remi, it's me. It's Oceayn!" she cried, taking a step toward Remi. Remi held up a hand as water particles began to form from the air. "Remi, please. It's me. You have to remember," Oceayn pleaded.

That's when Remi's emotions flooded through my shields, hitting me full force as confusion, fear, and pain consumed her thoughts.

"Stop! A lot is happening here, but the first and only priority is taking care of Sam," I insisted. No one else said a word as Remi dropped her hand down and picked up Meesha. She rushed away to do what I requested. My phone buzzed at that moment, and I knew it was Alex messaging me. He was on the way here to see about this Alpha in training, and I had a pretty good idea who she was now.

"Alpha? He's waking up," Howard sobbed. He removed his shirt and began wiping away the blood and the black fluid still leaking from Sam's body. I looked at the two shifters, who now stared at each other, then back to Sam. His fevered eyes opened and blinked slowly at us.

"Oh Sam, oh thank *Kunnuck*. Baby, we're here," Gina said, kissing his hand.

"Alp—Alpha," Sam coughed as he looked at me. I knew he must have felt my wolf and heard my voice as I called his wolf to me.

"Yes. It's okay, just rest. You're home now," I said as I released more calming energy. Sam shook his head as if he tried to form words.

"Son, don't try to talk right now. We have time. Listen to the Alpha and just rest," Howard encouraged. But I knew there was something that he had to say. I tried reaching into his thoughts to make it easier, but I was blocked. *How is this possible?*

"Lika, where did you find him?" Gina asked.

"We were on the beach, and I saw him walking along the road leading into town. I don't know where he came from, and no one else was around. I couldn't even scent anyone else, and I tried. We didn't waste time getting back here when we saw him close up. We really should get back out there and look for the others," Lika stated.

"He...he's coming. He's coming. He is coming. He is coming," Sam repeated until I touched his head to put him back to sleep. I looked up as Remi returned to the room with towels and water. She made sure she did not walk by Oceayn as she came to my side.

"Maybe we will get more information from him once he is rested. Right now, we have another problem to deal with," Remi said. She looked up at Oceayn and then stood up facing her, expressionless.

"Yes. Yes, we do. Gina, you and Howard both stay here unless you have other children you need to get to. I want Sam here for the time being, and Lika, I want you watching him."

"Yes, Alpha," Lika nodded.

"We should get back to the other children. I know they are worried. Howard, you stay here, and I will get the other kids together. We can trade-off in a few hours if that is okay?"

"Yes," I said, standing.

I knew whatever Sam had in his mind we were not getting until he could tell us. Someone or something has placed a spell on this boy. I looked at Oceayn, and she tore her gaze from Remi to look my way. The same feeling of unease, fear, danger, and evil rolled off her in waves. Just. Like. Remi.

She knew something, and it was about time that we all were in the know about it so we could deal with it. No more children would be taken from this Pack or any other Packs. We needed to make it known that this shit was going to stop, and it was starting right here and right fucking now.

I could feel Remi vibrating beside me because she knew something was coming just as I did. Whatever had been hunting for her had finally caught up, but it did not answer the question of why it was here. Why was it taking wolf shifter children from this Pack when Remi didn't even know it existed? On reflex, I grabbed Remi's hand, trying to soothe the fear and anger inside of her as we approached Oceayn, who held her head up high. I didn't stop and made my way to the opposite side of the house until I found a small sitting room where I could close the doors. I wanted answers, and I knew Remi did as well.

I closed the doors and turned to face the women when Remi attacked. A loud hiss came from Oceayn as she blocked Remi's attacks, but as I watched, I could tell she was doing everything in her power not to fight back. The tears in her eyes told a different story than the fanged mouth and snake-like eyes that flashed as she countered Remi. I almost took a step to stop it when I realized that Remi was not fighting as she usually would, either. I could see in her teal eyes that she knew something was off. She wasn't fighting Oceayn, truly fighting Oceayn. She was fighting her lost memory.

"Who are you?" Remi screamed. She ducked low and stuck out her leg, catching Oceayn off-guard, and then punched her in the chest, sending Oceayn slamming into the wall.

"Remi!" I growled, but Oceayn stood up again with a hiss. Remi's eyes flashed, but before she could move, Oceayn bowed low.

"Princess Rehema. I would love to say I finally found you, but it seems as if you found me," she sighed. I looked at Remi and saw the words slam into her chest.

"What did you say?" Remi questioned.

"Princess Rehe—"

We all turned suddenly. Remi launched herself at Oceayn. She shoved the woman back into the wall and her palm onto Oceayn's dripping fangs.

"Remi! No!" I shouted and grabbed her by the waist. She snatched it from my grasp and stumbled back before falling to the ground, shaking uncontrollably.

"No! No! You know my fangs are poison! What did you do? What did you do!?!" Oceayn screamed

Remi

I did not understand why I slammed my palm into the tip of Oceayn's fangs, but something inside called for it to be done. I screamed in my mind at the pain that burned through my veins as it spread through my body. I could hear Oceayn screaming and feel Thomas's arms around me, but I couldn't say a word. I wanted to pull away and wanted him to tighten his grip on me at the exact moment. I could hear him speaking, but it seemed to slip further and further away as everything went black.

I heard a pulsating noise as flashes of colors and lights surrounded me, making me squint after the sudden darkness. I almost felt like I was drowning and pushed, trying to find my way out of the water, when everything shattered into broken pieces. The colors faded and broke apart like pieces of glass and reshaped into a hallway covered in a thick black substance that should not be there.

What is this place?

As my vision cleared, I felt like I was slammed into a body that was running. The screams filled the surrounding air, but I didn't know why. I could see myself running and running, but I could also feel the warm stone beneath my feet and smell the sweet scent of the Bargandous sea.

Wait. I knew this place just like the creature who chased me. I cried out in my mind, wanting to wake up because I *did* remember. I remembered everything about this day, which broke my heart and soul over again. I let the memory play out as I re-lived the day my Kingdom fell.

I opened my eyes, expecting to see the study's white ceiling and the mess I made fighting Oceayn. Instead, I saw a soft blue and noticed the softness beneath me. I blinked a few times before realizing that something was tied around my wrist, causing me to awaken fully. Before I could pull on the thick leather restraints, Thomas leaned into my view. The teal of my eyes reflected on his face as he looked me over while placing a warm hand on my chest.

"What happened? Why are these things around my wrists?" I asked with a frown.

"Because you were going into convulsions after slamming your damn palm into a snake woman's mouth. Also, because if I didn't, I don't think I would have been able to control your shift," he stated. My brows furrowed because who the hell did he think that he was trying to control my Livyatan? At that word, it felt like something was trying to rip through my skin as power rolled its way through my body. My home, world, family, and people were either dead or captured! Everything and everyone I have come in contact with is in danger. I couldn't control the fear and anger that wanted to tear my body apart because I still could not remember how to handle the power inside of me.

What did Idhan do to me?

"Let me go! I need to stop him!" I roared. Thomas was over me, pressing his body against mine, trying to hold me down. I felt his clawed fingers wrap around my wrists as I thrashed. I wasn't in control of myself or my emotions to control this shift.

"Remi!" Thomas growled in my face. "You are letting your anger and aggression control you. If you shift now, you will hurt innocent people. You will hurt your Pack!"

I heard what he was saying and understood, but couldn't take the reins back. The other half of me had been dampened for so long, and now that it remembered, nothing would stop it. Now that I remembered, I didn't want to stop the shift. If I let go, at least losing control would help me forget seeing the people in my kingdom being annihilated. My Orcinus screamed for blood, but I knew there was a reason that I didn't stay and fight. Thomas was right, and I was letting my raw energy and emotions control me, but I couldn't stop it. I didn't know how to stop it. I screamed as my bones began to shift, and I saw a brief panic in Thomas's eyes before they went blank.

"Just let me go," I gritted. I knew my mind would become lost once I shifted into this out-of-control state.

"I think I remember telling you that if you couldn't keep yourself under control, I would need to teach you. I guess tonight will be your first lesson," Thomas grunted.

His body pressed hard onto mine, and I felt every inch of his muscles, skin, power, and intent all over me. Did he think it would be that easy? He did not know, but the look in his eyes told me he wanted my submission. That would never happen. He could never tame this ancient power inside of me. If I couldn't remember how to calm the beast, how would this young pup do it? I turned my head toward the window and saw the dark ocean calling me. I wanted to feel the waters along my skin once again. One leather strap snapped, but Thomas grabbed my arm and shoved it to the bed. He pinned my hand under his knee and used his clawed figures to turn my head toward him. "I always knew you were dangerous, Remi. I told everyone just how dangerous you were, but none of them would listen."

"So if I am so dangerous, you should let me go before I kill you," I gritted. My mouth began to stretch as my teeth sharpened. Thomas laughed, catching me off-guard at how dark the laugh became. He pulled back and looked at me with a slow smile that had me stopping all movement. I felt my core grow slick just as my nipples hardened. I didn't know what

Thomas thought he was about to do, but I knew he was not ready for anything like me. I couldn't help to rub myself on him when I felt his grip tighten around my wrist and when I felt his hand at my throat.

"I would love to see you try because you don't know how dangerous I can be. You will submit to me and learn control so we can do what we came here to do, Rehema."

The way my given name fell from his lips and the challenge he laid down cleared the rage and hatred in my mind. It even gave my Orcinus pause as it became fully aware of him. No, not him, but the Alpha wolf that growled the challenge at me as if I would take it lying down. All of my focus was now on Thomas, and I wasted no time as I broke the last strap and bucked hard so he would fall to the floor. I rolled in the opposite direction and got to my feet, but he was fast. He was faster than I had ever seen him be, because he was on me in a flash. I hardened my skin as I brought up an arm to block him, but he brushed it away and pushed me back. I narrowed my eyes, but he wasn't about to do me how he did me when we were home. I jumped sideways to launch myself over the large bed, but he caught my ankle and stopped my motion. I slammed onto the soft mattress, and he dragged me back toward him. I looked into his dark eyes and sucked in a breath as the indigo ring glowed. I felt a power slam into me, and I would have thought his hands and tongue were all over my body.

"Oh Gods," I moaned. I bit down on my tongue because he wasn't doing anything. It was just his hand touching the skin of my ankle, but my moan had him licking his full lips.

"You may have gotten some of your memories back, but I can tell it's not all of them. You are losing control over a shift because you feel out of control. To gain control, Remi, you first will need to lose all control over your mind and your body," Thomas said in a low rumble.

He released my ankle and, at the same time, pulled something out of his pocket that glowed white. He threw it over me, and everything around me flashed brightly, causing me to blink rapidly. Once my eyes adjusted, I realized I lay naked in a room that wasn't here a moment ago. My hands and feet were spread apart, but nothing held me down. I strained, but I couldn't move anything but my eyes and head. The room was dark and covered in deep shades of red from wall-to-wall. There wasn't any other furniture but the bed that I could see. But along the walls were things that made my clit pulse and breath hitch.

"Thomas," I whispered as I felt something wet touch my skin. His long tongue licked a trail from my ankle to my inner thighs. The slickness between my folds began sliding down, making me grit my teeth. I didn't have time for this or what he thought he was about to do, but my body told another story. I wanted to feel him all over me or one of those whips across my skin. "Don't play. Just make me cum," I said. My voice came out lower than usual and more commanding. I felt both sides of myself were trying to figure out a way to get free, so I could take what I wanted. Then I could shift and head for the sea.

"You can give me orders when you gain control. But you need to complete your first lesson."

I opened my mouth to snap at him when he slapped my clit hard.

I bit my lip as his rough hands kneaded my breasts, flicking and pinching my nipples till they were puckered and hard. His hands took their time to travel down my body frame like he was trying to appropriate and memorize every single part of me as he knelt between my legs.

"We don't have time for any of this, Tho—"

I felt him settle between my thighs, his face hovering over my core. His eyes gleamed as he inhaled my scent, and I was almost ashamed of how wet I was for him. A small moan escaped my lips when he gently pulled my slippery folds apart to get a better picture. Everything in my head seemed to go completely blank. This scene was something I wanted to happen, but I never believed it would. I shook my head, trying to remember why I was so angry and why I needed to—

"Oh shit," I groaned. Thomas bent his head and made a long swipe between my folds, tasting me. A groan escaped his lips while my body shook.

Fuck me. I wasn't one to submit to any *Being*, but—

My eyes rolled back as I felt my body writhe and buck under Thomas's as he continued to feast like a starved wolf.

"That's it, clear your mind. Focus on me," Thomas growled. He was drenched in my juices just the way he should because he was my mate, my *Aeternum*. Wait. This is impossible. When those words filtered through my mind, I tried to deny them. I was lying here, trying not to lose my mind, and he looked calm and collected. The indigo in his eyes seemed to glow at the moment as we both knew something had changed. Why couldn't I have sensed it before, and did he know? There was no time for any of this, but when I stared into his eyes, I knew he would fight to see if I'd submit.

No. He couldn't know, and I was not about to tell him. It would just complicate things when I needed to leave. We were from two different worlds. There was no way something like this would work. This connection should be impossible, shouldn't it? I narrowed my eyes and he growled, creating a vibration that had me twitching. My nose flared, knowing he wanted nothing more than me to surrender. Even knowing what I knew now, I was not about to let him win again. I was prideful, and there wasn't a chance I would allow this young wolf to dominate me so easily, even if he was my *Aeternum.* I was an Alpha and Royalty, so I would bow to no one. I raised my hips to meet his face. "Thomas, be a good pup and make me cum already."

Thomas's eyes went to slits, only allowing a slither of indigo light through, making me think he would give in to me. Instead, without warning, he thrusted two fingers deep inside me. I whimpered, my insides clenching around his two long fingers as if they depended on them for life. His other clawed hand gripped my hip, holding me down onto the bed as he continued to play with me expertly. "I'm not telling you again," I panted. I tried to remember what I was so angry about and why I wanted to be a part of him, but the sensations overtook me again.

"Good, because I will when I think you deserve it," he shot back with a growl. "You may be dominant, but when you are under me, holding onto that nature will feel like torture until you give in," he replied in amusement. He continued to pump his fingers slowly inside me like he had all the time in the world. "I guess you won't be cumming tonight, are you?"

"That's fine. I have shit I need to do," I shrugged casually, although I felt as if I would go mad if he did not let me cum. I swallowed, knowing I would only irritate him with my following comment. "A dildo would satisfy me if you can't get the job done."

He was annoyed, just like I was with him for not making me cum. I couldn't help the grin that appeared out of satisfaction. Instead of answering, he got back to work on eating me out in combination with his fingers. His tongue teased my slits, occasionally traveling to swipe at my engorged clit. His clawed hand dug into my skin, sending small sensations of pain and pleasure running through my body. How did he know what I liked? He said it before but—

Yet, it wasn't *enough*. Thomas crooked his fingers to hit that sweet bumpy and raised G-spot. But he quickly moved them as I cried out. I knew Thomas was hoping I would beg, that I would show my submission, but Thomas was in for nothing but disappointment. He sucked hard before pulling away and biting down on my inner thigh.

"Please."

He chuckled, the little rumble sending a vibration enough to cause me to almost climax alone. I knew what it was, and it was the fact if he bit any harder, breaking the skin, the mating bond would begin. Just that knowledge had my core clenching and my clit throbbing for his bite. Then, his tongue finally circled and twirled at my clit while he thrusted his fingers rougher into me. I let a small moan escape my lips as my head fell back and gripped onto the sheets. I wanted to touch and feel his hot skin under my hands, but I couldn't move. "*Thomas,*" I cried. I felt something inside me snap, and a wall went down, letting all his desires, emotions, and intentions rush through me. "Thomas!"

"You have my permission."

The tide came crashing down, like having his permission to cum was what my body craved. He suckled hard onto my sensitive clit while I moaned loudly, bucking my essence into his mouth. I clasped back with my eyes closed, trying to pull myself out of the sleepy haze he'd put me into. I searched deep inside myself for my Orcinus, but the contentment I felt coming from inside had me sliding into a deep sleep.

Awareness came to me slowly, but I could already tell something was different. I didn't feel the urge to run or fight. I knew that was unusual. I stretched lazily on the soft bed and breathed in deeply. I couldn't remember ever sleeping so well unless I was deep underwater. The thought had my eyes snapping open, and I stared into the brown eyes that watched me. Everything had changed, and I knew who I was even though things still seemed fuzzy. Thomas watched me, but I couldn't tell what he was thinking, and when I touched his mind, I found it firmly closed off. He licked his lips and lifted a hand to push my hair out of my face. I held myself still because his touch and scent made me want to push myself closer. I knew I couldn't do that. He didn't know about my thoughts or what my soul screamed. Thomas was an Alpha, and he would've known if I was his Mate. He would have known the day he met me.

"I think I know why I had a problem with you all this time."

I swallowed and worked my dry mouth before asking, "Why?"

I held my breath, knowing I needed to hear his rejection so I could do what I came here to do. I would help him figure out what was happening with this Pack then I had to get moving. I had to figure out where my brother was and take our Kingdom back.

"Because I knew you were death and danger rolled up in a sexy package. You seemed like a risk to my Pack and family. But now...I see. What is life without a little risk? You are Pack now, and once I finish my mission here, I will help you figure out whatever it is you came here to do," he stated. I wanted to ask what he meant and how he knew I came here for a reason, but he pulled away and rolled to stand up.

"That isn't necessary, Thomas. I will—" My words were cut off when we heard a light knock at the door. I knew this conversation wasn't over, but for now, I would push it to the side so we could do what was needed for now. "Let's handle Pack business and deal with my issues later," I said. I rolled out of bed, seeing that I was wearing a long tee shirt. Thomas moved to open the door, but I already knew who was on the other side of it. Guilt and shame rolled over me as Oceayn stepped inside and stared at me. I looked her over, not understanding what I was seeing.

"I am going to check on Sam. I think you two need to talk," Thomas said, shutting the door behind him.

"Rehema?" Oceayn whispered. She stood tall and rigid as she readied herself for another fight.

"Oceayn, I am so sorry," I said and moved. I pulled her into a hug and breathed in her familiar scent. "What happened to you?" I asked, pulling away. This was not the Oceayn I left that day, and I was still confused about how she was here.

"A little of this and that, but it doesn't matter right now. Are you crazy?" she shouted. Oceayn grabbed my hands and turned them over to look at them. I looked down as well but saw only smooth skin.

"I know, I know. I don't know what I was thinking or what I was not thinking. I was urged to do it, and I think I know why," I said slowly. I shook my head as my memories slowly began to wake and looked her over again. "Who did this to you?" I asked. I stood tall and looked down at her, expecting an answer.

"Nakeema," she grunted. "Never mind that right now. We have a bigger issue at hand. Idhan is here. He followed you, Remi, and I know for sure he hasn't left. Only your blood will open the gate safely, and only you know where it is," she stated.

My blood went cold the moment that name slipped out of her mouth. Idhan was here. If that was true, this realm was no longer safe. Thomas may have been right in his first thoughts about me. I was danger and death walking, but I was not at risk that he should endanger his life in helping. This was my fight and mine alone. I had already spent too much time with the Rayne Pack and could have placed a target on them. I wouldn't have even known it because whatever I was poisoned with stole my memories from me. My Livyatan was angry because I had a mission to complete. The poison not only suppressed my memories but my Orcinus.

"Do you know where he is? How long after did you follow me?"

"Remi, I have been searching for you for over one hundred years. There is no way that you would just appear here out of nowhere. Something isn't adding up, and I have a strong feeling Idhan has everything to do with it," Oceayn seethed.

"That's impossible! I have not been with the Rayne Pack that long, Oceayn."

"Well, it's true. That is how long I have searched, so I know he was doing the same because there is no way that evil piece of shit didn't make it through. So, where have you been?" she asked. Her pale blue eyes, which glittered like jewels, stared into mine.

"I…I do not know."

THOMAS

I stared at my hands, trying to figure out what I was thinking. I used pixie dust to take Remi where I'd told myself only my Mate would see. I felt my wolf shifting inside, wanting me to turn around and return and claim her as mine. I moved away from the door because I couldn't deal with that right now. If this was true, why hadn't I felt it before now? And, she was crazy as hell if she thought I would let her go.

Naw, that wasn't going to happen until I knew the truth.

I suppose helping her figure out why she was here and killing whoever made her run would get me to the truth. Then that was next on the list. But first, I had to figure out what was attacking my Pack and handle that situation. I returned to the living room to check on Sam but decided to check on Meesha first. I had already washed Remi's scent from my face and regretted doing it. I knew it had to be done because I couldn't concentrate when I tasted her every time I opened my mouth.

I pushed open the door to see Meesha curled up on a large bed, fast to sleep. I watched her for a few seconds, trying to figure out what was happening with her and how I couldn't feel her earlier. That should not have been possible. I shook my head as I closed the door and headed down the stairs. I rechecked my phone and was glad to see that Alex would be here in a few days. I also felt the darkness inside me no longer felt like it was trying to claw its way out of me. It was almost as if it were sated.

I caught Lika's gaze and nodded for her to come with me for a second.

"Is everything okay? Is Oceayn good?"

"Yeah, yeah, everything will be fine. Oceayn will be down in just a few, but I needed to holla at you quickly," I stated. We stopped at a large table that seated about fifteen people, reminding me of the table back home. I looked Lika over, feeling as though I should know her or like I knew her from somewhere. I brushed it off to Hayley telling me so much about the young shifter, and I could see why.

"The other children, how long have they been missing?"

"Right after Sam was taken, the other two went missing. It's insane, Alpha. Who would do something like this?" Lika crossed her arms across her chest as she bit the tip of her pinky nail.

"Many would do something such as this, unfortunately. I just don't know why and how. You have protections around this land, so how are they taking these children? Tell me what you think," I asked. Lika dropped her arms to her sides and began rubbing them along her thighs as if she was uncomfortable telling me her opinion. "Tell me," I said. I placed a hand on her shoulder, but she jerked back, almost knocking over the chair in the process. I frowned, but she laughed shakily before righting the chair.

"Sorry, sorry, I will..." She gripped the chair tightly as she closed her eyes. I cocked my head to the side and stared at her intently as I felt for her emotions. I came up against a wall that felt familiar and almost exactly like the shield I placed around myself.

"I think that place has something to do with it. Sunset Port," she gritted. I wanted to ask other questions about the shield, but I knew that would need to come later. She was still shaking, so I sent a calming wave without touching her and saw that she had relaxed slightly. "They were always weird, but it's gotten worse lately. Some Pack members visiting here visit that place because they have family defecting. Hayley didn't stop because it wasn't a problem until we started accepting shifters like Oceayn and the others. That's when the whole, 'not a wolf' and 'half-breed' talk started again. Then more talk of combining with Sunset Port, but Hayley stopped all that because they do not follow Pack Law. Not many of us even understood true Pack law until Hayley came, but now...now we can see how everything went wrong before. And now, it feels like someone or something is trying to start that shit again. I will not let that happen," she growled.

"So, someone who supports Sunset Port could be taking the children to them."

"But why do they come back? It's crazy! Why take them and send the children back? What are they doing to them?"

I crossed my arms over my chest, and so did Lika. It was almost like I stared into a mirror.

"It sounds like they are—"

"Looking for someone!" Lika finished at the same time I did. She looked up with a smile when we heard Howard scream.

I moved and stood next to Howard in seconds, noticing Lika was not far behind, giving credit to what Hayley said about her becoming a strong Alpha.

"Wh— what's wrong, Sam?" Howard cried. Samuel's form almost glowed from the moonlight coming from the Bay windows. I had felt energy like this before, and it was something that I would never forget. There was one difference. Whatever had taken Sam had far greater power than the demon that attacked my Pack. I knew demon energy, which surrounded the little boy, but so did another energy—something I had never encountered in my life. The black fluid came from his eyes and poured from his mouth.

"Howard! Move out of the way." I pushed the father aside, trying to remember everything I had been taught, but nothing came to mind. What in the hell was this stuff, and how would I save him from it? I placed my hand on his chest again and let my nails grow to enter his body. It was almost like the boy was drowning in ... some kind of poison. But why wasn't it affecting me?

"Thomas! Hold onto his wolf," Remi said. I felt her enter the room, but the moment she dropped beside me, I could feel the difference in her power.

"What is wrong with my son? I thought you got all of that out of him!" Howard roared. I vaguely heard Lika speaking to him when Remi's hands came into view. I saw a cream liquid on the tip of her finger and knew precisely what she would give him.

"That almost killed you," I gritted.

"This will kill him, and believe me, I know nothing from this world can stop it. Trust me," she whispered. I knew Howard was screaming and on the verge of a shift. I knew that just as I knew Sam would die if I let go of his wolf. Could I trust her?

"Do it."

The pain I felt was nothing compared to what Sam was feeling. Remi yanked me away, almost throwing me across the room. Sam convulsed just as Remi did, but it wasn't nearly as long or as violent. More thick blackish fluid flowed out of his mouth and nose before slowing down a few minutes later. I moved to pick him up, but Howard had already lifted him into his arms.

"What the fuck is happening? Who is doing this?" His dark brown eyes bled to amber as he shook.

"We find that answer out tonight," I stated. I was done with this shit. I hadn't been here for a day to even access these shifters, but I was done. We were finding the other children tonight and the ones responsible for placing them in this type of danger. I needed to know what Remi knew now and how poison inside her was now inside a ten-year-old pup. "Lika, you stay here," I said, moving to the doors.

"Wait! No, I can't stay here, Alpha. I promised those kids I would come and find them," she snapped.

"Lika!" I turned to face her, causing her to stop in her tracks. "Sam is here, Meesha is asleep upstairs, and right now, I only trust you to watch them. Do you get what I am saying to you?" I growled. Remi took a step forward and touched her shoulder. I noticed she didn't flinch but seemed to almost lean into it before she nodded.

"Just...just find them," she sighed. She pulled away from Remi, turning away without looking back at me. Remi looked at Oceayn, and she nodded once.

"I will stay as well. Rehema, be careful. You know what this means," she said as she ran a hand through long thick locs. My eyes met the teal of Remi's, but she pushed me before I could ask what the fuck that meant.

"I think I know exactly who to start with," she grunted. I fisted my hands and followed her out of the door.

"Thomas, can you try to keep the heads attached to the bodies? We will never get answers from anyone if they can't speak," Remi said.

"I always let my elders go first, then follow suit."

"You have no clue how much older I am, do you?"

"I am pretty sure I have a good idea, but it doesn't mean anything. As long as you can take orders, it's all good," I smirked. My senses were open, and I used my gift with emotions to push calm and the feeling to sleep throughout the Pack as I followed Remi.

"In certain cases, maybe, but I wouldn't get used to it," Remi murmured, but I could tell her mind was elsewhere.

"What was Oceayn talking about?" I watched her and saw when the muscles in her back tightened. She slowed down but never stopped moving forward. I looked at her and saw the differences in her body, skin, and power. I could feel the spirit inside her watching me, and my wolf stared back. Her scent curled around me, and I watched the sway of her hips as she moved gracefully.

"You saw it. I know you saw my memories when I passed out. I could feel you inside of me," she sighed.

"Yes, but it doesn't tell me everything I need to know. Is that green dude here or something? He thinks he can come and drag you back to your realm?" I asked. I heard the growl in my voice and felt the possessive wave that shot through my body. Remi stopped and glanced back to look at me. I came to stand in front of her, and I didn't look away nor was I going to hide the fact that I knew what she was to me. I knew I was right about her being dangerous, but she wouldn't be dangerous to us. It was what followed her that was another story. I stared into the large teal eyes and held them, letting her feel my emotions and what I knew to be true about us.

"Oceayn says he is here, and, to be honest now, with my powers returning, I can feel his evil, and he's close."

"What I do not understand is what he has to do with these shifters. How would he even know that you would come here with me? If he knew where you were this entire time, then why wait or play these games?"

I stood so close to Remi that it made her tilt her head back to stare at me. I didn't move as her hand came up and rested lightly on my chest. I covered her hand with my own, waiting for her thoughts because of none of this made sense to me yet. How did that poison get into Sam, and why?

"I don't know, but when I find his ass, I will kill him for touching these children. But I must agree with your pup. He isn't operating in his usual manner, so something is up. But our first clue to all this shit, I believe, will be with that bitch Grecia Jamison," she growled. Remi took her hand away and started a jog down the quiet street. "Let's go, Alpha."

"I like the way that rolls off your tongue. I want to hear you scream it next time."

"Don't get used to it. The only thing you will hear me scream is for you to get on your knees, Seahorse," she replied.

"Seahorse?"

"Yes, in my language, it means something completely different," she stated. We turned a corner and waited while she drew in a long breath.

"What does it mean?"

She let out her breath and turned to look at me. I stared at her lips as they pulled up into a smirk.

"It is what we call young males who believe they can hang with the big sea creatures."

"Good to know. That will be your new safe word," I growled.

I stepped forward and stood in front of her before she took another breath. I leaned down, breathing her in as I caught her lips, and she moaned. The rush of emotion that filled me felt like I had just done multiple sessions at Sinful Secrets. My wolf howled, and my thoughts went blank except for one word, Mate.

We came to the end of the road, and I cocked my head to the side as I studied the yellow and white ranch-style house. I knew everyone should be asleep or in such a calming state that they wouldn't be able to stand up from wherever they fell. This house was different, though. These shifters were not asleep, and they knew we were here. I was done wasting time, and it was like we didn't even need to speak as we moved as one. I took a step and shifted into my wolf form in mid-motion. We were all enormous in this form, and I towered well over Remi. I crashed through the door and pounced on the man who raised a shotgun. My large paws slapped the gun aside, and I didn't hesitate to rip out his throat. I turned, taking a step and shifting back into human form, and caught the wolf that leaped at me from the right. I threw the wolf to the ground but didn't release its massive head. I clamped my hand over its muzzle and growled.

"Shift! Now!"

The wolf whimpered, but it had no choice but to listen to my direct command. The male shifter began shifting back into human form. His pale skin was beading black droplets of sweat. The same black fluid I saw in Sam also leaked from his eyes and nose. I removed my hand from his mouth and shifted it into claws as I plunged it deep into his chest.

"Ahhh!! No! No! I do not belong to you. I do not belong to you! I do—do not—"

The man screamed the exact words repeatedly until I caught hold of the spirit of his wolf. I knew no one other than the woman we came for in this house, and I wasn't worried. Remi had her, but I needed to know if these people could be helped, or were they just pawns being moved on a chess board? His words cut off as I broke into his mind, and emotions sent him into a sleeping state. I called to his wolf and saw that it was rabid. Its eyes burned red as it growled, menacingly at my presence. I could spot the marking on his soul telling me that he was possessed. If his wolf was also in this state, he willingly went into this bullshit. I went through his memories, which were chaotic and confusing, but I saw the early morning when Samuel was taken. I saw the fear in his eyes and how Sam protected the other children.

"Tell me the name I need," I gritted. Another force was pushing me from his thoughts, making me lose hold of his wolf. I knew it was the demon. I saw the crimson eyes and smelled the evil like he stood before me. The giant Black Dog hid in the shadows of this wolf's soul. I caught flashes of crimson eyes as it watched me.

"I am the *devour*. That is all you will need to know, Thomas Rayne. Thank you for your contribution to my vessel," it hissed. I pushed my Alpha energy into the man's body and felt his back bow off the floor.

"Whatever you got planned, *Cadejo*, you will fail. You will die just like the one that came before you," I growled. I shoved my energy deep inside his chest, causing my claws to pierce through the rib cage to grab the man's heart. "You will not have this soul."

I opened my connection with *Kannuck* before yanking the beating heart from the man's chest. I felt my energy flow through his body so I could lead the spirit of his wolf back to its creator. I could hear the hissing and screams of the demon at the loss of a soul he thought he could claim. I crushed the blackened heart in my fist as it turned to dust. I brushed off my hands and stood just as a long, howling scream ripped through the house. At least I learned one thing before I had to pull out. I knew that the other children were still alive, and this demon was the same one that was fucking with Meesha. Now, I needed to know its plan and what it had to do with the *Being* after my Mate.

I found Remi inside the next room, holding Grecia down on the long wooden dining table.

"Took you long enough, Alpha," Remi smirked.

I knew what she was doing, but it wouldn't be enough to hold back this darkness inside me coming to the surface. I could feel her teal gaze as I looked at Grecia, who stared at me with fear. I let the energy and power of an Alpha roll off me, but I didn't stop there. I used that energy like a blade as I twisted it inside her emotions, finding any will she had to fight. I crushed the thought of any fight she had and ripped away any hope she held onto that she would make it out of this house alive.

"Plea—please. Alpha, Alpha, please. I had no choice. I had no choice," she cried. She was partially shifted, but her strength was no match for Remi. She held the wolf down with one hand on her chest. "My son called this demon here, and...it got into my mind. He took control—"

"Shut up," I growled. I stepped closer and breathed in her scent. I had to be sure, and now I was and shook my head. "You don't hold a trace of the taint of that demon. Traces, but nothing else. You did all this without being possessed but offered up whoever followed you as sustenance."

"I don't—" Grecia began to sputter, but Remi lifted her with one hand. Then she slammed her back onto the table, cracking it in half.

"My Alpha said to shut up."

Grecia groaned as blood erupted from her mouth. I squatted down, looking over the older wolf.

"I want you to tell me everything that you know, and then I want you to tell me exactly where those pups are being held," I commanded.

There was no way she could now defy a direct command from me. I mythically stripped away her free will and sent her wolf into a long sleep. A sleep that it would never wake up from again. The yellow bleed in her eyes faded as she lost the ability to hold her wolf form. That's when I knew she realized what had happened. I knew people always wanted to know what I did to interrogate my enemies. The power I held over emotions wasn't the only gift given to me at birth. I also had the power to tear the wolf's soul from any werewolf shifter and make their power my own. The energy and power were so thick in the air that I could taste its sweetness on my tongue. I heard Remi catch her breath and knew she realized what was happening. This was the second secret I kept from my family. The kind of darkness lives inside me that revels in stealing another *Being's* power. Except this time, it didn't feel as out of control as it usually would. I looked into Remi's large teal eyes, seeing curiosity and respect in their depths. I returned my glare to the woman who was now nothing more than a human.

"Speak."

REMI

The feeling that I got when I felt the power Thomas wielded gave me a new respect for the pup. I knew that he was powerful like the rest of his brothers, but I was not expecting him to be able to do something such as this. I wanted to know more about this gift, but I felt something was slightly off. If I could feel it, then I knew he could as well. I brought my attention back to the now human as she began emptying every thought, telling every action, and revealing intentions for this Pack. She told us all about the town called Sunset Port.

"I was told to bring the children. All we wanted was to be free to serve our Gods, so we made a deal. I wanted my Pack back, but some of the children were to be chosen as sacrifices. They would not be killed but given to our creator so that we would remain pure and blessed."

"Where are the other children, Grecia?" I growled.

"They are being held inside the grand white room in the largest building dedicated to our Gods. It stands in the town center, but you will never make it inside. Everything has already been set in place. None of this even matters anymore," Grecia laughed. Her eyes were wild, but Thomas raised his head when I was about to smash her head into the floor.

"Remember where we spoke to, Darlena?"

"Yes."

"That is where the children will be found. I saw it clear as day in her mind. We're done here," I stated. Thomas stood up and turned away. I knew that he wanted Grecia to have to answer for her crimes and to face the true Pack law. But I wanted to rip her head from her shoulders.

"I know damn well we are not leaving this psycho alive!"

"No, we aren't. She will face Pack Justice. They all need to see what that is so this Pack will understand," he said, moving to the open door. I followed behind him with anger radiating off me, knowing he could feel it. No way we were leaving this woman here alive. She may be human now, but she could still run, and I wasn't having that.

"What are we going to do with the bitch?" I snapped. I stepped around Thomas and caught sight of Lika. She stood there shaking with fury, and I saw the slight ripple over her skin.

"Talika! Control yourself. She will be judged by Pack law. I leave her to you to secure her until we come back with the children. Get who you trust and form a group to find out who else is following her bullshit. Once you have tasked those shifters, return to the house. Watch over Samuel and Meesha."

I watched as Lika stood straighter, and the teal ring in her eyes glowed brighter before she nodded.

"Yes, Alpha," Lika said. She looked at me, and I nodded my head and raised my chin. She took the hint and mimicked my actions. "It will be done, Alpha," she stated again, holding Thomas's eyes.

"Remi, let's go," Thomas growled.

Thomas took one step and began to shift into his wolf. He did it when we got here, but I didn't have a chance to admire the giant wolf. The sable coat looked soft to the touch, and I could feel my own shift wanting to burst through. His massive head turned to me and met my eyes. I was swallowed in indigo eyes that seemed to see into my soul before he bowed his head.

I didn't hesitate, knowing precisely what he wanted, and jumped onto his back. Thomas raised his head and howled before taking off into the night.

We moved through the night in the direction of the town where Idhan might be. There was no way that this was a coincidence, but I couldn't figure out how he knew I would come with Thomas. Hell, if he knew where I was this entire time, why didn't he come for me? I would have been vulnerable because I couldn't remember shit.

"Once we get to the town, the first thing is finding the children. We need to get them back to safety. Then we can come back and handle these rogue wolves."

"Thomas, I know you saw that bastard that is after me, and I don't know how he is involved with this mess but stay away from him if you run into him there."

"If you believe you can order your Alpha around, you're trippin', little princess."

I pulled back out of his thoughts because that word brought back so many memories it almost caused me to slip off his back. I didn't understand the feeling it gave me when he said it because I knew that when that word came from Idhan's lips, I felt like I wanted to gag. The loss at not being connected mind-to-mind with him had me opening myself back up to him needing that connection. I wanted to feel it as much as possible because soon, I would have to leave him so I could find my brother and save my Kingdom.

"Don't call me that."

"That is who you are, Remi. Don't let anything take away the title that belongs to you. It belongs not only to you but to your people who fought in your name."

I swallowed hard because he was right, and I didn't understand how he could see that, and I couldn't. I should have stayed and fought Idhan that day, but I knew there would have been no way I would have won. I had already been poisoned, my parents captured, and my people dying. I knew they counted on me to find a way to fight back and bring the fight back to Hyquadra. Escaping to this realm to find Atlantis was the only choice I had. Now that I remembered, there wasn't any more time to waste.

"You're right."

Thomas didn't respond as we slowed down, and the town of Sunset Port came into view. I took a breath, tasting the ocean that wasn't far away. I wanted to shift and finally release my Livyatan to feel whole. I turned my face back to the town as a scent drifted to my nose, and I knew for a fact that Idhan had been here. I slid off Thomas's back, but my fingers curled in his thick fur so he wouldn't move. Thomas's wasn't midnight black like Hayley's, but it was close to it. The darker shades of brown covered his entire body. It reminded me of rich dark chocolate, but the indigo eyes set it off. Thomas's massive head turned to stare into my eyes before looking back to the town. He growled low, and I felt his Alpha energy rise, making it known that we were here. The Rayne family was strong, and I knew they took on many enemies, but I didn't know an enemy like this. This was a darkness that could infect this world if I didn't stop it here. I refused to let what happened to my home happen here. I would not let him get hurt because Idhan was here for me.

Thomas took off, and if I weren't as powerful, I probably wouldn't have been able to keep up. If I were in the water, his speed would look like he was jogging compared to how I would move through the waves. I let my skin harden as we raced through the center of this town that smelled like death. When we first came here, I knew something was up with it, but this heaviness surrounding it wasn't present. We slowed as we walked down the same street we used earlier, and no one was in the streets. I couldn't see them by sight but could sense the surrounding wolves. The other wolf shifters stayed in human form, watching our movement. I felt the energy from Thomas build as he shifted back into his human form, but what stood next to me was something different. They called it the third form, and from what I knew, it had a time limit. I let a smile creep across my face because I knew we weren't taking any prisoners. Thomas was already about six-feet-two-inches tall, but now he was at least seven-feet-tall. The sable fur that covered his wolf looked inky black as his long, clawed hands flexed.

"The demon is no longer here, but everyone here is no longer alive," Thomas growled. My heart sped up, thinking back to the night we fought off the last rogue wolf and his followers. Are they possessed? What exactly happened here in only a few hours?

"What the hell does that even mean?" I asked.

"They are dead but still alive. Someone has reanimated them, and that *Being* has to be here. It could only be a Necro—"

We took one step toward where the children were being held, and a ripple began to form. It seemed to shape itself into a box, and I could feel the alarm coming from Thomas. The center of this space black box opened, and a tall, curvy woman stepped out. The black swirling markings covering her face, neck, and arms reminded me of Witch markings, but I knew that wasn't right. She pushed the mass of red-black curls back from her face, revealing clear gray eyes with pupils as red as blood. Even with those eyes, I couldn't lie and say she wasn't beautiful, but this woman was wrong. And how she stared at my *Aeternum* let me know she would be the first to die tonight. The smile that formed on her lips when Thomas growled stretched wide as she licked plump lips and showed pointed teeth. The warm brown of her skin with a slight red undertone was flawless as long as you could look past the tattoos covering her body.

"Thomas. It has been an age since I have tasted you. I see that you have brought back what escaped from my box. Tell me, do you require another gift from my box?" Her voice was melodic, and she held an accent that sounded familiar.

I almost took off in her direction if Thomas's clawed hand didn't captured my wrist. I wanted to kill her for even speaking to him, but her words lit a fire deep in my veins as more of my memories unlocked.

"I have brought you nothing, Necromancer. Just tell me, what the fuck are you doing here, Pandora?"

Once he spoke her name, the missing time from when I arrived in this realm to the day I washed on the shores of Maryland slammed back into my mind. The memories that filled my mind almost had me falling to my knees. I remember being taken from the waters and put in place with no lights, no warmth, and barely any life. The memories flashed as I remembered the torcher and the experiments as someone spoke of a prophecy. I gritted my teeth as this woman's voice whispered in my ear about the child I would never see and the love I would never have. My eyes snapped open that instant, and I stared into those eyes as her smile grew wider. Thomas's claws pierced my skin as the sharp pain brought me out of the misery I felt.

"What the fuck have you done, Pandora?"

I knew Thomas had seen everything in my thoughts because we were connected. I didn't know how they knew each other because this bitch stole the life from my very body.

"It seems that we have the same enemy, Thomas. I was summoned here, and when I saw you—"

I didn't want to hear anything she had to say. I ripped my arm from Thomas's grasp and roared. The blast from my sonar hit Pandora so hard that she slammed through the doors of the building. Then all I could hear around us were the howls of wolves as the people of Sunset Port stepped out of the shadows.

"Thomas! What the hell is wrong with them?" I grunted. The people of Sunset Port stared out of eyes as black as night and were covered in the same tattoos as Pandora.

"I don't know how this is possible. We will find your child, Remi," Thomas gritted. Pandora was back on her feet as red energy balls formed in her hands.

"*Zammiuntau* thinks of betraying me, but he is mistaken if he thinks a pup like you could kill me. Thomas, have you ever wondered about the essence? Has that ever crossed your mind? A Livyatan and the essence from the bloodline of a Dire Wolf. Such powerful children I created and ones you will never see again. Kill them!"

They spoke *Nahuatl*, an Uto-Aztecan language, and I knew it wasn't a language that was used in this realm any longer. I remember my brother telling us about this language and what it could do. I shook my head as the memories assaulted me.

"Remi!" Thomas growled. His voice snapped me out of my head and focused me on the here and now. The markings on her skin were glyphs that meant death. Which meant her loyalty was to the God and Goddess of Death. She was an acolyte of the R'lyehan!

"You were never supposed to wake!"

Before I moved, I heard a growl and saw Thomas aiming for a wolf's head that came at me. The others surged at Thomas as well, but I would be damned if they would touch him. I moved quickly and came up on the left of another shifter that tried to use curved claws to swipe at Thomas. I had the Hydranodic Blade in my palm in a split second. I didn't know how Oceayn managed to take this through the gate, but I wouldn't complain. I'd had it strapped to my leg, but it took nothing for me to grab it and slice one of the dead shifters across the chest. The shifter hissed in pain as the metal burned the flesh. This metal was the only thing known to be poisonous to the black fluid that ran through their veins.

"We need to get to the children," Thomas growled. I did a swift kick, knocking another shifter out of the way as I spun and dropped to a knee. I swiped out, slamming a hardened fist into the reaching corpse's stomach. The shifter flew into the crowd, slamming hard into a wolf that leapt at Thomas. I saw Thomas grab a large brown and gray wolf. He slammed it to the ground, making a path directly to Pandora.

I stood up from the ground quickly and darted toward that bitch as she began throwing energy blasts in our direction. I gripped the blade tightly as I dodged a large woman who tried grabbing me around the waist. I heard flesh tear as Thomas ripped the woman open. That was when I felt the power shift, and I ducked. Thomas had shifted into his massive wolf as he leaped over my head and crashed into Pandora, knocking her back inside the building. I stood up and spun around to face the dead shifters. I raised my hands, pulling in the water particles from the air. I waved a hand, creating a barrier between them and us. I was breathing hard, and I felt the drain on my energy. I knew I had been out of the water for far too long. This barrier would only hold for so long but should be long enough to beat the answers I needed out of Pandora. I ran through the debris to find an angry Thomas holding a smiling Pandora by the throat. He had the Necromancer against the wall, and I could tell by the imprint in the wall that she was slammed against it.

"What the fuck did you do?" Thomas growled. My entire body shook from the strain of holding the barrier and the knowledge of what was done to me.

"It's already too late. Either you can try to figure out how to kill me, or you can try to save your daughter."

I was in front of Pandora before I thought about it. I slammed the blade into her shoulder, causing her to scream.

"Where the fuck is she?" I roared. I could feel my mouth stretch wider as my teeth sharpened to points. Pandora's screams turned into deep, husky laughter as her gray eyes began to turn the same blood red as her pupils.

"You can not kill me this way, and you know that, Thomas. He has tried Rehema," she hissed. The black tattoos moved along her skin, and I wondered why the blade wasn't doing more to harm this bitch. "Either let me go or lose the chance to save your child."

"I think you have been in that box too long because you should know not to fuck with me. It would be best if you also never took your eyes away from your enemies. That could be deadly," Thomas growled. A pulse of blue energy burst from his hand, wrapped around her throat.

"Wha...what is this? You shou...shouldn't hav—," Pandora cried. Her eyes grew wider as she began to panic.

"Drop her! Do it now, or I will rip out their throats!" I was so intent on Pandora's pain and whatever Thomas was reading from her mind that I didn't hear Darlena behind us. Thomas and I turned around to see Darlena and two other shifters holding the pups we came here to rescue. "If I see a twitch, they are dead!"

"Thomas," I whispered. I knew he could reach for their wolves and make them submit.

"I can't," he growled.

"Let her go," Darlena growled. Her fingers dug into one child's neck, causing him to scream in fear. Pandora's irritating laugh made me twist the blade violently before pulling it free from her shoulder. Thomas released the Necromancer, letting her feet hit the floor before stepping away. I reached out swiftly and grabbed Pandora by the hair before looking at Darlena. I placed the tip of the blade on her chest.

"You let them go," I gritted. I didn't have time for this when I knew my child needed me. The thought was so outrageous that I didn't know how to keep it together. I could feel the same emotion coming from Thomas and the anger. I felt it when Thomas's anger won out, and all that was left was the wolf that took the heads of his enemies. I threw the blade before anyone saw my hand move, just as Thomas slammed a blue-rimmed hand into Pandora's chest.

"No!" Pandora screamed. I moved and slapped the wolf holding the other child as Darlena's body hit the floor. That's when I felt the barrier break. I looked back at Thomas, and we moved as one, just as all the undead town of Sunset Port came at us.

OCEAYN

My mind ran rampant once Remi and Thomas left the house. It only got worse when Talika came running down the stairs after a sudden sensation passed through my body. My anxiety went up another notch, putting me on high alert. Thomas put out a call for her to come to him, causing me to guess they found out the information they needed. I pulled out another blade, but it wasn't the same as what I gave to Remi. This blade was a typical metal, but with one difference, I poisoned the tip with my own venom. I sucked my teeth, feeling the curved fangs that hid in the back of my mouth. I hated what I had become, but at least it gave me the power to help Remi while in this realm. Giving Remi that blade was the only thing I could think of to give her every advantage to win against Idhan. What was his end game when it came to these children? I couldn't understand why he was messing with these shifters or how didn't I sense him this close. I ran my hands up and down my arms, hating the feel of my skin and wishing I had escaped long before Nakeema dug her poisoned tentacles into me.

I shook my head and went up the stairs to check on the little one, Meesha, and to see if Howard may need anything for Sam. Once I got to the top landing, I looked down the hall as a door opened and Howard stepped out, looking pale. I could tell all of this weighed on the male, and I wished there was something else I could do to help them. I knew there wasn't too much I could do in my state, but now that Remi was here, maybe we could lead Idhan away from these people. Howard looked up, and I could tell my appearance startled him slightly. I drew in a breath, and he walked toward me while rubbing his tired eyes.

"Is Lika here?" he asked. He stopped a few feet away from me like he didn't want to get too close. Howard and Gina weren't as bad as the other shifters. They didn't treat my appearance with disdain but were still wary.

"No, she had to run out and do something for the Alpha," I answered. "How is Samuel doing? I was coming to check on you all," I asked.

"He...he's resting. I haven't seen any more of that black blood, but...I don't know. Did Lika leaving have anything to do with finding those bastards that helped kidnap my son?" Howard growled. His slim frame shook slightly as he gripped the wooden railing tightly.

"I'm not sure, but we will know more when Lika returns. I can see if—"

"No, no, I understand. That isn't even the reason why I was looking for her in the first place. Do...do you mind watching Sam until my Mate or I come back? I want to check on her and my other pups. I need to update her in person and—"

Howard trailed off, but I understood what he needed without him having to say it aloud.

"I get it. We all need a moment to think by ourselves. I am not going anywhere and will watch Sam. Lika will be back soon, I am sure,"

"If anything happ—"

"If anything of the slightest happens to Sam, you will be the first to know," I stated. Howard hesitated for a moment but then nodded.

"Thank you. I won't be too long," Howard said. He looked at the closed door where Sam was sleeping and back at me.

"It will be fine. Do what you need to do and get back when you can. I will be here," I said. Another door opened, and the little girl who came here with Remi peeked her head out. Howard looked behind himself and then back to me with a nod.

"Okay. I won't be long," he said. He was down the stairs in a matter of seconds, and I heard the door close as I walked over to Meesha.

"Are you okay?" I asked. I didn't get too close because I knew my snake-like appearance frightened adults, so children weren't too much different. There were a few like Sam who wasn't afraid of me, but many who ran. I found it odd because these shifters turned into monsters themselves.

"Oceayn, where are Remi and Thomas? Did they go to the Ocean?" she asked with wide brown eyes. She looked almost afraid of the answer, and it caused me to rush forward. I lifted her in my arms and walked her back inside the room.

"Oh, they will be back, sweetie. They went to another town, not the ocean," I soothed. I lay her back on the queen-sized bed, but she grabbed my hand before I could pull away.

"Can you sit with me?"

"Of course," I said with surprise. I blinked a few times before settling on the bed as she scooted over, making room for me. "Tell me all about the water world," Meesha giggled. Looking at this little girl, I cocked my head to the side and tried to figure out why she would ask something like that.

"How...how do you know about a water world?"

"I dream about it every night. I swim and swim but never tire of it. I could stay under the water forever if I wanted to, just like you and Remi. She's always there with me in the dream, but she is so big, like a giant shark," she laughed.

"More like a whale in this realm. Well, the pre-historic kind," I said absently. Why was this shifter child dreaming of the sea or able to see the Livyatan? I stared into her eyes and saw something familiar as she stared back at me.

"Can you tell me about it?" I took a breath and realized I hadn't spoken of my home in so long that I forgot how much I loved it. I shook my head because whatever nibbled at the back of my mind seemed to fade away for the moment. I smiled at Meesha, unable to resist telling her what she wanted to know.

"Yes, yes, I can."

The more I spoke to this child, the more I felt as if I had known her once before.

"So, do you change into a water snake?"

I blinked a few times and smiled because, if only. I had never shifted, but that never stopped my developing gifts. I never expected that my *Livyatan* would be used in this way and able to change my outside appearance.

"Ahh, no. I could never shift," I said. Meesha's eyes got huge, but she reached out and patted my hand.

"It's okay. I can't change yet, either. I love my bear form, but I want to be able to change into my other form. But it is not time yet," Meesha sighed. I knew I was staring at her like she was insane, and that's when I saw it. Meesha turned her head to the side and began to play with her ear. She pulled at it, revealing a small, slightly raised symbol. The mark shouldn't have been there and not on this child. Remi's mark was barely noticeable unless you were looking for it, but it was in the same place but on the opposite side. The mark was a small sun with two circles on the inside with a straight line coming from the circle in the center. No one in this realm other than Rehema and her brother should carry it. I sucked in a breath because either she was the child of Yammi or Remi. If she was Remi's daughter, why didn't she know?

"Meesha, where are your parents?" I asked tentatively. Her big brown eyes, slightly larger than other shifter children, stared at me.

"My first parents died. I'm just waiting for my other parents to wake up," she whispered. I didn't know exactly what to say or if I should even take this seriously. I looked down but could not unlearn the knowledge I had just learned.

She had the royal mark of Zhavia.

"Do you know who your other parents are?"

"I'm sleepy now," Meesha yawned.

I swallowed as she snuggled into the pillows and closed her eyes. I stood up, and I pulled the blankets over her tiny body. I walked to the door but looked back, still not believing what I saw. Meesha's eyes were open, and she stared out the window into the night. I knew she stared toward the ocean because I would do the same. I turned away and slipped out of the room, closing the door behind me. I tried controlling my breathing when I heard the door open and could scent Lika. I could taste the anger and sadness that surrounded her as she made her way up the stairs. I had to stand guard at this door until Remi returned. If Meesha was who I thought she was, then the royal line had continued, giving me hope that all was not lost.

Thomas

Pandora slammed a burning red energy blast at my face, and I deflected it with the blue glow of my power. I had never openly used this gift before, but the look on Pandora's face told me she knew something about it. I always thought it was a taint leftover from her, but the reaction I had just gotten from her said that she was shocked. What the fuck did she know about this darkness inside me if she wasn't the one who put it there? I dropped to the floor as a male shifter swung a fist at my head. I came up with my claws extended and slashed him across the stomach before kicking him in the chest. He slammed back into another wolf that was heading toward Remi. I saw Remi trying to keep the teeth and claws away from the children hiding behind her, and it was getting harder by the second. The pups were screaming, but they used whatever was in reach to fight off any wolf that came close to their corner of the room. I dropped low as another wolf leaped at me with blood-slicked tan fur and maddened black eyes. I immediately met the giant wolf, ensuring it never reached Remi or the children. The growling rang in my ears as claws dug into my flesh. I slashed out with my clawed hand, taking its head off. Thick reddish black blood covered my hand that smelled of death and evil.

My mind was still reeling at what I saw flashing through Remi's mind and the words that spilled from Pandora's lips. It was impossible, yet she did ask for my essence in exchange. I thought nothing of it, just glad it wasn't a blood vow. I knew it was so much worse than my actions have put a child in danger, not just any child but mine and Remi's child. The thought was staggering, but I didn't have another second to think about it as Pandora screamed. Wings unfurled from her back, but Remi let another sonar blast rip through the space directing it to slam into Pandora's newly formed wings, and they collapsed. I had to do everything I could to stop her from escaping, but these pups came first. The children always came first, no matter what the hell was happening.

I twisted into the air as we landed on the ground in a crush of wolves' undead bodies.

"Remi!" I roared as I rolled over. I felt teeth sink into my legs as more wolves rushed inside, reaching out for me with black, soulless eyes. I could feel no souls inside them, just dead bodies used by that bitch Necromancer. "Remi! Get the children out of here!"

"I got this, Thomas! We need to end this and get her before she escapes," she growled. I looked up, seeing Pandora getting to her feet, helped by the dead she created. Remi was right. This needed to end here and now. We had to get these pups out of here alive and find our baby. I jumped into the air and began leaping from shoulder-to-shoulder of the shifters who stood between us.

"I'm coming! We will not fight alone!" I roared. I took the head of a wolf that leaped for my throat. I kicked at the soulless *Beings* and used the blue energy as a whip to take their heads clean off their shoulders. I didn't know how I formed this energy, but it worked effectively on the dead shifters. Remi's teal eyes grew darker, and I knew she saw Pandora. I could feel the energy in the space and knew she was creating a way out of here.

"Do not let them live! Fight until you are no more!" Pandora screamed. With those words, the dead shifters seemed to gain more strength than they should've been able to possess. I leaped into the air but saw Pandora turn in that instant. She smiled while raising her hands and sending two black bolts of power.

"No! No!" Remi screamed. I felt a rippling blast pass through my body just as something solid slammed into me. "Ahh!" Remi roared, and I knew she'd just taken the Necromancer bolts for me. Both of our bodies slammed to the floor at the same time. Everything went quiet except the whimpers of the children as they cried. I pushed myself up ad looked around, not seeing any blood, bodies, or Pandora anywhere. I knew she had gotten away, but the fine dust in the air that covered every inch of this place told me that Remi had killed them all.

"Remi," I growled. I turned around, looked at the floor, and saw her covered in white dust. The dark brown of her skin was covered, but I could see the dark magic seeping into her skin. She screamed from the pain and I knew I had to do something. My Mate was dying, and I didn't know what to do to save her from something like this.

"Get the children. We need to—"

Her voice faltered, but it was enough to snap me out of my thoughts. I moved to the pups, and they ran to me from the corner.

"Alpha!"

"We need to go. I will get you home," I told the children as I gathered them close. My heart was slamming in my chest because I could feel Remi's pain as if it were my own. I had to get us out of here and fast.

"It feels like it's trying to cover my body, or that bitch Necromancer is trying to come for my soul.

"I will never let it happen," I growled. I was the one who took souls, not the other way around. Pandora should know that Remi or I would never give up this easily. I saw the blackness creeping over her eyes as I lifted her into my arms.

"Alpha? We can shift. We will keep up," the young girl pup said. They were both shaking, but I could see the yellow gaze of their wolves shining through. After surviving something like this, I wasn't surprised they were willing to fight.

I could feel Remi's pain, knowing I would level Silent Hill to the ground. There wasn't a reason the True Alpha needed to come to Sunset Port any longer, and I knew he wouldn't want the evil here to linger. Ever since coming to this damn state, it had been one thing after another. Still, we were maybe one step closer to why we came here. But even with that, there were more questions than answers. I walked closer to the pups and squatted with Remi in my arms.

"We have to find her, Thomas. If Idhan knows about her, he will–" She gritted.

"We need to heal you, and then we will find our child. If I have to summon her ass, I will get the answers," I growled. I looked at the children and tried to smile. "Sam made it home, and you three will as well," I said. "Avery, can you shift for me? I need you to keep up with me, okay?"

"Yes, Alpha," she said. I looked at the other two, who were younger than her, and I knew they could probably not shift into wolf form long enough.

"Jonas and Kendall, I need you both on my back. Hold on tightly," I said. The two jumped as howling filled the night, and I knew the rest of the wolves were coming. There was no way the entire town was down, and Pandora made sure they would keep coming until they all died. "Hurry," I growled.

They both climbed on, and I felt arms and legs wrap around my neck and waist. I looked down, and the small tan and brown wolf stared at me with lemon-colored eyes. I ran out of the building at a fast jog, and Avery had no problem keeping up with me. We raced through the trees, trying to get far enough away before calling someone for help. It wasn't safe being on that land, and I knew at any moment Pandora could return. I couldn't help but think about why she was so afraid of a power I believed came from her. I was missing something just as I was missing the fact that I had a child. Where the hell was she, and how would we find her before the demon? I almost stopped in my tracks at my thoughts about the child. How in the hell did I not sense her in this world? I couldn't think about it until I got all four children to safety and saved my Mate.

They were all touched by the evil of that Necromancer and the demon. We still didn't know what Idhan had to do with this, but when I caught him, I would rip out his throat, too. Sunset Port was cursed, and nothing but the undead roamed this place now. We just had to make it off this land, and they shouldn't be able to follow. At this point, I was glad I did read Dimitri's books. I saw the shifters dipping in and out of the shadows. I could hear the other wolves behind us. I knew they were trying to cut us off, but I couldn't outrun them. If I did, I would leave Avery behind, and that would not happen. I felt the moment a wolf leaped toward us. I spun around and dropped to my knees as four more wolves leaped at me.

I pulled the blade from Remi's grasp and caught one shifter in the neck and another across the stomach. The smell of rotten blood spilled to the ground as Avery barked. At last, they fell to the ground as the rest of the undead wolves stood in front of me. They stared through me with their black eyes and fangs down at two wolves then turned back to face us. I noticed they waited for the others to get closer, so we were outnumbered with nowhere to turn.

As I did before, I felt for the power inside but stopped when I felt enormous energy that caused the wolves to back away. A gate formed between two shifters, making the temperature rise. It glowed a dark blue mixed with black symbols that seemed to rip a hole in reality. I knew it wasn't Pandora coming back to finish us off, just like I knew that the Succubus on the other side of that gate was good nor evil. She was something altogether different. Her long tail whipped out, striking the two wolves, causing them to disintegrate where they stood. One long honey brown leg stepped out wearing a red heel. The rest of Shannara Cane stepped through with eyes burning a laser blue as she flashed her fangs at the rest of the undead shifters. Her horns reached for the moon as if they could touch it, and her wingspan extended at least ten feet. She was taller than I was in this form, standing at least eight-feet without the heels. The red leather body suit hugged her curves like it was a second skin as she strolled forward with a scowl. Shannara held out one hand as a ball of intense blue energy formed in her palm.

"Die," she growled.

The light exploded out of her clawed hands. I felt the energy slam into me, and I thought she had killed us all. The power passed over all of us while slamming into the Necromancer-infected shifters. Their screams as they burned sounded as if being dead wasn't strong enough to hide from the pain of Shannara's fire. I didn't know where my power had come from, but after seeing this and feeling the energy, I knew exactly who to ask. I thought the darkness of this power came from the night I made the deal. It became present only after my night with the Necromancer, and that's when I knew what I had done was a mistake. I could feel the power and life that it could bring. But also, I could feel the death and destruction it could cause. The bright blue light died out just as suddenly as it lit up the night, leaving everything now bathed in moonlight. My skin felt cool, and the energy inside me seemed to quiet down like when I was inside Sinful Secrets. I knew that it wasn't Sinful Secrets that gave me that quiet now. It was Shannara. But how?

I searched my soul deep and felt my wolf, then reached out, feeling the creature that was my Mate's soul.

"Thomas, tell me why it felt as if you were dying, only to show up here and see creatures being controlled by a Necromancer surrounding you. I thought you would have learned a valuable lesson after dealing with them," Shannara said. She looked around and sucked her teeth when she saw the children whimpering. She rolled her laser blue eyes and let her wings fold away as she shifted into her human-like form.

"I don't have time, Shannara. Remi is hurt. My Mate is dying," I gritted. I got back to my feet and started moving once more. "Thank you for your help, but I need to get back and find out what I need to do to save her," I stated. I had so many questions but still not enough time. The raw dark power that ran through her veins should have given me pause but not tonight.

"Why didn't you just say so, Thomas? You know I like you enough to do you a favor," Shannara said. She reached down and scooped up the wolf pup as she waved a hand in a circle forming another gateway. "To the Jamison Pack, I presume. They smell of that Pack," Shannara smiled before stepping through the gate. I took the offered gift of help, knowing full well I would have to pay for it in the future. Shannara always collected on her debts. If you did not pay, your soul would be collected. We stepped through the gate, and everything went black before a burst of blue color filled my eyes, and we stepped out and stood in front of the house we were calling home for the time being.

"If you want to save her, then you need to accept all you are, Thomas."

"Who the hell are you, and don't tell me I already know?"

"These questions can be answered later. The only thing you should be concentrating on is your Mate."

Shannara looked from me and then to Remi as the door from the house flew open. I ensured the pups were on the ground as Lika and Oceayn came running from the house.

"You can not heal her here. You know where you should go."

"How the hell can I heal her?"

"You hold a power that may be dark in nature, but it also contains life with the right intent."

I turned around, but Shannara was already stepping back into the open gate she had created.

"If you pull through, out this situation, then you more than deserve what little answers I can provide."

The gate closed within seconds, and she was gone. I didn't give a shit about the answers if my Mate died. I would not let that shit go down because I needed her more than I'd believed. Everything was happening so fast, yet it was like we danced around it because my wolf and her Orcinus already knew we belonged to one another. Now we have a child to find, and I was going to make sure that happened.

"Thomas," Remi cried. A sharp pain filled my mind, body, and soul. I looked at Lika. I waited as her eyes met mine, and I saw something in them I couldn't understand.

"Get them to their parents. I need to save Remi," I stated. I turned and ran toward the scent of the ocean, knowing full well my Mate was dying in my arms.

The warm water crashed against my legs as I waded deeper into the ocean. Deep down, I felt this would be the only thing to help. I did not know what Shannara meant about intent or what the hell my power could do to fix this.

"You hold the darkness just as I do in your blood. It's something we have in common but doesn't define us. It can't have you! Listen to your Alpha, little princess. Fight back, or I will make you."

I could feel the inky blackness moving through her veins. My voice was guttural, and I heard a pain I never thought I would be capable of feeling.

"Fuck you, Thomas. I told you to stop calling me that."

"But it got you to listen. I need you to fight, or you can take the punishment if I have to save you alone."

I sank deeper into the black waters, not caring if I would never breathe again if I couldn't save her. I was a shifter and Alpha, so I could hold my breath for a long time but not indefinitely. I looked for the power deep inside my mind. Deep in my soul as my wolf stared back at me with glowing indigo eyes. The light inside me I used to push inside Remi faded as the darkness grew.

"Aww, the poor little Seahorse believes he can give his elder orders. Why fight? I have nothing left. No home, no family, nothing. Let me go."

The words Remi spoke weren't hers, and I knew it. Whatever was trying to take hold of her was twisting everything she had suffered into despair. Fuck that!

I felt my anger explode as I reached for that power one more time. It glowed and warmed at the pure anger I felt for Pandora and everyone who puts us in this situation.

"Thomas, it has me. I can't—"

I could feel my lungs straining and we still hadn't hit the bottom of the sea bed. It didn't matter if I couldn't pull her away from death. I grabbed ahold of the energy, and the darkness of the water lit up from the blue energy revealing everything around us as we sank into its depths. I wrapped her tighter in my arms as the energy, that felt strangely like what Shannara was using, built into my body. The light shone with my eyes and spilled from my mouth. I felt my shift into the third form, but I wasn't in full control over it. I was more like a man, but my hands were clawed, and my canines lengthened. My light brown skin turned the same shade as my fur. I leaned down, placing my mouth over Remi's, and pushed. I shoved the energy inside her body, and I could feel it beginning to burn. Remi's body felt like it was burning up from the inside out. I knew what happened when

Shannara released that attack, and those wolves fell to the ground. I knew I could be the one to kill her, but I also knew just how strong Rehema was, and she would make it.

"You will fight Rehema. You will submit to this power and live. Now, say yes, Alpha."

I waited for what felt like hours for her voice to fill my mind. I could feel the death magic eating away at her soul, but I refused to let it gain more ground. I pushed harder, not caring when my skin began to crack, and blue energy flowed from the wounds.

"Yes. Yes, Alpha."

Remi

I felt the pain in my body, mind, and soul. But what pushed through all that was Thomas's words and the feeling of the ocean's depths. I'd known him for a few years, which was a minute compared to the time I had spent alive. Not having memories of who and what I was blocked my Aeternum from me, and I didn't know. Thomas didn't know either, but our souls knew who we were to each other. That's how Thomas knew what I needed and brought me to the closest thing to home. Everyone talked about prophecy and fate, but this mission confirmed what we should have known all along. If we fought together and if I stood by his side, none of this would matter because together, our powers were more extraordinary than whoever came at us. We had a child that needed us, and they would be left vulnerable if I didn't fight through this bullshit. Not only would that child be left alone, but Meesha as well. I would not have that. Thomas wouldn't let me go. If I didn't eliminate this Necromancer's magic out of my body, he would die with me. Thomas knew that, and he knew I would fight for him. Idhan was still out there. If I knew anything, he would not stop until my bloodline was eradicated and he owned me.

"Nothing will stop the spread. You may be powerful just like Zam-miuntau has foretold, but your weakness will always be those you love."

Pandora's sultry voice filtered through my mind, making it harder to concentrate as a burning sensation began spreading through my body.

"You were nothing when I took you, and you will continue to be nothing now. I have taken the best of you and made the perfect vessel. One with the power from two realms."

What did Pandora want with my realm, and how did she know where to find me? I didn't have time for the questions because I knew that this was an effort to distract me from fighting through this magic trying to eat me alive. I could feel the death trying to claw its way to my Orcinus, and I could feel that spirit fighting. I knew my limits, and I knew my power. With Thomas by my side, I knew this thing could not get the best of me.

"I'm inside of you, and I have had the essence of your Mate. I have the information you crave and the knowledge you need for your child. You are on the wrong side of this fight, and it's time for you to choose. Join me, and I will reunite you with the child you lost," Pandora whispered.

I could hear the sneer in her voice and taste the lie she spoke. I could feel her moving through my mind and trying to capture my soul for her own, but I wasn't going out like that. I laughed at her play on my emotions and her willingness to dangle my child in front of me. She didn't fucking know the Alpha that was mine inside this realm, or me. Pandora didn't know Thomas as well as she believed. He would go after her until he took her bitch ass down. She would never give me any answers about my child. A child that Pandora stole from me when I was weak, but her desperation also showed. Whatever power Thomas possessed scared her enough to hesitate. I knew she could feel it coming. The burning in my body grew with each second. I felt like it would consume the entirety of my body, mind, and soul. Compared to this pain, her magic meant nothing to me.

"You think that wolf will come for you? Remember, he didn't trust you, so why would things change now? He has darkness inside him just as much as I do. You are a bottom feeder and a waste of power. You can't even remember how to shift. I took that away from you. You will never retrieve the knowledge of that again."

Her power squeezed my insides, but I pushed back, trying to clear my thoughts so I could set her undead-loving ass straight. I could still feel Thomas' power and my own power. The thought of him was helping me through this, meant I had to fight. I had to see him again, and I refused to let my child and Meesha down. I had to finish this mission because I knew if this Necromancer had her way, everyone and the thing I loved would crash and burn. I may have lost my family back in Hyquadra, but I had found another one. I couldn't let them down, or let the love I never expected down. I reached for the Orcinus as the teal light surrounding my inner thoughts flashed brightly. I fought back, knowing whatever else that bitch had to say meant nothing.

"You don't know me just because you had a few minutes in my mind, Pandora. You think you know all there is to a Being like me because you held me captive and used me to produce a vessel? You don't know my bloodline if you think you can take my soul. Well, you will learn something new today, Pandora. All Livyatan love the taste of dark magic, and now that I can truly feel my soul, I will love swallowing you whole."

I let loose a scream of pain laced with determination as I delved into the mind and soul of a Necromancer. I felt almost boxed in, but I knew it was just a construct of her energy. What I saw inside this *Being* was something more monstrous than I'd thought. She wasn't the first, and I knew she would not be the last. I saw endless and senseless death in a world covered in darkness as a black box blocked out the sun. I roared into my mind as the blackness tried its best to claw its way into my heart and soul. The healing blue light from Thomas was fading fast. I could feel him dying, and I knew

I had to hurry. As my body grew fifty feet long, I felt myself begin to shift. I dove into the Necromancer's thoughts and soul just as she did mine, and began to let my Orcinus feed. Their blood, bodies, and souls were tainted by the dark magic that filled them. That was the secret to Zhavia's family powers. Consume our enemies make their power ours. I could hear and feel Pandora chanting as she tried to break through to cause my brain to rupture and my heart to stop.

Bright blue and teal lights flashed. All I could feel was my Orcinus feeling freed. The rows of sharp dagger-like teeth in my mouth were ready to tear Pandora apart. I felt my jaws open so vast I knew I could swallow this energy whole. I felt the blast of power slam into me stronger than it was before. I saw a vision of Pandora holding a box that seemed more like a black hole. The markings glowed scarlet and vermilion as the magic slammed against me again. I watched this thing devour worlds after it subjugated and destroyed every living thing that stood up against it. I didn't know how they beat that bitch back the first time, but it took someone strong to hold that seal closed.

"YESSS. I like you. Mmmm, the box will be pleased and show you what true power truly tastes like. Your blood will serve well."

The voice came from everywhere and nowhere. The language was something not from this realm or mine, but it forced its way into my mind. I felt Thomas's power fill me as it rolled over me. I felt like it embraced me as it pushed Pandora and that fucking box out of my mind. I shook my head as I floated into the depths of the sea. The blue light burst around me as everything went dark again. I felt the moment the dark energy dissipated from my system, and the scent of Thomas seemed to settle inside of me. I felt my own power like I hadn't in a long time as I moved through the waters. I knew this much energy, and my shift would call out to Idhan. I knew I didn't have time to stay in this form, but the water felt so good and called to a part of my soul that I had forgotten.

Thomas.

I didn't know where he was, and the ocean was vast. I focused and knew I was further away from the shore and him. I did not know how far he sank below or what happened to him when I shifted. I knew I had to find him and get back to shore. We still had a mission to accomplish, a Pack to look after, but most importantly, a child to find. I felt energy much like my own, but it was softer and younger. I knew it wasn't Oceayn, but the familiar sense I got from it called out to me. I moved in that direction, making my way to the teal light I could see glowing in the distance.

"Remi!"

I heard a cry in my mind, but when I tried to answer back, I got nothing but silence. The voice sounded like it could be Meesha, but I knew that had to be impossible. Once I was closer, I would have thought I stared into a mirror. If the mirror only showed a miniature version of myself, I would have believed it. She had the same black and white coloration and the tiny dorsal fin with a sleek, streamlined body and teal eyespot located just above but slightly behind each eye. As soon as I looked at her, I knew what she was, and it took my breath away. How was this possible? How didn't I see this before?

"Meesha?"

I knew she could hear me. She had to hear me, but didn't know exactly how to respond. That's when I noticed the teal glow coming from her blowhole. Thomas's body was wrapped in that glow as she began to rise to the surface. I didn't know what type of power that was, but I knew it had to have come from both of us. I wasn't far behind Meesha, but I had already transformed into my usual form once I reached the top of the water. I began to swim toward Meesha as she tried to haul Thomas's body out of the water. She shook like a leaf, and I managed to make it to her before she fell to the sandy beach. I grabbed Thomas's body and pulled him further from the water. I panicked because I didn't know how long we had been in the ocean. I didn't know how long he could've held his breath. He may be an Alpha, but it didn't mean he was invincible.

"Meesha! Baby, wha—" I panted. My hands were rimmed in a teal glow, and I slammed my fist onto Thomas's chest. Meesha crawled toward us, and I still couldn't wrap my mind around what I saw and how she'd gotten here.

"He's going to live. I save him every time! He can't die!" Meesha cried. His light brown skin seemed pale, but his veins were black. The blackness crawled up his skin, damn near covering his entire body. I wasn't a healer, and I didn't know what the fuck to do about this. I would do whatever I needed to save him, even if that was making a deal with that bitch if she had his soul hostage. I turned, hearing a splashing sound, and covered Thomas's body from further attack. I was ready to rip off heads and tear some shit apart if anything else came at us. I wasn't about to let anything take us.

"Remi." I knew the teal in my eyes grew intense as my mouth began to stretch and my teeth grew to sharp points. "Remi, I can save him." I blinked at the words, realizing that it was Meesha speaking. I hadn't even noticed she'd moved as I tried shoving my own life force into Thomas.

Meesha fell to her knees beside us. Her tiny hands pressed blue, glowing water to his nose and mouth before her big brown eyes stared up at me. "Now do it," Meesha whispered. I swallowed at the intelligent gaze that looked more like me than I had ever noticed. I didn't question her because I could feel the power surrounding us. It felt like life.

"*Olo*, Goddess, please help me," I prayed. I reached deep inside and felt my Orcinus. I grabbed onto it and shoved what made me who I was directly inside Thomas. If I had to give him everything inside of me, that was what I would do. Nothing would ever keep me from my *AETERNUM*, my *eternal*, ever again. I looked down at his face as the black veins stopped moving. They were inches from covering his entire face but began receding. I held my breath and waited to see my Alpha's dark brown eyes with the indigo ring.

"You have only but to ask my child. After all that you have been through, there is no way I can deny such a request. An Aeternum *is an extremely rare thing to find. Do not linger but claim what has been gifted to you."*

I sucked in a breath at the hauntingly beautiful voice that seemed to fill my entire soul. The feeling of a storm at sea crashed into my mind as I felt a kiss on my cheek. I didn't know when I closed my eyes, but when I opened them, I stared at Meesha. She leaned away with a smile, and all I could see was brown with a swirling mix of indigo.

My mind was still reeling from what had happened as we approached the house. Thomas held a sleeping Meesha in his arms. I caught him staring at her several times but didn't say a word. We had one less thing to worry about, but Idhan had to be found. I wanted to get Meesha into bed, to pull Thomas into the room and look him over. I needed to see that he was alive, and then we could figure out what to do next. Thomas and I snapped our heads up to look at the loud door banging open as Lika and Oceayn flew out of the house.

"Oh my Goddess, oh my Godde–"

Oceayn reached my side with wide blue-green slitted eyes. Her bluish-green skin seemed to shimmer as it changed from smooth to scaley.

"It's alright. We are okay, Oceayn," I said. Lika wasn't far behind and immediately went to Thomas's other side. She reached out and pushed Meesha's wet hair from her face.

"We just noticed that she wasn't in her room. We didn't hear a thing and couldn't figure out how she got past us," Lika stated. I could see in her gaze the worry, fear, and anger, but I knew the anger wasn't for Meesha. That was toward herself.

"Lika, I am not sure you could have prevented her from leaving. This isn't your fault," I said. Lika looked up at me and then back to Meesha as she bared her teeth. I knew she heard what I said, but I could tell she was blaming herself for Meesha outside at night alone.

"Talika, you couldn't have known. Meesha seems to have some gifts none of us knew about, but everything is okay now. We have her back and the other children. Many things need to happen soon, but I need to speak with our True Alpha," Thomas said.

"No!" Oceayn shouted. We were at the top of the steps and about to enter the house. We all turned to face her, and I saw it. Oceayn's eyes met mine, and I could tell that she knew. She had figured out what I should have known when I looked at Meesha. My memories were still jumbled, and I was still missing pieces. I knew for sure Meesha was ours, but something still felt off.

"I know, Oceayn. I—"

"How about we get Meesha inside and dried off? We have a lot to talk about, but we understand, Oceayn," Thomas said. I felt calm surround me, and I saw when Oceayn relaxed.

"We will talk about it, I promise. But right now, we need to regroup," I said. Thomas stepped inside, but I still held Oceayn's gaze. I saw the hope and confusion written over her face. I opened my mouth to tell her something or whatever I could remember that was done to me when I felt a sharp pain. I looked inward, but the pain wasn't coming from me. It was

Thomas, and everything I wanted to say died on my tongue. He was still hurting, and I remembered what *Olo* said to me.

Claim what has been gifted to you.

I wasn't expecting to hear from my Goddess, and it surprised me that she answered. How are we all connected? More and more questions but very few answers. It didn't matter right now, though, because she gave me back the life that had just begun.

Thank you.

I took in a deep breath, and Oceayn smiled slightly.

"I have something for you. I knew when I found you that you would like something familiar. We can talk about all this later. The children are safe. You are safe," Oceayn said. She moved and was standing in front of me. She reached out and pulled me into a tight hug. I hugged her back, but I pulled away quickly to go to Thomas and fix the pain.

"Thank you, Oceayn. Thank you for coming after me," I whispered before heading towards the house.

"She has the mark, Remi. Meesha is in line to rule after Yammi and you."

"Goddess. We will make sure she will have a Kingdom to rule one day. We will destroy Idhan, find my brother, and take back our realm."

I smiled at Oceayn before entering the house to find my daughter and my eternity. Lika wasn't downstairs, and neither were Thomas nor Meesha. It didn't matter because now I could feel them both like they were my heartbeat. I hadn't felt my power in years, and now it rushed through my veins. I could feel the difference deep inside my body. Whatever poison Idhan had could take it away again, but I refused to let it happen. When I got to the top of the stairs, I saw Lika leaving the room where Sam was sleeping. Even though the pull to go to Thomas was strong, I couldn't move until I spoke to Lika.

"Sam is still sleeping. I need to check on the prisoners and—"

"Lika, this was not your fault. None of this is your fault. You can not protect everyone," I said. I placed a hand on her smooth brown cheek, and she leaned in slightly. She blinked a few times and pulled away.

"I know I will be an Alpha. If I can't take care of anyone here now, how will I take care of a Pack?"

I stared into her brown eyes and saw the teal ring surrounding her pupil glow for a second.

"You still have ways to go, Lika. No one expects you to be able to do all of this yourself when you become Alpha to a Pack. That is another reason why we are here," I stated. I could feel Thomas's presence behind me before I felt a hand on the back of my neck. It trembled slightly, and I had to find out why.

"Remi is right. You will have training and guidance to become the Alpha we all know you will be. Now, I need you to get the word out. We all will meet in the hall at dawn, and Pack Law will decide the fate of those Pack members you gathered."

Lika stood straighter and was taller than me by a few inches. I could see her doubts clearly as Thomas spoke and knew this was what she needed.

"Yes, I can get all that done, but...but I am worried about Sam."

"Oceayn will be here, and I am sure his parents are coming back soon. He will be fine here until you can return," Thomas said. I saw Lika's eyes glance at the cracked door of Meesha's room. She shifted her feet and bit her lip.

"It will be fine, Lika. Your Alpha needs you to do something for your Pack. What are you going to do?" I asked. Her hard brown eyes looked down at me, and I saw the Alpha rise inside her.

"I will take care of it," Lika said, looking at Thomas. I felt his nod, and Lika made her way out the door.

"Will she be okay? She is taking this hard as if she failed," I sighed. Thomas turned me around, and then I saw it. The pain in his eyes seemed to scream at me.

"She will do what is needed. Lika will be fine, and once Alex gets here to begin her training, she will be great. She will be an Alpha we will be proud to know. I can feel it," he said.

"What about Meesha?" I asked.

"I don't think we will know anything until she wakes up. I only know that she is ours, no matter how it happened. We need to get cleaned up, and then we need to plan out the next steps. Let's go," he said. I followed him into the master bedroom and then to the white marble bathroom suite connected to the room. "Get in the shower, Remi. I need to check you over to ensure you have no wounds," Thomas growled. His eyes watched me, but he was trippin' because I needed to look his sexy ass over. He was the one who died! My heart lurched and then stopped for a second. I could have lost him when I just got him.

"Thomas, I need to check you out," I scoffed.

"Rehema, take off those wet clothes and get your ass in the damn shower. Do you understand a command when it's given?"

I raised a brow, but his growl was low, and his power caressed my skin, making my clit throb. His eyes traveled down my body as he took in a deep breath. He reached around me and turned the knobs so the water would flow. The shower was massive and could probably fit at least six people comfortably. The heat from his body made my heart speed up, and I knew if I just did what he said right now, I could do what I needed to do. He was hurt, and I was going to find out where.

"Yes, Alpha," I moaned. I didn't mean to moan it that way, but when his hand snaked up my chest, and his hand closed around my throat, I couldn't help but do what he asked.

"Good."

REMI

I removed my clothes and dropped them on the floor as Thomas watched. I ensured he could inspect my back as I stepped inside the shower. I let the hot water run down my body as I turned to face him. He began to strip, and I watched him barely breathing as he revealed smooth honey-brown skin. I didn't see a mark on his body, and I ran my eyes over his muscled chest, thick arms, and slim waist. I didn't realize that my hands began roaming over his body as I searched for the cause of his pain. Thomas washed my entire body. His strong hands in my hair prevented me from looking for what caused the squint in his eyes. He pulled my hair back, and I stared up at him.

"You saved me," he whispered against my lips. I ran my soapy hands up his back, and the low growl caused my core to ache for him as his claws grazed my scalp. Thomas pulled my hair tightly and leaned down to capture my lips with his. The kiss pushed a calm inside of me, but I could also feel the raw energy of need. I could feel his wolf growling and pushing against his skin to claim me, to mark me, to make me submit. I wanted all of that, but I was also an Alpha in a way.

"You saved me first," I panted. He pulled away, and I caught him as he swayed. "Thomas?"

"I'm good, little princess. Finish up here, and I will check on Meesha," he said. His fingers slipped from my hair as he stepped back and out of the shower.

"I will check on her as well once I am finished here," I said. I stood under the spray and watched him walk away. Something was up, but I was about to fix it tonight. I had to, because I did not know what tomorrow would bring. I knew what Thomas was to me, and I was sure he knew the same thing. So what was keeping his wolf from claiming me?

After getting out of the shower, I saw something lying on the bed. I already knew what it was and couldn't believe Oceayn had made this. The simple clothing brought a sense of peace because it reminded me of the good days in Hyquadra. There's just something about wearing my natural clothing that made me feel sexy and powerful. It reminded me of where I came from and of who I was. I had no clue how Oceayn managed to make this, but the material was so close to the original that I wouldn't have known the difference if she hadn't told me. The mesh netting of the dress left nothing to the imagination, and I knew wearing it in this realm would cause a commotion. The netting was a different shade of blue that reminded me of the different oceans back home. It clung to my body like a second skin—the design around the nipples resembled the sun, making my nipples the only thing you couldn't see clearly. The tiny white lace thong didn't help much either, because I could still see the trimmed teal hairs between my legs.

I knew Thomas would go wild when he saw it, but I also knew this piece would stun his ass enough that he wouldn't be able to speak. I know it would send him into a frenzy when he saw me. I didn't know what was holding him back, but that shit was going to stop. I wanted his mind on me to push that building darkness inside of him away. He was punishing himself for something that was out of his control. Everything could be managed when you had someone be the light to guide you through it. For him, now that we'd finally caved into accepting that we were made for one another.

Tonight was the night that I was going to take what had always been mine, mine.

The one that was made for me.

The love of my life.

My *Aeternum*. My *Mate*.

I grabbed that light robe and slipped out of the room to check on Meesha. Thomas wasn't there, but I could hear his calming voice below, speaking to other shifters about what would go down in a few hours. I closed the door and moved over to the large bed to find the miracle that was Meesha. I felt the tears on my cheeks, but I brushed them away quickly. She was still asleep, but I couldn't help but push the brown curls from her face and kiss her cheek. She shifted slightly, and a small smile formed on her lips.

"Mama," Meesha whispered.

My eyes widened at the word, but she was still fast asleep. I looked out of the window and noticed that it was cracked. I looked back at Meesha and trembled slightly. The drop from this height was steep, and I didn't know how she managed it. I could still scent her on this window, and I smelled blood. I pushed away from the windows after closing and locking them. I gently pulled the blankets back and saw a deep gash on her left calf. It was already healing, and for her age, that was unusual. Thomas must have cleaned it already, and there wasn't a reason to bandage it. She was already in a healing state, which made sense why she slept so deeply.

I leaned over and kissed her again before I made myself go back to the room so I could get ready for her father. I knew it had become harder for Thomas to hide his emotions from me, and I knew what he was thinking, but I was about to stop that shit here and now. I chose to jump in front of that death strike of Pandora. There was no way I would let more darkness touch him in any way. He believed that darkness lived inside of him, but if that were true, where did the light come from that gave him life? My Livyatan waited for our souls to merge, patiently, to claim what belonged to me. I walked inside the room, closing the doors behind me as I ran my hand over the silky material of the dress.

This mesh dress is like no piece anyone in this realm had ever seen. It was styled like a high-neck dress but made entirely from something close to spider silk. I knew without a doubt that Thomas would probably have difficulty keeping himself in check once he took one look at what I was wearing, and I didn't even blame him. I even did a few poses to ensure it looked good at every angle, loving how it wrapped around my form in the mirror.

It only came down slightly above mid-thigh. I was trimmed, my breasts were fully displayed, and my nipples puckered through the mesh. It made my dark skin stand out alongside my teal eyes while I bit my lip.

Why am I so nervous?

He wanted to teach a lesson, but it was his turn to sit and listen. My orca let out a small cry, seeming to swim in the murk of my brain. She'd been rather anxious the whole night, her animalistic senses telling me something was going to happen, and I wasn't entirely sure if it was good or bad yet. Whatever it was, I knew we could handle it. I knew who the boogeyman was, and now that I had my powers back, I was ready for his ass.

Taking a deep breath, as the doors opened, I immediately met deep brown, impatient eyes. Thomas's gaze whipped over to where I was, almost as if he was scared I would have left. I saw Thomas' eyes widen when he took in what I was wearing.

The temperature rose by a hundred degrees despite the AC being on max to combat the Miami heat.

After seeing all the lingerie in this realm, I knew it couldn't compete with the things we wore daily. It left little to the imagination, to begin with. The blue mesh encasing my luscious, large breasts tightened almost painfully upon hearing a low growl rumble from Thomas's chest.

My nipples protruded through it, aching and calling for his attention as his eyes found mine. His wolf seemed to rise, front and center, by the way his chest let out a low rumble in response to my advances as well.

"Remi, what the *fuck* are you wearing? When did you get that?" Thomas demanded, his nose flared, and his jawline clenched as he ran his hand over his low fade with a growl. The ever so possessive Alpha of my life made me laugh as I swayed my hips toward where he was standing. I pointed to the bed and raised a brow. I waited, but it didn't take long for that pup to get the picture. I moved over to him while he was sitting on the edge of the bed.

"Does that mean you like it?" I said softly, tilting my head playfully to one side while walking closer to him. "It was made for me. It's something we usually wear when we are home. So don't worry. No one saw me naked by any means. Well, aside from myself. Now stop being so Alpha-like and ready to pounce on imaginary people you believe are looking at me. You never cared before."

"I *am* an Alpha, and you fucking know I cared. A lot," he huffed, narrowing his eyes until they were slits, the indigo ring in his pupil seeming to shimmer brightly. "You're lucky that I love you, but you really do know how to play with fire, don't you? Tempting your Alpha like that. Did you want to be tied up and fucked senseless again?"

I shivered, my core clenching rather painfully at the memories of his tongue and the slaps against my clit. I almost immediately thought about those clawed fingers wrapping around my throat. It didn't make it better when he hoisted my long legs over, so I was straddling his lap, his sweats being the only thing separating him from my heated, dripping core. "Thomas..."

"No, I suppose you're in the mood to be disciplined and punished for teasing me, huh?" he snarled, his nose flaring. Then, to punctuate his words, he dug his nails into my thighs, and I could feel electricity zapping through my body.

My body is already accustomed to the pleasure and pain that came with my Alpha. I could feel him inside me as if he still breathed life back into my body. I wanted to give in, and I refused to stop fighting for those I loved.

"Oh, God," I whispered breathlessly.

"That is what you want?" he questioned as his hands slowly went to my hair, fisting and pulling at the end, making me shudder. I could feel his length rocking into my core, making me ache in need of him but not wanting to submit. "You want to be fucked right here, don't you, little princess? You are so wet that you can't wait to be taken hard and deep. You need your Alpha's cum trickling down your thighs?"

"What if I say yes?" I challenged. "Will you fill me up, my *Alpha*?"

His eyes seemed to go even darker before a mischievous smile made it to his face. A whimper escaped my parted lips in the process as his possessive arms snaked around my waist and pulled me down on his thickened member.

I could feel his erection up against me; the rising heat in my core seemed to pulsate as he licked and lapsed on my neck teasingly. My hands slowly made their way over to his hair, tugging him closer.

"You wanted me to live so bad that you gave up some of yourself. How can I repay you for my life and for giving me a daughter?" Thomas whispered in my ear. His nose trailed up the side of my cheek, and then he bit down on my earlobe. The sharp pain made me gasp and crane my neck to the side for more. His canine was extended, and it was as if his tongue grew several inches longer. His warm tongue licked my skin where I knew he wanted to mark me.

"Repay me, but stop thinking me getting hurt is your fault. I can feel the anger about what happened but I chose to do it. You are mine to protect just as much as I am yours to protect. Don't get it twisted, Thomas. You aren't the only Alpha in this room."

His mouth closed on my collarbone, and I felt his teeth hit the spot where his teeth should pierce me. I leaned closer to him as I panted.

I seemed to beg him to claim me for the world to see because I was ready. I wanted to spend eternity with my calm, overbearing, possessive Alpha. He grabbed my wrist, pulling me toward him. Before I could get another word out, my eyes widened as he slammed his lips onto mine. His kiss was powerful, his tongue gliding at the bottom of my lips before I moaned, our tongues meeting in an erotic dance, but he would submit to me. His wolf and he still weren't sure about something, and I would find out.

I was pretty sure I stopped breathing, and I felt him shudder, a growl escaping the back of his throat that made my Orcinus counterpart want to come out and play. My nipples beaded against his broad, muscular chest, and if he swiped right between my legs, he would already notice how embarrassingly wet I was for him. Instead, he deepened the kiss, the rush of heat boiling in my stomach.

We were *maddening* together.

His rough hand cupped my breast through the mesh fabric, and I knew he was seconds away from tearing it soon. I lifted my hips quickly when I felt him tugging off the silky straps of the mesh dress, and I knew he needed me badly as I needed him. I took control of the kiss and pushed him down to the bed. I reached for his arms, using my strength and power, that matched his perfectly. I held him down and lazily licked a trail up his abs to his neck. I knew he could feel the bond, just like I knew the feeling inside him was the need to be one. *Olo* was correct; I needed to claim what was given to me. My teeth began to sharpen into needle points, and I covered his neck. I sucked lightly and bit down just enough to make his thick-length jump.

He knew what I wanted and would take it with little struggle.

My dress pooled down as we pulled away to look at one another. I didn't think Thomas's eyes could even go any darker than they did right now as he stared at me, his eyes lingering over my breasts before he leaned down to capture a hardened bud in his mouth.

His other hand wasted no time kneading one mound with his giant hands. I could only writhe in pleasure as he sucked the nipple in his mouth before letting it go with a loud pop.

"Fuck, Remi! You taste like heaven and sin. This taste is something I will never give up. If we do this, there is no turning back. This is it, Remi."

I leaned away and rolled to the middle of the bed. His eyes followed my every movement. I leaned back onto the pillows and raised one leg. My foot hit his chest, and I reached down to spread my lips as my juices slid down my thighs.

"Hurry up, I need to be fucked," I confessed through heavy eyelids. The command in my voice got his attention. It also brought the Alpha forward. We would see who won this round.

"Do you now?" Thomas growled, his hands slowly slipping between my legs, and hissed. "Fuck, you're so tight and wet for me already, and I barely even touched you, Remi," he groaned, plunging two fingers into my wetness, causing me to cry out. "Who's my good little princess?"

His dirty words make me almost putty underneath him as he went for the other nipple. He alternated between the two, making sure both were lapsed and pointed from his talented tongue. I couldn't help but jump when he nipped me, causing jolts of pleasure and pain to go hand-in-hand. I was practically feeding my breasts to him, wiggling and dancing as his fingers worked an orgasm out of me, yet right before he did, he'd always stop.

"Thomas, hurry," I demanded. "Fuck me already."

Sometimes, both of us being an Alpha, really would be the death of me or would be a source of endless fun. The problems and danger seemed so far away. I only saw and heard Thomas, and my clit throbbed just thinking about his bite, mark, and claim.

"Soon," he murmured against my nipples before resuming what he had been doing before. "When you're coming, it will be around me first, before anything else. Your body needs to know that it's fucking mine. You understand me?"

His length was pressed to me at this point as he withdrew his fingers from my wetness. I watched in a daze as he groaned, lapping up my juices as he slowly teased over my wet folds without the satisfaction of entering me.

Two can play it at that game.

With a loud growl, I push away with force. I moved so fast that I knew I had caught him off-guard. My hand was not as wide and long as his, but I was just as strong. I sat between his legs with my hand wrapped around his throat. I squeezed as my tongue darted out to lick his soft, thick lips.

"Remi," Thomas groaned.

"Someone likes a little pain. Am I right, pup?"

When I moved, I put myself in a position that could force him to the mattress.

"I didn't think I would until I saw you," Thomas said with heavy eyelids. He leaned forward and captured a nipple in his mouth. I gently pushed his talented mouth off my nipples and moved down until I hit the floor. I grabbed his thighs and squeezed, letting him know he needed to move or I would do it for him. I got on my knees, and as he slid down, a hiss escaped his lips when I tugged his sweats off. I wrapped my hands around his hard-as-steel shaft and gave him small, slow pumps. His hips jerked forward against my tiny hands gripping onto him. "You are breathtaking on your knees for me, little princess."

"Alpha," I breathed out. The appraisal only made my muscles clench, the tingling on my clit intensifying. Grabbing the base, I took him entirely into my mouth. The salty taste of his pre-cum flooded my mouth as I eagerly swiped my tongue in hopes of more. I pulled back, and he damn near cried out in protest. My teeth were still sharp and needle-like, so I ran the tips lightly along his length and he bucked up. His hands found their way into my thick curls as he began to try to take over. I sucked hard from base to tip and swirled my tongue over the head while rolling his balls in my hand. I squeezed them slightly.

"Remi! Fuck! Remi, remember what I...oh shi—"

I smiled to myself because I knew he was at the edge, and when I said he could come, it would all be mine.

Mine.

My Mate.

My everything.

My *Aeternum.*

He thrust his hips into my mouth, making me take another inch of him. A whimper escaped as I hummed around his length, making him groan and throw his head back. His large hands tangled into my hair and pulled gently.

"You were teasing me this whole time, so I'll lose my damn mind, huh?" Thomas questioned darkly, and I could barely hear him because I was so focused on what I wanted him to feel. "You want me to be extra rough with you because you want me to show you who owns your mind, body, and soul? You want me to pin you down, fuck you hard, pump my cum into your tight core and remind you that you belong to me, isn't that, right?"

I had something for all that mouth. I began to bob my head, taking him deeper, twisting my hand, and making sure my tongue would touch his sack. I pulled back, sucking hard, and saw his eyes flash indigo.

"Remi!"

I pulled off with a loud pop, letting the saliva with a mix of precum drip down my chin. I used my hand that was stroking him and gripped him at the base. I glared at him, knowing my eyes were glowing a bright teal.

"No!" I growled. "You don't get to cum until I tell you that you can. You need to ask me if you can cum. Do you understand, Thomas," I growled.

"Yess. Yes, I understand, princess," he groaned. I licked the tip and was satisfied with the jerk.

"Hm."

Without warning, I bobbed my head, taking as much as possible into my mouth. It was a warning for not asking me for permission to cum. The more I sucked, the more brutal he became and the thicker and longer he got. He was so enormous that I was practically gagging on it. It caused him to hiss, and I hoped my action would show him how much I wanted him.

How much I wanted my AETERNUM. How much I wanted to be his Mate.

I hummed again and clicked with my tongue as I licked each ball while stroking him faster.

I worked on him with my hand, jerking him off since I couldn't get all of him in me while my other hand went to caress and massage his balls. In response, Thomas lifted back his head to stare at me, dazed. It amazed me that I was the only one to make him like this. He swallowed, not saying a word until my lips met the bottom of his shift and suckled at the underside of his head that I knew was sensitive.

"Fuck," he groaned, further fueling my blow and hand job as I worked at a pace that had him growling. His eyes burned with the indigo glow, and his clawed hands gripped the sheets as he fought not to nut. At this point, I knew every single nook and cranny that made him give me this reaction. My heart thumped, wanting to mark him for the world to see. He squeezed his hand tighter against the lock of my hair, trying to take control of my movements. "It's so fucking sexy watching me disappear into your hot mouth, little princess."

I took a deep breath at his compliment before pushing it further down my throat and humming lightly. I fought against my reflex to gag, and tiny tears formed around the corners of my eyes. I could feel my throat tighten around him, and a string of curses came out of him.

The usually calm, collected, and direct wolf Alpha was losing control because of me. Honestly, I was quite surprised he had let me take control for so long without taking over, and I loved every single second of his submission. I knew how hard it was for him not to be able to control the situation, but I also knew he wasn't thinking of anyone or anything else. All the emotions he could feel belonged to only me.

I continued, letting my tight lips move up and down his shaft as his eyes closed in pure bliss.

That was enough to motivate me to continue.

His forehead puckered together, sweat running down his face. As I continued, he twitched in excitement, the saliva dribble frothing down my chin in rapid session. The slurping sounds I made had my core clenching in anticipation. I licked around his mushroom head and let saliva drool down my chin, but I was too wrapped up trying to please this man even to care.

In fact, it only seemed to drive him wilder.

I could feel my wetness seeping out of my slits and down my thighs, but I continued. The need to please, own, and bring him to his knees was higher than my current needs. When he tightened his grip on my hair, I expected him to shove my mouth till my nose hit his skin. Instead, I was surprised his other hand cupped my face and pulled me away from what was now mine. I tried hiding the frown on my face because I knew he was close.

I couldn't fight the pout anymore. "Why did you stop me?"

"Because I'm not cumming in your mouth right now," he answered in a low and gruff voice.

I opened my mouth to protest, but he settled comfortably on the center of the bed and hauled me along. I thought he would flip me over, yet I was shocked when he settled me right over his throbbing shaft. For a moment, I blinked in disbelief, tilting my head to the side of our position.

"Thomas? What—"

"I love you, Remi," he professed, his eyes landing on mine as he was filled with something that looked like lust, love, and adoration that made my heart thump. He had said it before, but something about it in this moment felt more intimate. It felt like something finally settled between us.

Suddenly, tears welled in the corner of my eyes, especially when I felt the rest of the walls around us starting to crumble, and his soul was laid out before me. He bore his neck in submission, much like a wolf would, which I didn't think an Alpha would ever do in a million years.

It would be similar to his wolf showing me his underbelly, trusting and allowing me to be in control.

His Mate. My Aeternum.

"I...I love you too," I whispered. Our eyes met, and I remembered our time together back home. I could see myself watching him, and I never knew why. Idhan had stolen my ability to remember and to know who I was. I could have lost Thomas because I didn't know. I shook my head as Thoms brushed my face.

"The fact that you remember now is all we need. I never felt this type of peace, which was what scared me. It's you that gives me everything I need and the only one who could turn the darkness inside me into light," Thomas said.

"I will always be the only one. Do you understand that?"

"Yes, I do. Now fuck me," Thomas instructed. His claws dug into my hips as he plunged his length into me. I reached between us, wrapping my hands around his length, stopping the motion so I could stroke him once. Thomas watched my juices slid down my thighs before sliding him through the wetness and back inside my core.

Not once did he take his eyes off me as I sank down.

A groan escaped his lips, his hips rising to bump against my swollen clit as he stretched me out to accommodate his shallow penetration. Using my hands to steady myself on his chest, I raised my hips, dropping back down and taking more of him inside of me.

So fucking full.

So fucking good.

"Rem— fuck!" he choked out when I slammed myself down until I was seated on his length. I don't think I would ever get tired of how sore he makes me as my core drew him in again, always seeming to seek more.

Leaning forward to rub my clit against him, I took him as deeply as possible, my hips moving and my swollen core clenching and unclenching. Thomas groaned loudly, and it was as if he wasn't just inside me but part of me at this point.

"Goddess," I breathed out. "I love you so much, Thomas."

"Good, because you're getting it for the rest of our lives together," he snarled. "There are so many things I want to do to this body. So many ways I want to tie you down," he grunted. He smiled as I lifted and sat back down, ultimately taking control of the pacing. His eyes rolled back in his head as his clawed hand moved to my ass. He lifted my ass and spread my cheeks apart as he began to thrust hard.

"Oh...my...Thomas! Oh damn...baby, please! Please, Thomas, harder! Harder!" I screamed as I ground down with each thrust. All too soon, I knew from the way he growled that I was using him as my personal dildo.

I love him.

I want him.

His pace slowed, pushed me down on him, and I began to rock slowly. One large, clawed hand slapped my ass as the other pinched a nipple, hard.

"I want to claim you," I finally confessed while leaning forward, touching my mouth to his gently as I frantically rode myself closer and closer to my own relief. I swore that he throbbed and grew even thicker and longer, hitting my cervix at this point. "I want you to mark me, Thomas."

It almost felt like those words made him snap as he devoured my mouth, driving in and out of me with hard rolls as our wet slaps filled the room in rapid session. At that moment, it wasn't about who was more in control as we became drunk on one another.

"I'm close," I warned.

"Does my Mate like a little pain with her pleasure?" he questioned, shoving it so deep inside me that I was breathless.

"Yes," I gasped, staring at him with wide eyes, everything becoming more and more intense by the minute. His indigo rings glowed brightly at this point, and I couldn't look away even if I wanted to. "A—Alpha."

"Look at my little princess, trying to take all this like she can handle my essence. Are you trying to make me submit? Fucking make me, princess. Ride your Mate," he grunted and slapped me hard on my ass. I moaned, especially when his free hand went to wrap around my throat. He was showing me that although I was in control, he very well still owned my very breath, and it was enough to set me off. "Remi!" he gritted, and I smiled.

"You can cum for your princess, Thomas."

My tight heat clamped down hard, strangling him while he roared his release, his warmth flooding me that never seemed to end, either. It didn't take long until his thick seed trickled out of me as he kept shoving his thick member back inside me, pushing through the messy aftermath he'd filled me with. The feel of his claws pressing into my skin further pushed me over the edge. I reached out, gripping his throat as well. His eyes flashed with heat, love, and a determination I couldn't decipher.

Thomas began to pump harder and faster as if he was filling me up to carry another one of his children. Except for this time, it would be our choice.

Fucking mine.

Then he ripped his mouth away, nuzzling into the crook of my neck, and I did the same. With no warning, he clamped down hard, and I did the same, his blood instantly filling my mouth, and something inside me seemed to settle finally—

The warmth that came with a home.

That my soul knew home was wherever he was—he was part of my family.

The ocean, my Livyatan, seemed to settle as it fed. I could feel myself growing stronger, and I could feel the changes happening inside of Thomas. We were one, and nothing would even dare to try to split us apart.

Thomas.

Thomas' thick essence filled me to the brim as he continued to spank me, giving me the pleasure and pain that we needed to get off as we allowed our markings to center us—that we're forever. He never once stopped biting my neck with his sharp canine teeth. The pain erupting when it hit the bone felt like a new bone began to grow. Thomas moaned long and loud as he pulled away from my neck. He lapped up the blood, sealing the wound shut. I bit down hard, more toward the back of his neck. I licked his neck and stared at the circle marking that begun to glow a lighter shade of teal. It was my energy, my love, and my life. Thomas was all of that plus more, and I knew it now. I could see it so clearly.

He continued to fuck me until he softened inside me and the feeling of him moving through his release was enough to send me into another frenzy, but I was just too tired. Nuzzling into his chest, he finally slipped free, pulling me into his arms.

I sighed in contentment at how his chest rumbled through me.

"Mate," he said, burying his hand into my hair and pulling me so that I was looking up at him.

"Eternity," I smiled, completely lost in how I could feel his every emotion and thoughts coursing through our connection. I could feel his emotions before, but now we were connected on a level no one else could reach. I knew I could conquer just about anything as long as Thomas was next to me. We would take care of Meesha and kill the ones who threatened her safety. I knew it as a certainty as emotions raced through my veins. I felt I could do and accomplish precisely what I set out to do when I came here. I looked at Thomas, and he stared into my eyes. I could feel, see, and hear his questions and wish I could answer them all.

"We both have questions with very few answers, but I know we can figure this out together," I said. Thomas blinked slowly, and he raised a brow before speaking.

"We will figure out everything that we need to know. I know that for sure. The only question that is screaming in my mind is that our baby girl shifted into a water creature and a black bear. What the fuck did Pandora do?"

That was one question I didn't think we would get an answer to until we tracked that bitch down and beat it out of her.

"I don't know, but we will find out. Isn't that right, Alpha?"

Thomas squeezed my ass and slapped it before nodding.

"Exactly, and the first person we need to start with is Sam. As soon as he wakes, we find out everything he knows."

"Agreed."

There was no need to say next on the list would be Meesha.

IDHAN

I was done with this deal. I was done with this entity's evasion and lies. Not only did he know where Rehema was hiding, but he also knew about these abominations she gave birth to. I seethed in the back of my mind while I watched *ZAMMIUNTAU* walk through the dead town of Sunset Port. There were barely any wolves left to worship him, but I had the sense it didn't matter. He wanted to kill two birds with one stone, which meant dealing with the Necromancer. She was something to look at physically, but where I bled poison, she was poison. She was poison to the mind, body, and soul.

"I knew you would show up here again, you bastard! How dare you have me create the perfect army for them to be destroyed by that wolf and his bitch!"

Zammiuntau stopped walking, and I could feel his amusement. Pandora stood ten feet in front of us, seething with a handprint that wrapped around her neck burned into her flesh.

"Pandora, I only sped up the process of them being dead, dead. It isn't my fault you were outmatched," Zammiuntau laughed. "Clearly, so were you."

Zammiuntau shrugged.

"You knew she would be here! You and whatever body you are wearing, like clothes, knew she had survived! If this messes with my plan for my vessel, I will destroy you, demon," Pandora growled.

"No faith in me? I have everything covered for us all. It has all worked out according to the prophecies. They all gathered on the land that is a peninsula. It sits between the Gulf and the *Aethiopain* Ocean, now known as the Atlantic. This is the place where we all came through. This is where I will claim what has been made for me. Do not forget, Pandora, that if it weren't for me, you would not be who you stand before me today."

"Just keep up your end of the bargain, demon, and I will not choose to use the power that I now control against you," Pandora gritted. "The girl belongs to me. Do not forget that."

Pandora took a step backward, disappearing into a void that held no light. I didn't care about the child or what happened. All I wanted was Rehema. She alone could get me out of this realm and open the gates to allow the rest of our forces inside Hyquadra.

"Idhan, are you ready for the final phase? Once we lead the child to us, I will relinquish control and give you the power to stand in this realm as I possess the body made for me."

"If you think for a moment that I trust you to carry this out, you are crazier than I believe."

"Why would I not help someone who has helped me remain in this world?"

"Because if it were not beneficial for me, I would not help you, either. I understand your thinking because I think in the same manner."

"Then why let me stay? Why haven't you shoved me from your body yet?"

"You already know the answers to your questions, Zammiuntau. You know what I seek, and I knew that you could find it. I have always known that you would leave my body once you received what you have been waiting for all this time. You didn't think I would know it didn't matter how much time I spent in this realm. I could never stand it here without being attached to another power source. You took me to be a fool."

"There was always a 50/50 chance. It doesn't really matter to me one way or the other. Just do not get in my way once the transfer is complete."

The hissing growl he used to call the wolves his way grated on my senses. I watched as at least twenty wolves came running toward us. A tall, muscular man ran beside them and stopped before us, dropping to one knee. It was always odd when Zammiuntau used my body. My arm was raised as he sliced it through the air, causing the wolves to fall on their bellies and whimper. These wolves and this man had been the only ones not killed and brought back by the Necromancer. They were the last and the most loyal. Edwin stood up with glowing yellow eyes tinged with red and stared at one side of my face. His lips were pulled back, showing his teeth and the blood that coated them.

"When do we attack? My daughter is in place and is ready to give you entrance into where you seek to destroy," Edwin growled. If I had given a shit about these lower *Beings,* I would have pushed through to tell them to run. These wolves would be nothing but a source of power to ZAMMIUNTAU once he got what he wanted. None of them mattered in the least to him, and neither did they matter to me.

"I want all of you waiting in the trees beyond the barrier. No one attacks until I am present and have lifted the barrier," Zammiuntau stated. I felt my arms move once more, creating a portal revealing a wooded area in the early morning. "Go, wait and stay far from sight until I call for you. Those who disobey will not know the peace of death," Zammiuntau growled. Edwin bowed, but I knew he would be the one that would be the problem. Zammiuntau had left him with too much willpower, but I understood the need for it. Someone had to control the mindless while their master wasn't around.

"We will wait until your call, then destroy the false God *Kannuck's* wolves one Pack at a time," Edwin rumbled. He slipped through the portal, and it snapped shut. The last of Zammiuntau's plan had been set, and now it was time for the end game. I came here for a purpose at the beginning. That was to retrieve Rehema. But now that I know of the Livyatan city in this realm, I shall conquer that before dragging the princess back to submit or watch the rest of her people die screaming.

I sat on the beach closest to the Pack and closed my eyes. It was still early, and this place was secluded enough for what needed to happen here. I pulled to the front of the mind space, but Zammiuntau did not pull back as usual. It would take both of us to use the boy and the other children to start the events. My poison and his blood possession were what we perfected and used for this moment. I hadn't understood until now why this would bring the princess running without that wolf beside her. I also needed to deal with him because her thoughts should not be clouded by him but full of my face. I should haunt her thoughts, her dreams, and her nightmares. I will ensure that I am the only *Being* she sees when she closes her eyes.

"Focus, Idhan. She will be yours soon, and I will even give you a parting gift of knowledge once this is done."

"Knowledge or a riddle of lies and half-truths?"

"Atlantis was destroyed long ago when one of your kind tried crossing into this realm over a millennium ago. There is no need to try to find this place that is now more myth than reality. Take my advice and leave this place before your body gives out here. We both know it will not be long once we are separated."

I took his words for what they were. They were a half-truth at its best, but I knew the Zhavia people. They were resilient and masters of hiding. I would not put it past Rehema and her family to make the call to shield the city, even from themselves. But I knew Rehema would have a way to contact them, and I would use that to my advantage.

"I will consider that. It wouldn't matter what I do because once this is over, you will be gone."

"I just like to ensure I help a friend out before departing."

I would have laughed but felt the instant connections to young minds now tensing in fear. I knew the entity had no friends. Not even other entities like him would be considered something so mundane. He wanted me out of this realm because he wanted the knowledge for himself.

"Your lies taste like death and despair. Stop while you are ahead, or do you forget how closely we are related? Different Beings may have created us, but they are one and the same. The only difference is that we are far superior to you or any of your kind in this realm. So don't bullshit me, Zammiuntau. Our partnering was convenient for us both and has worked until this point. You are finished with me, just as I will be finished with you."

This hissing laughter and the bright red eyes that glowed in my subconscious seemed to burn into hatred before turning their attention to the matter at hand.

"We shall see how that plays out for you, Idhan. Now, let's do what we came here to do."

The altered poison and blood in the boy called Sam were barely there, and it seemed like someone had managed to rid it of the child's body. But not all of it was gone, and it was just enough for our minds to slip through and begin to speak.

"Samuel. It is now time to wake up. It is time to do what is promised and bring the vessel if you want to save your family. You will know when the time is right to slip off the land and bring Meesha to me. You will do this or lose everyone you love. Is that a deal?" Zammiuntau growled.

While he spoke to the boy, I sent out the instructions to the others who were still possessed. Those were the adults who followed the Port's teachings and the children who were taken and sent back. No one ever suspects the children, making it hard to contain the madness. I activated the other children to begin attacking and killing all they come across, starting with their families. Chaos, confusion, fear, and heartbreak would rule over this Pack, and the Alpha would be engulfed in saving them. He would not only watch this Pack fall but realize that he had lost his child, Rehema, and his entire bloodline. I could appreciate the thought process of Zammiuntau's plan, but the only thing I wanted to know was what did he need on that land so badly that only a member of the Rayne bloodline could access it?

I stared through Sam's eyes and watched as he moved through the house. I could scent what he scented, and the smell of Rehema crashed into my senses. Her Livyatan was awake and growing stronger now. I did not smell any lingering effects of the poison, so I knew now was the time before she could put up much of a fight. I gritted my teeth at the mingling scent of the wolf that consumed her thoughts. I was hoping he followed her so I could end him where she could witness it. Once he opened the door to a room, we saw a large bed and a small child sitting up, blinking. She rubbed at her large brown eyes, and I could tell she knew what would happen. Her appearance reminded me of the child Rehema held an attachment to so much that I would have thought she had been reincarnated. She blinked once before swinging tiny brown legs to the side of the massive bed. Zammiuntau was now in control of the boy. By the way, the girl had looked at him. She knew it too.

"If I go with you, will you let Sam and the others go?" Meesha asked.

"Why? Why do they matter to you? I can just force you to go with me right now," Zammiuntau growled.

"No."

"Well, I will have Lena kill the other pups and cubs, along with Jessica. How does that sound?"

I saw the tears forming in her eyes, but I also saw a fierceness in them that reminded me of Rehema. Even though this child reminded me of the girl back in Hyquadra, I could tell this was not the same child. She was nothing like the scared little shifter girl who should be dead or transformed by now.

"I can't help them now. I am here. But I can help these kids just like Thomas told me to. So that is the deal."

"What does a child know about deals? I can accept this deal as long as you understand the cost."

"I don't have mone—"

"Our deal was that you would come without complaint, and I would let your old parents' souls free. Now you add more, so what shall I get in return?" The girl's brow furrowed but cleared as she looked back into Sam's eyes. She was young, but the intelligence I saw hidden deep in those eyes was something ancient.

"Let all the other kids go, and once my Thomas kills you, my other mommy and daddy will go free."

I felt Zammiuntau's rage, and I knew the child's defiance grated on him, causing me to laugh. She was her mother's child, whether I wanted to admit it or not.

"She knows you can not hurt her, and your plan will fail without her. A mere child is playing the Devourer of Children, eater of souls."

Why would she let him take her would be my question, but I knew the answer before I voiced it. The child truly believed that this Thomas would save her, and by doing just that, he would leave Rehema alone with me. Zammiuntau was correct about it being time for us to separate. It was time to bring the princess back to Hyquadra to open the gates for the rest of the R'lyehan to come through.

"You know nothing! Once I am done, I will savor the taste of her soul, along with all the rest."

I felt his attention shift back to the girl, but she had never taken her eyes away from us.

"A deal is a deal, child. Once I have your body, they all will go freeee," Zammiuntau hissed.

THOMAS

My first thought when I woke was of the Mate I held in my arms. The next thought was of Meesha, my child. Remi and I had a child together. But how was that possible? How did I not see Meesha for who she was, and why hadn't my brother or I sensed something like this? That wasn't my only question, though. I knew I had to get answers. How could I use power similar to the Succubus Shannara, and how did she know I was in trouble?

"I can feel you thinking," Remi whispered. Her soft lips moved against my throat, and I had an urge to mark her once more.

"We have a lot to accomplish today, and I wanted to get started," I yawned. We barely got any rest, but it was enough for now. "I need to see Meesha," I said.

Remi sat up and stretched. I followed suit as I mentally prepared for the day's events. I watched Remi's hips roll as she entered the bathroom. I started to go after her but stopped when I heard my cell. I dug through the pile of clothes on the floor and pulled out my phone. I was surprised it still worked, but I knew Journee had done her witchy magic on it and told me everything I needed to know.

"YES," I answered. I didn't even look at the caller ID. I gathered up the clothes while making my way to the bathroom. I wanted to get all the clothes just to be sure none of that poison still lingered.

"THOMAS, I'M SORRY I AM JUST CALLING. IT'S BEEN ABSOLUTELY INSANE ON MY END. WHAT'S UP?" Quinn asked. I dropped our clothes in a hamper, knowing I would be burning every piece of clothing we wore to that town after I went through them.

"QUINN, SHIT. EVERYTHING, EVERYTHING IS UP. DID CAMRON TELL YOU ABOUT THAT TOWN SUNSET PORT?"

"DAMON GAVE ME A RUNDOWN ON IT, AND HAYLEY TOLD ME ABOUT SOME OF THE WOLVES DEFECTING THERE. ALL THAT LONER AND ROGUE WAYS WILL STOP UNTIL THINGS IN THIS NATION ARE PUT BACK HOW THEY ARE SUPPOSED TO BE. *KANNUCK* IS NOT PLEASED," Quinn grunted. Knowing that our creator was not pleased with us made what I would say to my True Alpha worse.

"THAT TOWN AND ALL WOLVES ARE EITHER DEAD, INFECTED, OR POSSESSED. THAT PLACE NEEDS TO BE LEVELED TO THE GROUND. ONCE I FIND THE REST OF THE SHIFTERS RUNNING WITH THAT CREW, I WANT PERMISSION TO ERADICATE IT. A DEMON MADE ITS HOME THERE AND WITH THE WOLVES. THEY NO LONGER FOLLOW PACK LAW OR THE TEACHINGS OF *KANNUCK*."

I heard the long sigh and low growl that made my wolf fall back, and he wasn't even in the room.

"THERE HAVE ALWAYS BEEN SOME WHO DO NOT FOLLOW *KANNUCK*, AND AT THAT TIME, IT WAS THEIR CHOICE. NOW, WITH EVERYTHING HAPPENING IN THIS WORLD, THERE IS NO MORE CHOICE. ALL WOLVES ARE BORN WITH THE KNOWLEDGE OF WHO CREATED US AND WHO HE IS. THE ONLY WAY TO TRULY TURN YOUR BACK ON KANNUCK IS BY LETTING ANOTHER INSIDE TO FEED OFF YOUR SOUL. BECAUSE YOU KNOW JUST AS MUCH AS I DO, THOMAS, OUR SOULS WILL ALWAYS RETURN TO HIM. GOOD OR EVIL, WE BELONG TO *KANNUCK*."

I sat on the edge of the bed and rubbed a hand down my face. I knew that to partially be true because I had stolen my fair share of souls from wolves.

"There is more, Quinn. So much more," I sighed.

"The Necromancer?"

My eyes opened, and I sat up straighter as if he were in front of me.

"Ahh, yeah. How did—"

"Shannara. She told me some cryptic stories about you and Remi. Then she said, if I spoke to you, then you were still alive, and she owed you an explanation about something."

I wanted to hang up and call Shannara but restrained myself.

"That sounds about right. But that isn't everything," I said. I let my senses stretch and could feel Meesha close by and awake. I felt like she had always been a part of my blood, but I had no clue why I didn't sense it before. I was so intent on hearing her heartbeat that I didn't know Remi was beside me until I felt her hand on my shoulder.

"Tell me now so we can work out what needs to be done. We must find this demon, destroy it, and get this Pack back on the right track."

"I...we...Remi and I have a child," I stated. The phone went silent, and I thought the call had dropped until I checked it.

"That was actually faster than I would have thought possible, but—"

"Wait, wait, what the hell do you mean? Why would you even think we would have a kid?"

"Thomas, I am your Alpha. I think I would know when my wolves have found their Mate," he chuckled.

"I didn't know, Quinn. Neither of us knew what we were to each other and why are you laughing."

"Everyone could see it, Thomas! I mean, others may not have been sure, but I knew. I'm just not sure about the child thing. How?"

"It's Meesha."

"What! Little Meesha. The bear shifter Meesha that had parents," he said skeptically.

"Yes. I know it like I know the back of my hand. She is mine, Quinn. Meesha is our child," I said. I released a breath and realized I had been holding it this entire time.

"Okay, okay. Meesha is Pack, and she belongs to you, so she belongs to me. We will figure out how it all happened. But for now, we need to deal with what is happening. Alex should be arriving soon, and he will help with judgment. I will leave that in your hands, and the town of Silent Hill—"

"Seriously?"

"Fine, the town of Sunset Port and anyone still living or unliving left in that place must be wiped out. You have my permission to do whatever you need to do. I want this done, the demon sent back to hell, and my Pack secure. Nothing else comes before that," Quinn demanded. I looked up at Remi and shook my head. I knew what she wanted to say, but what was happening to her, we would deal with it. If Idhan had anything to do with this demon, we would follow orders anyway.

"I will see it through. If the wolves of this Pack who aren't tainted but followed along would like another chance, is that still my call?"

"They will have to see me before they can join any Pack. They may not live or be a member of the Miami Pack."

"Understood. Since we know it is a demon, any advice on how to kill it? It's not like I have a Hunter around," I asked.

"Yes. That's why it was taking Alex so long to join you. There aren't many demon blades, but I am close friends with someone who seems to have one to spare. He will bring it to you and assist with whatever is needed. Once that is fin-

ISHED, HIS OBLIGATION WILL BE TO TRAIN THE NEXT ALPHA OF THAT PACK," Quinn grunted.

"I UNDERSTAND. TALIKA WILL MAKE AN EXCELLENT ALPHA ONE DAY SOON," I said. I felt that deep in my gut and saw the slight nod of Remi's head. She felt it just like I did that the girl was special.

"GOOD. TELL ME EVERYTHING THAT HAPPENED WHEN YOU WENT TO SUNSET PORT FOR THE CHILDREN," he growled. I told him everything that had happened, including the part about the blue light and what she had said about Meesha. The only thing I didn't let on was how she got my essence from the jump. There wasn't anything to say about Idhan or that we would take him out. Well, as long as he was a threat to Remi, I would not rest until he was put down.

"THAT'S ABOUT ALL I GOT."

"I HOPE SO IN LESS THAN TWENTY-FOUR HOURS. SHIT, Y'ALL RAYNE BROTHERS' LIVES ARE WORSE THAN MINE. I THINK YOU AND REMI MISSED SOMETHING PANDORA SAID," Quinn speculated. I raised a brow, and Remi stopped messing with the shirt she'd pulled on.

"WHAT?"

"SHE SAID CHILDREN AS IN MORE THAN ONE. FROM WHAT PANDORA SAID, I DON'T BELIEVE MEESHA IS THE ONLY ONE. THERE IS ANOTHER."

"What the hell? This...I..." Remi stammered. "We have Meesha, but how do we find and keep the other safe if we do not know where they are?" I could feel the anger and fear rolling off Remi in waves. I clamped my jaws closed as I forced back the growl. If we didn't know about Meesha and she was right under our noses this entire time, how the fuck would we find this child?

"LET ME SEE WHAT I CAN COME UP WITH ABOUT THIS NECROMANCER. RIGHT NOW, YOU HAVE MEESHA. ALL YOU CAN DO IS PROTECT HER AND DO WHAT YOU HAVE BEEN SENT TO GET DONE. WE WILL GET THIS ALL FIGURED OUT," Quinn stated. I knew he was right, but I also knew that the child wasn't only in danger from Pandora or this demon, but Idhan as well.

"I WILL HANDLE THINGS HERE, BUT SOMEONE ELSE WILL NEED TO TAKE MY PLACE ONCE THIS IS FINISHED. I NEED TO FIND OUT IF THIS IS TRUE, AND IF IT IS, WE HAVE TO FIND THEM."

"IT WILL BE DONE."

The call ended, and I looked at Remi and could see all the fears and pain in her teal eyes. I stood up, but a familiar tingle went through my body before I could say a word. Remi's head shot to the door. Just a knock sounded.

"It's Shannara," I said. I wasn't ready for anything else to be revealed, but if it helped me defeat my enemies and save my family, I would have to deal with it.

I walked over to the door and pulled it open. Shannara stood against the side of the door, leaning against the wall. She was fully clothed in a sheer black body suit that, if she moved the right way, I was sure I would see everything every man and woman would love to glance at. She smiled at me and then looked down at Remi. I watched as her laser blue eyes danced as she looked at us both.

"Thomas!" I snapped my head to Remi, and she stared at me like I was losing my damn mind.

"What?"

"You're naked!"

I looked back at Shannara, who was still smirking and shook my head. I turned away, not worried about the nudity, but knew if it were her, I would react the same way.

"It ain't like I didn't change the pups' diapers," Shannara laughed. I walked into the bathroom, trying to figure out precisely what she was talking about. How would that even be possible? I knew she knew my parents, but I didn't think they were close. What was I missing? I took a quick shower and dressed in the clothes Remi brought into the bathroom. I walked out, trying to wrap my mind around Shannara being here, and she wasn't taking a soul or killing anyone. Neither Remi nor Shannara were in the room, so I went downstairs to see them sitting at the table. Shannara watched Remi as she tapped long blue nails in rhythm on the table. Remi sat beside Meesha and watched her talk animatedly about what happened last night.

"Thomas!" Meesha pushed away from the table and ran over to me. She jumped into my arms, and I caught her like usual. Something inside of me seemed to settle with her in my arms. I looked at Remi as Meesha kissed my cheek, and she nodded. She felt the same thing I was feeling, and it pained me that another child could be out there alone, and we had no clue where to look.

"Well, this is all nice and happy-go-lucky, but I can't stay much longer," Shannara purred. Meesha wiggled out of my arms and dropped to the floor. She returned to the table and pushed her way into Shannara's lap.

"Meesha, hold up, I don't think—" Remi started, slightly panicked. I couldn't act like I wasn't already moving because the Succubus didn't seem like the kid-friendly type.

"She is fine. She just likes to be close to greatness. Who wouldn't want to be close to me?"

I stopped moving as Shannara settled Meesha in her lap and pulled the plate of fruit Meesha had been eating over so she could finish.

"I didn't expect that you—"

"Thomas, I have taken care of these things before, okay? Let's get down to the business of why I am here. You want to know the truth about that darkness inside you, right?"

It was early, but I knew soon enough it would be time to deal with the wolves Lika had rounded up.

"Just tell me what it is, Shannara. No games or riddles, please. I don't have time for it," I said. She stared at me with sadness, but I saw when she came to a decision.

"I promised your parents I would never speak of this unless I had to do it. We never thought it would become a problem because you grew up normally like the rest of your brothers. You never seemed to have any side effects, so I didn't see the need to say anything," she defended.

"What do my parents have to do with what I let happen? I went to that Necromancer because I couldn't handle the emotional strain of my gifts. I let that darkness inside of me."

"No. No, that isn't completely true. Thomas, when your mother gave birth to you, you took one breath and died a minute later," she sighed. I looked at Meesha, but she was quiet with her head down.

"What? I think Dax would have said something about that if that were true. Right, Thomas?" Remi asked. I didn't answer as I stared into eyes so blue that there was no pupil or end to the deep pools. Shannara blinked and turned away, dropping her intense gaze when I saw the truth in her statement.

"What did they do?" It was like I had to force the words through a throat suddenly dry.

"You know the story of your parents, correct?"

"Some of it."

"Well, Ransom and Saniya called me. I have very few *Beings* that I call friends, and let's just say when they died, the pool grew smaller. If your mother or father summoned me, I would always come. That night, they didn't call their friend. They called a demon."

"They wouldn't do that. They would never do anything like that!" I felt my anger build as I pushed from the table. Remi was up and grabbed hold of my wrist in a second. Her touch seemed to drain away the sudden anger and denial.

"Your mother, as you know, practiced magic and had tried everything. I refused to make the deal for them because I knew if I pulled my soul back, it would be brought back to us altered in a way you would no longer be their child. Instead, I offered a piece of my soul or myself to anchor your soul back into your body. I forced life into you from the many souls I had taken. We watched you grow and saw no changes or side effects of the exchange. We thought that we were in the clear, and we were until the night I spotted you in my club. I could feel my power inside of you, and I knew that it would consume you one day if you didn't get help to control it. That is why I made you that offer. I just couldn't figure out why suddenly it was so strong and virulent in you when it wasn't before. Now, I think I know the reason," she said. She leaned her head to the side and raised a perfect brow. And it all snapped into place, and I believed it was because of the Necromancer. Why did I think it was from Pandora?

"It was because I had been in contact with Pandora. If I had just gone to Dax or my parents for help instead of trying to figure it out alone, none of this would have happened?"

"All things happen for a reason," Shannara said sharply. I followed her gaze to Meesha, who stared up at me.

"When that bitc— when you and Pandora did what y'all did, she exposed you. She exposed you to the raw evil inside of her. The piece of my soul that lived in you rose to feed from her. Since then, it has needed fuel to survive. It needed to—"

"It needed to stay fed. Since that night, that part of you is now awake."

"But, like I said before, I used that power to save your life. It only knew darkness because that is what it first tasted. Nothing would have been able to change that until...until you had to save a life. The life that could handle or bury the dark parts of you," Shannara asserted.

My mind was everywhere, but I didn't have time to process it all, and Shannara told me everything she knew. I looked at Remi as the sun began to peek through the blinds, and I could hear the Pack begin to rise. It was time to handle business and figure out the rest of this shit later. Shannara was right about one thing, and that was Remi. What lived inside me didn't crave the pain or violence like normal, but it craved the touch of my Mate.

I sat there trying to process everything I had learned and was still no closer to all the necessary answers. Shannara was already gone, but I knew there wouldn't be anything else I could get from her right now. We had other problems, and honestly, this darkness inside me seemed less like an issue.

"Thomas?" I looked up, catching Remi's eyes before looking at Meesha.

"Yes, Meesha."

"Are you mad at me?"

I had been around pups, cubs, and normal children all my life, but I felt like I did not know what to do now. I always held myself responsible for the children of the Pack, but this was different. Remi came over and smiled as she got to her knees. She pulled Meesha into a hug before kissing her on the cheeks.

"I am not mad at you, baby. You could never do anything to make me mad at you," I said. I could feel the changes in the air and mood in the house as Lika and Oceayn began to stir.

"Meesha, can you tell Thomas and me how you knew when to come to help us? Have you known all this time that we were your parents?" Remi asked.

"I had the same dream over and over. I could just feel it when it happened. I don't know. It just happened like my dreams," she whispered. Her tiny arms wrapped around Remi's neck as she pressed her face to her neck. Remi touched a spot behind her ear briefly and then looked at me. She pulled her ear back and revealed a raised marking.

"How did you know you belonged to us, baby?" I asked again.

"Can't you feel it? I felt it, but you weren't ready to feel it yet. That's what he told me," Meesha smiled.

"Who told you?" Remi asked.

"The big dog, man. He is so big! He's bigger than Alpha Dax! He's like this big," she said, flinging her arms wide. I raised my brows because if it were who I thought she was talking about, that would be amazing. She was young, and even though she was my child, I sensed no wolf inside her. I could hear movement outside, but I already knew who it was before the front door opened. I stood up and was so glad when Alex walked through the door.

"Thomas! You have been gone for one damn day, and you already have kids on the way," Alex chuckled. "I told Malic you had some kind of mommy kink going on but—" Alex stopped talking when he saw Meesha smiling at him. He opened his mouth to say something when we all looked at the stairs. Lika and Oceayn stared down at us, with Sam standing beside them. Now Sam was awake. We needed to get down to business to look for the missing piece of our new, small family.

Remi

I stood up with Meesha in my arms as Lika and Oceayn brought Sam downstairs. I flicked my eyes to Alex, but he stared at Oceayn with a look I couldn't understand. I couldn't tell if he liked what he saw or looked at Oceayn the same way everyone else in this bullshit town did. It didn't matter, though, because we had so much we needed to do.

"Sam, how are you feeling?" Thomas asked. The boy looked tired and wired all at once. His light brown skin seemed slightly pale, and his light brown eyes still looked glassy. He tried for a smile, but I could tell it was forced.

"I want to see my parents, Alpha. I feel better, but not. I don't know. Everything still feels like it was all a dream," he said, rubbing his eyes.

"Lika, you should get one of his parents here to see him, and then we all need to head for the hall. It's time to get this done so this Pack can move on," Thomas said.

"Little brother, you should introduce me to everyone. Especially Talika, since I will be the one in charge of her training," Alex grunted. His words were directed at Thomas, but he kept looking at Oceayn while he spoke. Alex seemed confused while squinting at Oceayn. Alex didn't joke around a lot, and he definitely was not an asshole, so I knew I could pull him aside and ask him what the hell was wrong with him.

"My bad, Alex. It's been a lot happening and—" Thomas began, but Alex held up a hand.

"Yeah, yeah, I got you. I get it, Thomas. I feel you and know you have a lot on your mind. Demons, crazy ass Pack members, new or old love, and a baby mama," Alex smirked. That's when I got it. He knew exactly how much had been happening and was trying to gauge if Thomas was ready to blow.

"Lika, this is Alex, and he will be training you once we get everything sorted out here. Oceayn, this is my brother. He doesn't mean to stare at you the way he is looking at you," Thomas said pointedly.

"My favorite color is Verdigris."

"Verdigris? Really, Alex? So turquoise is your favorite color?" Thomas asked as he folded his arms.

"Oh, most definitely now it is," Alex chuckled. His usual terracotta eyes seemed to glow a bright topaz slightly, and I saw Oceayn step back slightly as she looked away. I leaned back and raised a brow before shaking my head.

"Well, okay then. Alex, don't you have something for us?" I asked. I moved and placed myself in front of Oceayn because I couldn't tell if she was uncomfortable or... shit, did she like it? There was another knock at the door, but Lika opened it to Gina and Howard.

"Alpha, is Sam...oh baby, how are you?" Gina cried, rushing over to the boy. Sam hugged his mother, but it was almost distant. His eyes flicked over to Meesha, then settled on me. It wasn't the first time I noticed it, but now it was creepy as hell.

"I am exhausted. Can I lie back down for a while?" Sam asked. Gina and Howard looked taken aback for a second but smiled at him.

"I'm still sleepy, too. Do we have to sit for the grown-up stuff?" Meesha whined. I looked at Thomas and then at Meesha.

"No, baby. Get some sleep and when we are done, let's go to the beach for a bit," I smiled. Meesha's eyes lit up, and I could see the happiness, but it faded too quickly.

"I will stay with them," Gina said, reaching out for Sam's hand. Sam pulled back, making it seem like he didn't see his mother trying to grab his hand. Something was off with the kid, but I knew he'd had a traumatic few days. Who could blame the pup for being a little strange?

"Gina, that would be appreciated, but Oceayn can stay with them both until we deal with Pack business. You know, as I know, that it is time for judgment, and all will need to attend. Are you okay with that, Oceayn?" Thomas asked. Oceayn was no longer worried about Alex, who stared at her like she was the last glass of water in a desert.

"Yes, yes, of course. I don't see the need for me to be there," Oceayn smiled. Sam had moved closer to Meesha. She grabbed his hand, and they raced up the stairs. I heard the door close.

"What are we going to do about him, Alpha? I know my child, and he is not acting normal," Gina sighed. Her entire body was tense, and I looked at Howard, who stared at the stairs.

"I understand what you are saying, Gina, but the boy has been through more shit than any adult shifter in the past few days. We will get this judgment taken care of and then figure out the best ways to help Sam and the other affected children," Thomas stated. I felt the calm move through the room as he spoke.

"We understand, Alpha. Let's get this done. I want to know why they would target our children and their Pack members! They need to answer for what they have done," Howard growled. I moved and stood in front of the parents, fully understanding their feelings.

"We will find out everything, and they will pay for the things they took part in doing. We will help Sam and the others and make sure something like this doesn't happen again," I said. I looked at Thomas, and he nodded. Lika stared at me with a slight smile before pulling open the door and walking outside. I turned to Oceayn before following Thomas out of the door and caught her frowning at Alex. I looked at him and saw him hand Thomas a long, bone-like knife.

"Oceayn, I don't know where Idhan is, but he is close. I can feel his eyes on me, and I don't know why or where he is, so be careful. Once we finish with all this mess, I am going for him," I said.

"Remi, you must ensure he does not get his blood in you. Wherever you go, I will follow," Oceayn vowed.

I caught up with Thomas and Alex just before entering the hall. Everyone was there, and the fourteen wolves that Lika rounded up were chained to the floor, with three other shifters standing behind them. I came up on Thomas's side, and I could feel the tension and anger rolling off him in waves the closer we got to them. The Pack was just as angered, but some seemed to think it was a bit much that they all needed to be here. Some of the shifters did not understand why it was anyone's business if a wolf wanted to leave the Pack. Some blamed the parents for not being strong enough to protect their children from running off. I sucked my teeth and tried not to go off and start attacking the idiots. I could tell that this was how they'd lived previously and how little they knew about what it was to truly be a Pack.

I calmed myself, knowing that it was only a few shifters spitting that nonsense. I knew Hayley must have gotten through to most of the Pack because I saw a few glares and confrontations with the ones who were talking bullshit. My eyes caught on Harmoni as she stood to the side, but when I followed her gaze, I noticed she was staring at a group of pups. They were all sitting there quietly, and I wouldn't have thought anything was wrong or chalked it up to everything they had been through, if I didn't see a thick black fluid coming out of Avery's ear. I breathed deeply as we reached the wolves that would be judged. I caught the scent of citrus, salt water, and death. The top layers of that scent were something I had only smelled once before, and that was the night my kingdom was attacked. Idhan was somewhere, and if that is true, no one here was safe. I didn't want to alarm everyone or let Idhan know I was onto him, but I had to warn Thomas. I touched his arm, and all his attention went to me, and he stared into my eyes. I could see the brightness of the teal glow reflecting off his brown eyes.

"Thomas, something feels off. Idhan is close, but I do not know where. This could turn bad fast."

"Tell me what you sense."

His growl in my mind was deep, and the indigo ring around his pupils grew in intensity. I looked back at the table where the missing pups sat, and my eyes widened. Every last one stared directly at me as black and obsidian green lines began covering their faces.

"Oh shit," I whispered before they all attacked.

I almost stumbled to a halt when I saw Avery leap from her chair and attack Harmoni. Her mouth formed into a deranged smile. The other children attacked adult shifters, who looked stunned at the sudden violence. I knew that some parents or other family members hesitated in even fighting back. The adult shifters, whom we thought were chained down, seemed to gain more strength than they should as they ripped the thick silver chains from the floor.

"Thomas!" I screamed before letting out a sonar blast into the crowd. The children began to attack, intending to kill. The blast knocked the children back along with Harmoni in the process.

"Stop the children! We can't let them infect anyone else!" Thomas roared.

I felt his power rise along with Alex's. Alex went from man to wolf in a split second to engage two wolves that seemed crazed, eviler than Garcia's people. Thomas was right, and we needed to get a handle on the kids before things really got out of hand. The only problem was how we would keep them alive and save them simultaneously. I heard a growl from Lika before power exploded all around us. It hit me with a force so hard I thought I would pass out. The power felt more like Thomas but with elements from me. As Lika moved through the crowd, a bright teal wave appeared in the air. I was behind her, grabbing one child by the ankle before he tried to leap in the air. Wolf shifters and water shifters screamed from the front of the hall. Six more wolf shifters roared loudly as the obsidian green and black lines crawled along their skin. I turned to Lika and saw her create a barrier to keep the children on the other side. She used her other hand and pressed it over Harmoni's wound as blood seeped out. The bite on her neck wasn't healing; if we didn't do something, she would bleed out. The pup I held thrashed in my grip, but I slid him on the floor to the other side, and he passed through the water barrier that was keeping the other children inside. I moved to Lika quickly and knocked her hand out of the way to try to save Harmoni.

"Lika, how in the hell are you doing this?" I asked. I sent in a wave of healing I could feel dwelling inside me. I could feel it was a holdover from when I saved Thomas.

"I don't know. I can't do it all the time, but it will hold until I take it down," Lika said.

The power was so similar to what I could do I didn't know what to think. Was it possible it was Lika? Could she be the other child? The bleeding slowed enough that I could pull my hand away. Harmoni stared at me, and I could see the blackness in her eyes beginning to fade.

"Lika, that isn't...has anyone seen you do this before?" I asked. Lika shook her head as she pressed a torn shirt to another shifter's stomach. I looked her over and could see that she was healing.

"No, no, never," she said, looking around. She scratched at her ankle, and I saw raised marks on her skin, but something slammed into my side before I could ask more or look at it. "Remi!"

I heard Lika scream my name as I was thrown across the room. I rolled to my feet just seeing the fighting all across the space. The shifter that slammed into me stood on shaky legs, but the wildness in his eyes told me all I needed to know. I dropped low as a muscled arm flew out. I came up under his arm as I hardened my skin. I used the tips of my fingers to slam into his chest. I held onto the arm he tried to hit me with and flung him simultaneously as my finger struck his chest. The whole created center mass should take weeks to heal, but whatever these wolves were infected with could be fast. Then I felt the power of two Alphas slam into every shifter in the hall. Most fell to the ground, including those infected, but a few still managed to pull themselves to their feet.

"Lika, get up. You're strong enough to shrug that off. I'm okay, but we need to take them all down, and I can't do it without you. You need to get up and fight. Your Pack needs you," I shouted. Lika shook her head and pushed to her feet. I looked at the barrier and saw it still held, even as the children threw themselves against it. Another wolf launched at her, but she moved away in time, throwing him through the barrier as well. Her eyes glowed the same indigo shade as Thomas's when she spun back toward me. My heart stopped. Just a faint teal glow shimmered over her skin before it settled back to normal.

"Lik—" I was knocked to the side, but I didn't fall. I turned into the punch, crushing the hand of the shifter.

"You belong to the R'lyehan! You will join the rest of your people after you submit, bitch!"

His crushed hand healed rapidly in front of my eyes. I knew I would need to get close. I would have to break every bone in his body and get him behind Lika's barrier. The only way we would stop this madness was if we stopped Idhan. This Pack was becoming just like the people of my kingdom long ago. He was changing them. It would be too late if we didn't stop it now. I reached for my Hydranodic Blade as I smiled at this twisted version of a wolf.

"Are you watching, Idhan? Is that him talking, or is it you?" I asked. The obsidian green of the shifter's eyes flashed, and I saw the instant change. The wolf seemed to stand taller as his facial expression we blank.

"Princess, I finally get to speak to you. I will give you the same bargain as before. Come to me and submit. I will let these creatures go free. They are insignificant to me," Idhan chuckled. He was out of his damn mind if he thought I would ever believe anything he said. I didn't give it any thought and just moved. I went low, bringing the blade up, trying to cut this bitch in half. He was fast because he jumped back, just missing my blade. "Oh, where did you get that? I thought they were all destroyed," Idhan sneered. I flashed to him, bringing my blade down and cutting his arm off. The scream was piercing through the chaos of the fighting. I prayed Thomas would leave me to this and he wouldn't come near me.

I did not want Idhan to see him or what he meant to me. It was a mercy that none of these shifters knew that Meesha was my child. He could have used her as leverage. I could tell Idhan was controlling the body by how it moved. His other arm flashed out, but a dark green glow shot from his palm, hitting my shoulders and blasting me away. It was like a punch to the gut, and I flew back, hitting another shifter. I kept moving until arms wrapped around my body before slamming into the wall. We slid to the floor but were rolling as more blasts came at us.

"Thomas, it's him! Idhan is doing this shit!"

"I figured. Not all the wolves are completely taken over. The ones not responding to my command need to go behind your barrier."

"It's not my barrier. It's Lika's barrier."

"What! Wait, could she—"

"You will come to me, Rehema," Idhan growled. Thomas and I faced the shifter, noticing that the arm had already grown back.

"No! I will come for you," I gritted. "You may have that body, but you won't for long. This ends here, Idhan. I will not let what happened to my people happen here. You are alone, cut off from your family and the traitors that helped you enter my realm. Without them, you are nothing, and I will kill you," I spat. I gripped the blade tighter.

"Alpha! Remi! Help!"

I felt a shift in my soul and heart at Lika's cry for help. I saw her gaze land on us, and I knew. I knew like I should have known when I met her, that she was ours. Why it was just snapping into place, I did not know. The more my Livyatan woke, the more I could feel those connected to me. I just knew without seeing that mark that Lika belonged to us. Thomas and I both looked over in that instant and saw Lika. Two wolf shifters had her cornered, and I could tell they were long gone. They had fully transitioned into R'lyehan puppets, and I knew they would be stronger. They would be too strong for Lika to handle on her own, and it wasn't because she wasn't powerful enough. It was because she would hesitate to kill Gina and Howard.

"Thomas! Save her! I can handle this," I shouted. I didn't look at him, but I knew he would go to her. If I knew anything, I knew Thomas trusted I could handle this alone. We had to save this Pack, which couldn't happen if we didn't trust that we would get it done separately. I needed him to save our child while I dealt with my past, threatening my future.

I had tunnel vision as I moved to take this puppet down. I would kill Idhan's ass this time and make sure he couldn't do this shit to anyone else. All I had to do was take care of the body he controlled so the Pack would be safe. We collided together in a flurry of fists and kicks. His smile looked manic as it grew wider. The black fluid dripped from his canines, and I knew he wanted to sink those teeth into me. I refused to let that shit go down. The shifter moved, and its eyes flashed from green to crimson. It seemed like two different people in one body. His eyes seemed to focus, and I could tell Idhan was watching me.

"I didn't think I would find you or figure out why you ran here. You will tell me how to find that outpost, Princess," Idhan said as he kicked me hard enough for me to lose my grip. The blade fell from my hand, but I managed to kick it so that he couldn't get to it. How the hell could he know about Atlantis? No one but my family knew where that outpost was, and the only other *Being* that knows was Oceayn. I knew he couldn't have gotten that information from her, so where?

"There is no need to tell the dead anything about the living," I roared. I formed energy from the water in the air while simultaneously sending out a sonar blast. The energy slammed into the shifter's body, blowing him across the space and slamming into a table. I could hear screams from other shifters and the crash of his body. I went after him, determined to take him down even if I had to stand there and burn him alive. I followed the path of destruction, catching up to him as he stood. His eyes flashed obsidian green as he growled at me.

"Enough! I am finished playing with you, Rehema!" He rushed me faster than I thought that body could move. He was throwing combos with punches and kicks, but I knew he aimed to get that poison inside me.

I kept up with the sonar and energy blasts, pushing him further away. After a strong blast, the shifter's body flew through the doors leading outside. I wasn't worried about the rest because I knew Thomas and Alex would have it handled. They would save who they could and deal with the rest. The green and black marked body landed on the ground but immediately stood again. His foot came down on the road, making a crater and causing the ground to shake. He held his hand out again, and I saw the green energy forming, but it wasn't pointed at me. It was directed at Oceayn. "You may have saved one child, but not the other. Come to me, and I promise to help you get her back."

Idhan let go of the blast, aiming directly at Oceayn, who was running toward me with fear in her eyes. She didn't seem to see the blast coming. I screamed mentally and physically for her to move. I rushed towards her, trying to get to her before it hit her, but that power was moving so fast I was unsure if I would make it in time. I heard him laughing behind me. I pulled in every bit of water as I formed a teal ball that moved like a wave and threw it behind me with such force it pushed me closer to Oceayn, causing me to crash into her. The obsidian blast sailed over our heads and slammed into a storefront, shattering glass everywhere.

"You want to save her, Rehema? Then you will submit!"

Then it hit me what he said and why Oceayn would even be outside. He had Meesha!

"Oceayn, where is Meesha?"

"She's gone! Both her and Sam are gone!"

THOMAS

Alex was beside me as we ran up to the two wolves. We had taken out the captured shifters before they managed to affect anyone else.

"What the hell is going on here, Thomas?" Alex growled in my thoughts.

I saw Alex leap in the air simultaneously as I went in for the attack. The slate gray of his wolf transformed into smoke before crashing into Howard. I reached Gina just as her claw went strike Lika across the stomach. My hand shot out, grabbed the obsidian and black veined arm, and slammed her into the wall. I heard bones and the crack of her skull, but I knew she wasn't down.

"This is how it's been since we got here. This entire Pack needs to be cleansed," I growled.

I moved to Lika and grabbed her by the chin, looking her over for scratches or bites before stepping back. I hadn't reached into anyone here for a claiming to meet their wolves, but I took the second right there to do it to Lika. Her eyes widened, and I saw the ring in her eyes that I should have paid more attention to when I first met her. I should have known, and

I couldn't understand why any of this was happening. What in the hell was Pandora, this demon, or fate, planning?

"Wh—what are you doing?" I stared down into her eyes as I felt for the soul, the wolf that lived inside of her. I saw a snow-white wolf with teal-tipped ears and tail. Her burning indigo eyes lowered in submission as she bowed her head. I pulled back sharply and heard the loud gasp from Lika, but I was already moving. It only took seconds, but that was enough time for Gina to get back up with her wounds. I turned, catching the shifter by the throat before pulling out the demon blade Alex had just given me. I felt the power of it vibrating against my skin, and I wasn't sure what it meant. Right before slamming the blade into Gina's chest, I saw the shifter's true self for a split second. I saw the plea to end it, and quickly. I didn't know everything about demon blades, but from what I knew, once stabbed with it, there was no saving the possessed. I knew it was too late for the two shifters and ending it quickly would be best. The blade slammed through her chest, and I caught her body before it hit the floor. I pulled out the blade, flipped it around in my palm, and threw it behind me exactly where Alex tossed Howard's body. I heard the blade hit its target as they both screamed and the obsidian and black veins burned crimson. I let Gina go as her body consumed itself, leaving nothing but a thick black fluid that seeped into the floor.

"Lika," I growled. I moved over to her as she stared at the floor. I grabbed her and looked her over once more before turning to Alex. He stood in front of the barrier, looking at the thrashing children and other shifters who hadn't been taken completely.

"Who did this?" he asked. Lika looked at me, and I could feel that she knew. I didn't have time to explain or to answer Alex as a soul-crushing pain gripped my heart.

Mate

"Alex! I need you to get everyone together in one spot. This isn't over, but I can't leave unless I know you have her," I said.

I wiped the tears from Lika's cheeks as I stared at Alex. His eyes glowed as he stared at me for half a second and then at Lika. His brows raised, but his nod was all I needed. I wanted to say so much and ask many questions, but something was wrong. Whatever the fuck was happening, it was tearing my Mate apart.

"Go," he grunted. I was gone and out of the door without another thought.

"Remi!" I roared. I saw her and Oceayn getting to their feet. I saw the look on Remi's face and the feeling of pure hate. "We will get her back!"

I knew even though Meesha was not a wolf shifter, she was still our blood. We knew she was ours, so with that knowledge, nothing would stop us from finding her anywhere she had been taken.

"She's ours, Remi. Feel her," I growled.

I let my mind go as I felt along the newly formed bond and the old bond that was built before knowing who she was. Then I felt the pull, but it was faint like I was cut off or something was blocking me. The scent of the ocean filled my nose, and I knew Remi stood in front of me. I felt her hand on my chest, and the bond grew stronger as I pulled on the thread in my soul that connected to Meesha.

"There she is. She isn't far," Remi said before breaking our connection. I opened my eyes and looked toward the ocean just as a power surge rippled through us.

"We need to go," I growled. We were both moving toward that massive amount of energy, and it was like nothing I had ever come in contact with.

"Oceayn! Protect Lika! Do not let him come after us, no matter what," Remi shouted. The distance we traveled was in the blink of an eye. We were past the house and made it to the cliff, looking at a deserted beach, but surrounding it were ragged rock formations. "Oh no! Goddess, no," Remi screamed.

The man stood in the shallow end of the water, holding Meesha above the ocean. He was the same shade of green as the veins covering the infected wolves in the hall. His long jet-black hair seemed to move on its own, and it wasn't because of the wind. It snaked around his body like the tattoos covering his arms and face. I knew this was Idhan. He was the one who hurt Remi, and now he had my daughter. Idhan held up his palm to Meesha so casually that it made it seem like she was hanging suspended over the water on her own.

Words between Remi and me weren't necessary because we both jumped from the cliff.

"Thomas, get Meesha and get her out of here."

"I will get Meesha, but if you think I will leave you alone to fight, your ancient mind must have snapped."

We landed on the beach, and I shifted into the third form in one step. I knew I would have to make it count because there was a limited amount of time. Remi and I moved as one when black smoke that crackled with a crimson glow began streaming out of Idhan's mouth, eyes, and nose. I knew this energy because we had faced something like this recently. As the energy shifted and the closer we got, I could see the smoke began to form in an outline of a large black wolf, and when its massive head turned our way, I saw the crimson eyes. It was a *Cadejo*. The *Black Dog* would cause disease, destruction, confusion, chaos, and death. It was once a shifter that opened itself up for possession and became the very thing we all despised. This *Being* was the reason my brothers and sister existed. Our prophecy was to send every single one of the *Cadejo* back to hell.

"This vessel will serve us well."

Hissing laughter from every direction felt like spikes to the brain. I roared and picked up speed, leaping toward Meesha. The black smoke rippled and streamed toward Meesha. Idhan had fallen back, but he wasn't down. Before I could grab Meesha, Idhan flung out his outstretched hand, causing Meesha's body to fly violently further down the beach.

"Our deal is done, demon," Idhan roared. I landed in the water and felt something coming toward me. I ducked and rolled to my feet as the loud, thunderous crash of two blades met each other. Remi's blade came up against diamond, hard obsidian green skin.

"Thomas! Go! Save Meesha," Remi gritted. My heart was split in two, but I knew the faster I got to Meesha, was quicker I could help Remi end that bastard. I moved, but so did Idhan, who effectively blocked my path to my child.

"So you're the one that occupies her every thought. I cannot allow you to keep breathing," Idhan concluded.

"My thoughts exactly," I growled. I let down my walls and let the emotion slam into me. My claws lengthened while I moved, going for Idhan's head. I covered my clawed hand and arm in the blue energy I put my faith in to keep me safe from his brand of poison.

Idhan was more skilled at fighting than I wanted him to be. I struck a blow, making him jump back as he reached for something on his back.

"Don't let it touch you," Remi yelled. She was past me in a second, sending out kicks and sonar all at once. Idhan pulled out a long black staff, spinning and, blocking Remi's attacks. I could tell she was giving me a chance to skate, which I decided to take. I could feel Meesha's pain like it burned in my veins. I reached out mentally to her but was blocked. I could see her writhing on the sand. I had little time, and I had to make my move. I took a step and was by Idhan when I felt a blast of energy coming. I threw up blue energy, deflecting it. He sent another my way, but I somehow dodged it. I rolled enough to see Remi give him a two-legged kick to his midsection and land by rolling into a crouch. She stood back up with the unusual-looking blade, pointing at Idhan. Idhan slid backward while twirling the staff that changed into a spear. Remi had him occupied, and I had to trust she could hold it down. I moved, making my way to Meesha just as her body stopped shaking, and she sat straight up, Michael Myers style.

I could feel my blood rush through my veins and the energy gathering around us all. I heard the hissing whispers that came low and fast. I didn't know the words being spoken, but the ground began to shake as rough waves began to crash against the rocks. Meesha stood, but where a little girl had once been, she was different. As I walked closer, she turned to face me with a deranged smile and crimson eyes. I could see a tear in reality forming as Meesha's lips moved. The crazed smile never left her lips as I approached.

What the hell was I supposed to do?

How am I supposed to kill the demon that was now trapped inside my child?

"You can't do it, can you? You know you would have never been in this position if you had been more like your brothers, but you couldn't control your gifts," it hissed. The voice was old, deep, and stank of evil. But the words...the damn words were valid because this wouldn't have happened if I were strong enough. My parents would still be alive if I were strong enough. Meesha would not be suffering if I were strong enough!

"What do you want?" I gritted. I was glad for the blade Alex handed me before leaving the hall, but now...now, I hated it. I wouldn't need to use it if I had been the Alpha everyone thought I would become. I raised the blade to strike a killing blow, but my thoughts had me frozen. I lost the third form as I stared at Meesha, unable to do what needed to be done again.

"Thomas!" The scent of the ocean and crashing waves seemed to dig its way into my mind. *"Thomas, stop it! It's using your emotions against you! That is not Meesha! We need to get Meesha back, but you have to fight. You overcame this once, and you can do it again. Use the power given to you and get our fucking baby back!"*

I heard Remi scream in pain, but her words snapped me out of whatever Zammiuntau was trying to accomplish. The skies were obscured by thick, dark gray as the opening behind Meesha grew wider. My grip tightened on the blade's hilt as I refocused my eyes. Meesha stood three feet away from me, and I hadn't noticed that she had moved. I shook my head because I had to think of her as Zammiuntau, not Meesha. That was what it was counting on and why it almost had me.

"If you think I will let you take my daughter from me, you are insane. If you believe you can use my gift against me again, you are sorely mistaken," I growled. I brought my other arm up, which was covered in the blue light. I saw the widening of crimson eyes as Zammiuntau jumped back. I let the energy go, praying it wouldn't harm Meesha in the process, but a tanned arm with a tattoo of a dog with red eyes reached through the tear, grabbing hold of Meesha's body and pulling her through.

"Too late yet again," Zammiuntau hissed. I could see trees through the portal that seemed familiar. I leaped for the closing rip, but it snapped shut, sealing me out and Meesha on the other side.

"Tell me what you want! Tell me what you want!" I screamed, but I knew it couldn't hear me. My mind raced to figure out how I could track them and the purpose of all of this shit. My head snapped to Remi when I felt a sharp pain in my chest. I felt something with tremendous power coming toward me. I turned around as a hail of obsidian power came directly at me.

"Thomas, move now! Get out of the way!" I moved slightly. I shifted into wolf form, twisted away, and landed on the sand. I was already back in my human form as I rushed at Idhan. A gust of wind hit my face as Remi slammed me down, using her hardened body to cover mine as a wave of diamond shards came crashing down around us.

"Shit! Damn it! What the hell is this," I grunted. Remi was off me in seconds, forming a barrier as she used the coming storm to cause a rogue wave.

"This is going to hit us all! Get ready, Thomas," she gritted. The massive wave hit Idhan, but he managed to send another blast at us that caused the barrier to buckle. Remi was already using so much power that she knew she would need to release the shield. "Here we go!"

The water crashed into us and felt like bricks slamming into me as it came down and around us. I felt myself being pulled and knew it was Remi from the teal glow that surrounded me. The touch of Remi's mind in my thoughts cleared any doubt and enabled me to focus on what needed to be done.

"Thomas, AETERNUM, are you okay? What happened? Where is Meesha?" I saw the pain in her teal eyes as we floated underwater. I could feel the water receding and knew this brief moment would be over. This wouldn't have stopped Idhan.

"It has her, and she is gone. I will find out where she has gone, and I will get her back, but—"

Everything inside me screamed not to leave my Mate, but I knew it would be the only way. I had to go after Meesha, and Remi needed to deal with the situation here because as long as Idhan was still around, neither of our children would be safe.

"I can deal with the R'lyehan. All I need to know is that you will bring our baby back to us. None of what I do here will matter if we fail Meesha."

I could feel the sand beneath my feet as her words settled in my soul. The trust, faith, and love she had in me demanded the same in return, which I had no problem with.

"You will defeat him, Rehema, and remind him who you are. Do you understand?"

"Yes, Alpha."

I pushed to my feet, knowing we had little time, but I already had a plan formed in my mind. I had to contact someone who could trace portals or gates and also has the ability to create their own.

"Good. Now I need to get to Alex," I growled. Idhan rose from the water, and his long hair moved like tentacles. They wrapped around his body as the tattoos on his face turned from black to a burning liquid green.

"I am finished with these games, Princess. It is time for you to submit and time for this wolf to die."

"You forget who I am, Idhan. Your blood no longer poisons me. I have regained my memories, power, and reasons to erase you from existence."

I could feel the difference in Idhan like a switch had been flipped, and his power grew. I didn't know what it was, but his cyan-colored eyes glowed brightly before turning an inky black.

Remi and I stood side-by-side. I pulled out the demon blade, palming it in my hand. I readied myself for the fight I knew was coming.

"When I move, get the hell out of here and go to Meesha."

Again, there wasn't any debate because it was what had to happen. I pushed a calmness into Remi, and I saw her relax. With everything running through my mind, I knew I had to time this shit right.

"I love you, Remi. I will get her back."

Those were the last words before Idhan raised his spear and roared. Remi slapped her palms together as her teeth sharpened and her mouth began to grow wider. I knew this would be it once she drew in a breath. Remi sent out a blast just as Idhan's spear came spiraling at us. I moved in the other direction. I had to leave my Mate to deal with a past that had been following her since the first day our eyes met.

"And I love you, Alpha. Now Go!"

THOMAS

My claws dug into the rough stone as I climbed up the cliff. My mind ran into different scenarios, trying to understand the logic behind taking a child and going to such lengths to have her created. Nothing made sense to me for any of this to be happening or how Meesha and her family had found their way to us. Is it a coincidence that they joined our Pack, or is it something else altogether? I felt another presence in my mind, causing me to stop moving. I felt like I was falling, but I wasn't moving. My vision went black, and when I opened my eyes, I stared at a wolf that was more than a wolf. Kannuck tilted his head, and I lowered my gaze. The power surrounding me felt immense, making me feel insignificant in the grand scheme of things. Even with all that, I felt my irritation rise because I did not have time for this shit.

"Time moves differently here, Thomas Rayne."

"How do I stop this? How can I help Meesha?"

"You seek answers to the knowledge you already possess. You were created for this purpose, and your powers were granted to you so you may succeed. It doesn't matter how you gained them, but how you will use them to prevent what is to come. Clear your mind and remember

things read long before now. You know what it seeks, why it seeks, and how to destroy it. Learn to trust in your power just as others trust in you."

I blinked and stood on the cliff's edge as rain poured down. I turned back, but I couldn't see anything but flashes of teal and obsidian green. Where the hell was Zammiuntau going? How would I get there in time to stop what he had planned to do?

"Thomas! Where is Remi?" Lika asked. I looked up and saw Alex, Lika, and Oceayn running toward me. I balled my hands into fists, making myself move. Lika's eye grew wider before she ran to the edge. I caught her around the waist and pulled her back toward the house.

"No! Remi will handle it," I growled. As he studied me, Alex cocked his head to the side, but I didn't stop walking.

"No! We can't leave her to fight alone! What is wrong with you? You're the Alpha!"

I stopped and turned Lika to face me. The more I looked at her, the more I saw the blend of our features.

"Talika, your mother will handle it. She is trusting us to save Meesha. She needs us to save your sister," I grunted. Her eyes widened, and I saw when my words snapped her out of the anger she felt.

"Wa—wait...where...Meesha? Where is Meesha? Where the hell is Sam? What happened down there?" Lika stuttered. I let her go and began walking once more.

"We don't have time to waste. The demon threatening this place has taken Meesha, and Sam is missing. The demon has taken possession of Meesha's body."

"What the hell? Thomas, this...for what? This can't be happening, not again. We need to call Devana or Dali. Hell, call Quinn and see if he can get a Hunter," Alex seethed.

"And how long will that take? I need to find her now before it's too late. That bastard is planning something and using Meesha to accomplish it. I just...I don't know why and I fucking should!"

I could feel my thoughts slipping into the darkness inside myself. Without Remi close, I could feel it urging me to feed it. It wanted to kill everyone here for all of this happening. If these shifters had been better or stayed on the path of Kannuck, this demon would not have taken root. I felt a large, strong hand on my shoulder, pulling me back before I let it take hold. The smoke curling around us seemed to clear my thoughts, and I managed to think clearer.

"I will make the call, but it does not mean we can't figure it out, either. We will need help, either way, to get the demon out of Meesha. We will do whatever it takes for family," Alex gritted.

I looked behind me, but Alex was staring at Lika. My gaze flicked to hers and Oceayn. Oceayn's skin rippled into scales as she fought to control her transformation. I only knew that because her nose was now flat with slits, and her eyes seemed to do the same. She turned away as she shook, but her garbled hissing words managed to kickstart my brain.

"Remi will not let me help her. She is keeping me from being able to even come to her aid. We must find Meesha and protect Lika, for they are in line for secession," Oceayn stated.

"Okay, so what about Silent Hill? Would he take her there?" Alex asked. He moved closer to Oceayn but didn't reach out to touch her. His smoke began to surround her, and I watched as she swayed in it and relaxed.

"Silent Hill?" Lika frowned.

"He is talking about Sunset Port. Alex make the call to Quinn. Either way, someone will need to get down here and hold it together until we return. We will need whatever help is available," I said. I inclined my head because it was a thought. We hadn't killed everyone, but there weren't many left. "We killed the leader of that cult. Darlena is done, and most of her pet shifters."

"What about Edwin? Even their daughter would've been a problem if she didn't run off with some fake ass Alpha. He tried to come through here, but Darlena and Edwin claimed they stopped them from advancing but lost wolves in the process. I always thought it was odd because Lena learned about dark magic from her mother, so she wasn't the type to follow anyone weak. From what Darlena had said, the wolf was nothing, so it was weird, but whatever. Then Hayley came back here after taking care of a few things out of state, and that's when they began to leave. We were all relieved by it, mostly. They were followers of Jace, the old Alpha. He was into the evil shit, and they were deeply involved with that, so it was good they were gone," Lika said. Something about what she said caught my attention.

"Wait...wait, what now? What does Lena look like?" I asked, facing Lika. I heard when Alex ended his conversation, and he turned toward me. He folded his arms across his chest, but his eyes burned into mine.

"Oh, ahh, Lena is a slim chick with a tanned olive skin tone, I guess. She has coral-colored eyes and keeps her hair dyed that same shade. She also has a tattoo on her inner wrist of a Hellhound," Lika finished, but I was already moving.

"Shit! I'll call Malic," Alex growled.

"Lika. How long will that barrier hold?" I grunted.

"That barrier will not come down until I touch it. If someone else touches it, they will be pulled through with the others. It will also dissolve if the threat inside of it is neutralized," Lika said.

"Even if you aren't around? Is it that powerful?"

"Yes, but I can't always make it happen. It just happens at times," she said. The rain began to pour out like a hurricane was incoming. I could hear and feel the battle going on, but I had to keep my mind on how to find Meesha and Sam. If anything, Sam was freed and ran away, but we would find him.

"No one is answering! Something is up, and I can't get through to anyone," Alex shouted. I knew that would be the problem, but none of it mattered because it would be too late when any of us could make it there.

"What about Quinn? Camron or Hay—" I was cut off when a scaled hand touched my shoulder. I turned and looked into the slitted eyes of a viper.

"I need to stay here and wait for Rehema. I know she will have regained all her memories and knowledge, and she will be able to open a gate to get to you. I can open a gate for you, but it will be short, and it can only be done once, so you must hurry through it. Doing this could cause someone else to find this realm, and they will come to investigate," Oceayn stated.

"Will it put you in danger?" Alex growled. He had moved and invaded Oceayn space. She stepped back, meeting her angered gaze with his.

"None of that matters as long as we protect Zhavia! This is my duty and what is expected of me. If something comes for me, you better believe I will handle it," she snapped. Oceayn seemed to slither backward as she held her hands to the sides. "Send me your thoughts of where you need to be, and I will get you there close by it."

"Thomas," Alex growled low, but I knew what he was saying. To most, Alex was difficult to read, but his emotions did all the talking for me.

"Stay with her and make sure you bring my Mate when you come."

"You know I got you, little brother. I will contact someone. You know your brothers will not go down without a fight."

"Yeah, but what scares me is that they won't know to fight. It's wearing Meesha's body, and now it can pass through the wards. She is a Rayne, Alex. She can get through any ward on the property."

Nothing else needed to be said as I turned back to Oceayn and sent thoughts of my home and the people living there. I sent the surrounding land and houses into her thoughts.

"I am coming with you! I need to come with you," Lika persisted. I stared into her eyes, opened up to feel her emotions, and saw the pain. Things had happened to her in the past, but the thought of losing Remi, Meesha, or even me when she just met us seemed to eat her soul alive.

"Do not leave my side, Talika. Do you understand me?" I could tell that wasn't the answer she expected, but if she believed I would let anyone else that belonged to me out of my sight, she was trippin'.

"Yes, Alpha," she smiled. The wind began to pick up as Oceayn made a series of signs with her hands. She moved faster while the wind and rain picked up. It whipped around us as she mumbled words I couldn't understand but heard in Remi's thoughts. Suddenly, the rain and wind stopped as colorful lights seemed to form out of nowhere. It began to stretch into a shimmering sphere that blinked in and out. Oceayn held her hands together as she shook from the force.

"Go! Go now!" Oceayn cried.

I could not see anything but smoke inside the gate, but I trusted that she would get us where we needed to be. I moved, and I could feel Lika just behind me. The sphere was getting smaller by the second, and I knew I had to make this quick. I grabbed Lika and leaped. We slammed through the sphere, and everything flashed brightly with color before it went black.

We fell a few feet to the ground as everything returned in sharp focus. I rolled to the side, coming up to my feet as I stared around. Lika hit the ground hard but pushed herself up and dusted the dirt and leaves from her pink and gray tee-shirt.

"Where are we?" She coughed. Everything was silent as I opened my mind to reach out to Malic or the Enforcers. Something was wrong as I breathed in the air and could taste death.

"We need to move. Shift," I commanded.

Lika began her shift without hesitation, and I could tell she would be just as fast as one of us in time. I started running toward my home as I mentally screamed out to anyone in my Pack that was listening. Something was nagging me in the back of my mind about why Zammiuntau would want to risk coming here. I just couldn't see it, but whatever the reason, that would be where he fucked up. We are a family of all Alphas, and nothing would cause us to fall.

Maybe, except for a child that everyone loves.

We were close now, and I could see the house through the trees and knew we would be coming up on the back end of the main property.

A deafening roar broke the silence, emitting a powerful shock wave that spread throughout the woods, reaching the heavens. My eyes widened when the sky suddenly turned gray as a vast portion of the land was wiped out. Homes and other buildings were just gone. Howls ripped through the air, but I still could not contact anyone. Some kind of spell was blocking mental speech, but I had no time to find it and get rid of it.

"Oh My God, Thomas! We have to stop her!" Lika cried. I felt her pain and anguish in my soul at the knowledge of what we may have to do. She had shifted back, panting hard as her eyes took in the devastation.

"We need to find Meesha and get her away from here!" I growled. My heart started racing as mixed feelings of shock and rage got ahold of my senses. I sprinted towards the source of it while countless thoughts came to mind, yet I knew exactly what this was about. My Pack had no clue what was happening, and they would not think twice that it would be Meesha. Lika ran behind me, but even she couldn't keep up with my speed. I had to slow down because I refused to lose her, too. She wasn't far behind as she raced after me and soon came up behind me. We approached the scene as a screen of dust covered our vision. I dashed further into it until I felt the grass beneath my feet. It was suddenly harsh and cold like life had left that area entirely. I opened up to the emotions on the land and could feel pain, confusion, anger, and sadness, but they were further away from where we were. Nothing was left alive here in this place.

"This can't be happening," I whispered.

The scene almost matched what happened the night my parents were killed. The same feeling and scent as my vision suddenly cleared to a scene straight out of hell. A dark brown wolf with long spiked fur stepped around the body of one of my Pack members, but I could not tell who it was by looking. I could feel their wolf and could tell they held on, but it wouldn't last much longer. The brown wolf was covered in blood, holding another wolf in between his fangs. Another tan wolf stalked the grounds, and a tall broad-shoulder man stepped out of a house holding a young male wolf shifter. I felt my anger build when he threw My'kel to the ground, but the young shifter rolled to the right.

"That's Edwin," Lika growled.

"Help My'kel and leave the rest to me," I grunted. My'kel came up in a crouch, hitting a wolf that tried to come for his throat. I shifted between forms like it was nothing. I stayed in my third form as I ran toward the pup before they killed him.

"My Alphas will kill you," My'kel roared.

I let my Alpha energy be known as I pushed out fear, pain, and the force of my *Will.* My'kel's eyes widened as another large wolf attacked. The massive smoke gray wolf slammed into the boy. He went down, and the man that came out of the house leaped into my space. I reached for the wolf inside of him but found his energy and soul closed to me.

"Aht, aht, that is not for you to control," he growled. I saw a blur of white and teal fly by me to crash into the wolf that took down Mykel. I had faith in Lika to deal with them until I could take out this man. I stopped moving and stood a few feet away as more wolves with crimson eyes came to surround me.

"You are not protected by this demon just like your Mate was not. If you think I can't harm you, you need to think again," I snarled. These wolves were neither Alphas nor strong without the evil coursing through their veins. I may not be able to control their wolves, but their emotions were mine. I pushed the fear inside them, causing some wolves to fall, but Edwin stood. He began to shift, but I refused to give him a chance. I need this over quickly so I could find Zammiuntau and save Meesha.

"You may put down the weaker wolves, Rayne, but not a wolf like me," he roared.

The wolves still standing attacked as soon as I moved. My clawed hand swiped out, gutting a leaping wolf. I used my other hand to catch a wolf by its front leg and threw it at two others. Edwin was even taller as his skin gleamed with sweat. The light fur that covered his chest didn't hide the tattoo of the giant Hellhound. More wolves came from the tree line as shouts and screams filled the air. His massive fist came at my head, but I dodged it and struck out, hitting another large wolf on its head. I spun around, dropped to a knee, and brought up my fist, hitting Edwin in the thigh. I opened my hand, and my claw dug in deep. I reached the bone and pulled, snapping his thigh bone in two. He roared, and more howls came from all around us. Shifters I knew and shifters I didn't begin to come out of homes and buildings. They all held the same dark gaze. Some eyes glowed crimson, and others were black as open space.

Edwin leaped back, and I turned to find Lika and My'kel. Another howl crashed through the sounds of the grunts and growls of the wolves that were closing in on us. I moved to Lika, who ripped the throat out of a shifter, and My'kel used a blade to stab at any wolf that came close. I rammed my way through the wolves to get close to them just as Lika was hit. Her howl of pain flipped something inside me, and I went on a rampage. I didn't know how many wolves I cut down, but I was covered in thick, black blood. I slid across the grass and used my claws to cut tendons and muscles in the legs of the wolves that tried keeping me from my child. I reached Lika just as she pushed up on all fours and saw the long gash on her side.

"You can't protect them and kill me simultaneously," Edwin sneered. I felt a shift in the air, and scents I knew as well as my own filled the space. I smiled, letting go of my third form as I lifted Lika in my arms. My'kel stood as well, holding the bloody blade as she tried keeping all the wolves in his line of sight.

"Oh, but he doesn't need to deal with you. Let us handle this, Thomas. It's what Enforcers are for," Ezra growled. Edwin spun around just as a large platinum gray wolf with a white diamond on its back took him to the ground. Jamel howled as he slammed Edwin repeatedly to the ground. Ezra smiled as he took in the rest of the wolves and cracked his neck.

"We got this, Thomas. You have to go now," Ezra growled. His canines lengthened, and his claws grew out as he roared a challenge and more of my Pack came running.

"Meesha?"

"That is not Meesha. Find Malic," Ezra growled. I wasted no more time. I knew the Enforcers trained with Devana and could handle the possessed. With Lika in my arms, I took off as I pushed healing energy into her wound.

"My'kel, keep up."

Remi

The water crashed against my legs as Idhan came at me repeatedly. I had to block out everything and the pain of knowing my child was gone. I had to trust Thomas to find Meesha and deal with the demon riding in her body. I leaned back as his staff flew at my head, then struck back with the blade, managing to cut his arm, but the moving hair absorbed the blow. Idhan jumped back, landing in the shallow waters, and sucked his pointed teeth. The black marking on his face seemed to move around as he watched me for my next move. Idhan began to wade through the water, causing it to suddenly became agitated. Waves started forming at the horizon, getting bigger and bigger each second. This was not coming from me, but the power surrounding me felt familiar and all-knowing. It followed me, opening the last of my lost memories and revealing who I was. I remembered the full scope of my power, and I could feel it returning to me.

"It seems I am not welcomed here, Rehema," Idhan shouted, raising his arms high. The waves gathered, coming from all directions, drowning the beach with their power. Idhan smiled at the scene before disappearing suddenly into the deep. Numerous water tornados emerged from the ocean and standing at the top of one of them was a beautiful woman with very distinct traits. She had white spots spread all over her brown skin and a coral crown above her long, dark locs that only added to her beauty. She raised a long, oddly shaped spear with four points, and I instantly knew exactly what it was. I had only seen it once when my mother held it in battle, but soon after, it was gone. The endpoints were shorter than the other two in the middle. The white-gold gleamed when the lightning flashed. The storm raged as the woman threw the Trident toward me. I knew right then my mother and father were dead. Now it was up to me to save the rest of my kingdom, even if I had to get it done alone.

Olo.

"This Trident belongs to the Queen of Hyquadra. It is now yours, Rehema Remi Zhavia."

The waves pushed me forward and into the air as I reached for what belonged to me. I caught it in one hand and turned my body around as the waves brought me back to the beach as it receded. I landed on the sand on one knee, and my Trident slammed to the ground.

"Thank you, Goddess," I whispered, knowing she heard me. I stood looking toward the sky. I carefully looked around the deserted beach until the ocean calmed back down. I saw the R'lyehan floating in mid-air with an energy shield around him. The water ran down the shield and revealed my enemy's handsome, deranged face. He raised a brow at the Trident in my hands before he let a slow smile creep across his face. Idhan bared his teeth while licking his lips as he let the shield fall away. His obsidian green skin began to glow as he pulled his staff from his back.

"Queen," Idhan chuckled. "I have come to claim what is mine and take this world. But I shall start with finishing capturing your kingdom. You alone will give me the power to pass through these gates and allow me to bring all R'lyehan through. You will learn to submit, Princess, and I will have you by my side and down on your knees," he added.

"You cannot have this realm, this world, nor keep mine," I growled.

"I know what it means when one gets the Trident. Nakeema will be disappointed, but that isn't my problem. Lucky for you, that snake managed to return it into the depths for you, weak Goddess. Now let's end this, so you understand your place. You submit now and deliver your brother to me, and I will give your people the option of conversion. But the people in this realm...are a lost cause. You can either save this realm or your own. The choice has always been yours, Princess," Idhan taunted. As he spoke, I used the Trident to call the storm and stir up the surrounding water.

"Enough, R'lyehan! I won't follow you even if the world around me crumbles to dust! But I am not worried, Idhan, because you will die here this day," I replied. I pointed my Trident toward him, and all the waterspout vortex advanced, crossing the water's surface.

"Fascinating attack, but it has to reach me first," Idhan said, holding his staff with both hands. I used the Trident to move the waterspout, which, once merged, would form tornados because Idhan was moving at an unbelievable speed, and I had difficulty following him. I pulled on the ancient power of my *Livyatan*. I raised my other arm, letting the teal light glow from my palm as I kept him in sight. I slammed my other hand onto the Trident and pushed power into it until the tornados caught up with him and circled him completely. Each tornado kept closing in on him until they reached their target, merging into a mega waterspout vortex that spun uncontrollably before vanishing into a cloud of droplets dropping from the sky. I let out a long breath, closing my eyes and seeing Meesha's face.

"Well, well, you thought you got rid of me? I know you didn't think it would be that simple, did you? I think I like this side of you, Princess. I'm getting hard just at the sheer power I will possess," Idhan chuckled, showing up from behind me. I hadn't even heard or felt him close to me. I froze at his voice and felt his breath caressing her neck. A cold drop of sweat slithered down my back with each word he spoke. The snarl that escaped my lips before his hand clamped around my throat was full of hate and disgust that I had let him get this close. I wasn't focused and needed to be so I could return to my family, my children, and my *Aeternum.*

"You really hate me this much that you can't stand my touch? But you would let this youngling, that wolf, touch what is mine," Idhan growled. I turned swiftly to strike with my Trident to find that he was right beside me this time. He put his hand over my hair, and I reached towards him to slap it away, but he caught my hand. Idhan had the nerve to hold onto it like we were some loving couple.

"Ahh, so you finally accept that you're mine now, don't you, Princess," Idhan said.

"I won't repeat myself, and as I am now queen, I never go back on my words, R'lyehan," I gritted.

"All that pride, and you are still here holding my hand," Idhan smiled.

"Yeah, it works better when we are up close and personal," I roared. I reached for the blade in my waistband and, moving, sliced upward, causing him to let go of my hand. When he dodged my blade, I clenched my other hand into a fist, turning the water droplets still falling into flying daggers. They headed directly toward Idhan. He wielded his staff expertly, blocking the flurry of attacks I used to try to overwhelm him. I gathered a large quantity of water above his head as he deflected the blasts I'd sent. I pointed my Trident toward the floating water, instantly turning it into freezing water. The darkened sky flashed with obsidian green lighting. Idhan raised his head and saw the water forming rapidly into ice. I let go of the power, which shattered and dropped spears of ice over his head. Idhan unleashed a shield that expended even more, this time disintegrating all the ice daggers around him. A giant ice spear and shield collided, causing a loud shock wave. When it erupted from the impact, the massive ice spear pierced through the shield as it burned a bright teal. Idhan suddenly slit his arms open, making his green blood pour down. I was confused at his actions, but then it managed to dispel his shield, making the ice fall directly over him. He raised his bloody hand to the sky like he would catch it barehanded.

"No way! This can't be happening!" I roared. The teal energy and his blood met and burned brightly for a second. I stepped back when I saw the ice spear stop moving at the contact of Idhan's blood. He smiled as his blood spread through the ice, almost like it ate away at the energy I'd poured into the water. The teal struggled against it before turning obsidian green. Idhan turned toward me and pointed his hand where I stood. The ice switched targets and went directly for me instead. I held a hand and panicked when it would not respond to my call. It was water, and everything dealing with it should bow to my *Will.* I put my hands together, causing a whirlpool to form between me and the ice spear. A drop of sweat fell down my forehead because I knew my defense wasn't gonna do anything to prevent me from getting injured. But as the ice flew toward me and was about to hit, I closed my eyes. I readied myself for the impact when I heard a deep chuckle. I could feel Oceayn trying to call out to me and felt her wanting to come to me. I blocked out her calls and stopped her from coming. This was between Idhan and me. I would take him out and stop the plans his people had for all the realms. Idhan was just one piece on the board and would be the first one to go.

"Giving up already, Princess?" Idhan laughed.

I opened my eyes to see him bring his hand down, making the glowing obsidian green ice explode into a glittering green fog. My eyes widened because I knew this shit was mixed with his blood. His poisoned blood now floated around like an airborne virus. The green fog floated around me before disappearing a second later.

"I'm not trying to kill you, Princess. That is not my aim," Idhan said calmly. I stared at him, giving no response because I knew this was all a game to him. Destroying lives and taking away homes from people in different realms meant nothing. I needed to fight hard, and I had to demand my power return to me. This was my power, and I was the only *Being* to control it. "However, I am gonna make you beg to save your people since you ran from me," Idhan growled.

Suddenly, I felt a sense of dizziness come over me and burning in my veins. "You see, blood is exceptional in different ways. First, the color differs greatly from yours as I contain a highly concentrated poison that can be lethal or cause other side effects, as you know. But, you know you don't need to worry about all that, Princess. I also have the ability to control its doses and move it as I will. That's how I managed to control your attack," he explained.

"Why are you telling me this," I asked while grabbing my head.

The numbing feeling spread through my body. My vision became blurry to the point I couldn't keep them open. I dropped to the sand and reached toward the sea. The water pulled me deeper as Idhan laughed in my mind. Flashes of Meesha, Lika, Oceayn, and Thomas came one after another as my body sank into the ocean's depths. How was I supposed to do this now without my Trident? Why am I even fighting him because I know they will always win in the end? Idhan always delivered what his Goddess wanted. My body entered the shadows of a vast ocean as I recalled my memories of Thomas. Thoughts of him stormed through my mind peacefully until a vision hit me with force. A vision in which Idhan controlled my people and reigned over my realm while invading this realm. I watched as Idhan pierced Thomas with his hand and hung his lifeless body for everyone to see. Thomas stared at me, and the indigo ring in his eyes faded to black before pulsing an obsidian green. After seeing those visions overwhelmed my thoughts with mixed feelings of sadness and complete rage. Thomas was fading, but I could hear an echo of words.

You will defeat him, Rehema, and remind him who you are. Do you understand?

I snapped my eyes open as a blue glow seemed to burn through my veins, then poured out of my eyes. It felt like Thomas, intense, filled with life but hidden darkness. My Livyatan fed as I regained consciousness. I let the power flow through me as my body transformed. The blue glow spread wider over my body as a glowing teal mark of alternating rings of sea and land appeared on my forehead. The symbol of Zhavia pulsated as a long, sleek, black fin emerged from my back while my legs turned into a large Orca's tail. I flapped my tail, bursting out of the water at an incredible speed and into the sky.

"Finally, the true power of the Queen of Hyquadra. It's an honor witnessing a power that I will soon control," Idhan growled in my mind.

Even in this form, I couldn't beat him alone, but I sensed the lives of the surrounding ocean, all kinds of beasts traveling to be by my side like they had been waiting. They were waiting for my return and my command. As I thought those words, multiple water jets splashed over the surface, showing numerous whales coming to surround me.

"You got some company, Rehema, but it will not be enough."

"Let's end this here and now, R'lyehan. You will never make it back to tell anyone about this realm. And when I get back to my kingdom, I will decapitate Idh's head just as you did my mother's, and she will join you next!"

I began communicating messages to all creatures that came to defend their realm. I let the power fill me to the brim as I shifted once more into my final form. I could now swim in the deep and also walk on land. The sleek black fin was smaller on my back, and the fins on my arms gave me the speed I needed to glide through the waters. I reached out my hand, calling to my Trident and blade. I put my hands together as I crashed to the surface and back into the air. Idhan came at me quickly, but I dodged and blocked his staff, matching energy to energy. He flew back, and I landed on one of the water jets. I clapped my hands together, forming a *sign*, and pushed power into it, causing the ocean itself split in half, dividing into different parts around me before rising into the sky, forming into floating sea mid-air, and trapping Idhan in the middle of it.

"Your mistakes will cost you a lot, Rehema. I can also control any creature with my blood inside," Idhan smirked. His sharp pointed teeth gleamed as he raised his hand and lengthened his nails. Idhan clawed his massive chest so profoundly that blood poured out, making a sphere around him.

"You are in my domain, no. I have control over everything in here! Nothing in this realm or mine belongs to your kind," I said. My Trident slammed into my hand while the blade slammed into the other. I made a powerful current hit through Idhan, dispersing his blood and making it pour more and more. This made Idhan forcefully heal himself with his staff as the sea creatures swarmed him. His blood may be poisoned, but I had something for all that shit. I looked at my Trident and connected the blade to it, watching it sink into the white gold, causing it to flash teal before settling back to its usual color. I wasted no time and pointed my Trident toward the ocean, raising it high before throwing it into the waves.

"Bring him to the deep!" I roared. The first to attack was the swordfish that dived directly at Idhan, piercing him in his shoulder. He used his staff to block their sharp edges and dashed away into the water. I smiled because he was now panicking and had done exactly what I wanted him to do. He had no more surprises and no one to help him. There wasn't a Nakeema here to help with his plan, and I would make sure he never used that poison again. I brought my hand down, and the divided waves crashed back together as I dived into the deep.

His speed decreased drastically, causing him not to be able to keep up with their attacks. As Idhan struggled, I moved through the waters, sending a blast his way. He was deflecting them but hitting him was not what I wanted. He needed to pay for the things he had done, and I needed to know he would never come back out of this sea alive. I pushed him further into the abysm and directly to an underwater volcano. As sharks, whales, fish, and other creatures attacked him, I flashed by him, sending more energy, causing him to turn and shift. I reached the area that I knew housed a mighty volcano. I could feel the heat in the sea and the power of the elemental inside of it. I hadn't thought I would find one here, but I was grateful.

I floated right over the opening and called out to *Being*. I showed it what Idhan has done and what he would do to this realm if he wasn't stopped. For long moments, I heard nothing but a whisper of sound in my thoughts, and the burning of fire answered my question. I had the go-ahead to do whatever needed to be done. I waited for the right moment and stormed in toward Idhan. I hit him, but he blocked me with his sword. The collision caused him to fly toward the top, but a mighty whale awaited him above and dived with all its might. He put his staff between him and the whale, trying to absorb the attack, but to no use, as he was at a significant disadvantage inside the water.

This world was mine, and he knew they would have never taken Hyquadra if it weren't for the traitor in our kingdom. The whale swallowed the R'lyehan whole but then he got brutally expelled. Idhan flew out of the whale's mouth, but his staff caught the blue whale and cut it open. He regained his balance and floated away from the other creatures but did not see me. My Trident came crashing through the depths and slammed into his stomach. I moved and grabbed the Trident, yanking it free just as I hit him in his chest. His screams were muted under the water, but he saw the volcano. He noticed the volcano was right beneath him and his eyes widened at the massive lava hand reaching for him. Idhan never noticed me as I swam beside him with the Hydranodic Blade. I stabbed him in his eye, slamming it so deep that I felt it hit the back of his skull.

"Enough!" Idhan shouted.

He swung his staff with all his might, driving me away. He turned towards the volcano and, with his own blood, formed a more extended staff. I could tell Idhan was weakened at that point after using so much energy and losing that much blood. Still, he raised his head and saw me floating there, smiling wide, surrounded by floating spheres of water holding my Trident over my head. I pushed power as it began to transform into a colossal four-pointed Trident. Idhan forgot about the lava as he stared at me with hatred until it wrapped around his body and began to burn his flesh.

"You should've never threatened my realm or this one, especially my AETERNUM*. That's where you fucked up. Even if you use the whole blood inside your pitiful body, you wouldn't have any chance of controlling the power I now hold. You would never have been able to because, as you can see, I have a bit of a problem holding on to it!"* My arm shook from the power. *"Now, VANQUISH!"* I moved at speeds under the water I could never do before, heading directly to Idhan. The colossal Trident pierced through him violently as I pushed him down inside the fiery depths of the volcano.

As I rose to the surface, I felt a vibration spread through the ocean. Before breaking through the surface, I froze, floating in the water, trying to feel where it had come from. The power seemed familiar, and it was like it was answering the amount of energy that I had put out. It didn't happen again, and I didn't have the time to wait for it. I reached out to Thomas and got nothing, so I contacted Oceayn and got an immediate reply.

"Meet me on the beach."

I broke through to the surface and felt the calmness of the ocean. The storms brought on by the fight left a sun-filled sky. It was peaceful, but I knew it was all an illusion until I was with my family. Nothing will be at peace until I had my daughter back. I swam to the shore and searched for Sam. I hadn't seen him when we got here, so I was hoping he was back with the Pack, but a foreboding in my gut told me something was wrong. That child did not deserve all that had happened to him, and I knew that we would do whatever was necessary to find him as well.

"Remi!" Oceayn waved me toward her and Alex. I shifted to human form as I stepped out of the water and made my way to Oceayn.

"Where are they? Is..."

"I used a gate to send them to where Meesha is," Oceayn stated. I could tell by the resignation in her eyes that she understood what she had just done. Without her telling me everything, I knew the form she was in now was because of a spell. If she used her powers, it would be like a beacon to the one that cursed her to look this way.

"Whoever comes, we will handle it, Oceayn. You are not alone in this," I stated.

"Yes, I know," Oceayn sighed.

"The demon took Meesha home, Remi," Alex specified. I looked into his eyes as they glowed with unrestrained anger. Again, the Rayne Pack had been attacked, but no one would see it coming this time until it is too late.

"Now that Idhan is dead, only one thing is left threatening my family. Let's move," I said. I raised my hands in front of me and began reciting the ancient words that connected one place to another. I spoke words that I hadn't spoken in years. The language of our Goddess rolled off my tongue as if I had never forgotten how to speak it. The colorful light of the gate began to glow as an opening formed in front of us. I looked back at Alex and Oceayn and they stared at the gate as it expanded so we all could fit through.

"Go, Remi. We need to stay here and care for the Pack. It is broken and needs an Alpha here to heal the others. Tell my brother, to bring my nieces back," Alex gritted.

"I will remain here with Alex but make sure you come back, my Queen," Oceayn bowed. I dropped my hands and gave them both a nod before stepping through to help save everything that I cared for in the world.

THOMAS

The howls and screams came from the main house. That told me where I would find Malic, and whoever else was here. I still couldn't reach out to anyone on the property, but I could feel Malic not far away. I raced through the grounds and came to a scene I would call straight from Hell. Shifters from my Pack were everywhere, fighting wolves with crimson or black eyes. As they fought, some shifters stood in their human form, and I could clearly see the tattoos carved into their flesh. They all had tattoos of a Hellhound. Except I began to notice that the Hellhound looked like the normal but had two heads. The one Hellhound had crimson eyes, and the other a burning orange.

I had seen this particular hound somewhere before. Lika twisted, and I let her down as a wolf came from the side of a house. I reached out and slapped the wolf to the ground. I moved just as another leaped in the air, but a white and teal blur took down a wolf coming from my left. I was already ducking as another jumped from the roof. I grabbed it in the air as the wolf used its paws to slash across my chest. I snapped the neck of the wolf and saw My'kel fall to the ground with a giant wolf over him. My'kel stabbed the wolf before kicking it off of him, but I knew it wouldn't stay down. My'kel rolled to his feet, and Lika moved to flank him. Her mouth was covered in dark blood, but she was good. They both looked at me, and I pointed toward Max. Max was fighting four of the possessed shifters. One of them was a wolf, and the others were in human form. They fought relentlessly, but Max had no problem keeping up with the shifters. His problem was he was protecting three pups and a few cubs.

"Max!" I roared. I threw the demon blade, hitting one of the wolves in the neck. Max raised his head after stabbing another wolf in the chest. The shifters screamed as their bodies began to burn and turn to dust. I was moving just as Max struck another shift in the thigh and yanked. The possessed shifter went flying and slammed into another house.

"How...how the hell did you get here? What the fuck happened in Florida?" Max panted. Lika leaped for the wolf's throat, coming up behind Max. He spun around, grabbed Lika, and pulled her away. His blade sank deep into the wolf's head.

"Where is Malic? Where is Meesha?"

"Bruh, that is not Meesha," he growled.

"Where, Max?" I said, picking up my blade. My'kel came up beside me but moved to the children hiding behind Max.

"I don't know. Shit got crazy, and I lost Malic during the fight. They keep coming unless you take them out with a blade. They are changing our shifters, Thomas," Max gritted. "This was the worst fucking time for Dali to go on a mission!" A roaring howl ripped through us all, shaking the ground beneath us. I reached out and held Lika in place before deciding I knew she would hate it.

"Lika! Shift and take my blade. Do not leave Max's side, do you understand?"

Lika began to shift, and Max looked at me like I was crazy. I didn't have time to explain shit, but I knew where I was going. I had to know Lika would be safe.

"Who is—"

"My daughter."

"You work fast as shit! I mean damn."

"Max. Do not let anything happen to her while I save Meesha," I said.

"Thomas, you can't leave me here. She is my sister and—"

"I can't have you in any more danger. I don't know if he will also try to get inside you. I won't take the chance. I need to go," I growled. I looked at Max, but there were no words that needed to be exchanged. I knew he got it. I looked Lika over one last time and saw all the best parts of Remi and me. "Stay with Max. Keep these children safe because it will not be over until either the demon or I am dead."

I turned away and began running toward the screams and growls. I knew once I reached my brother, everything would change. I would get Meesha back even if I had to die in the process.

I saw Malic with a few shifters from our Pack fighting other shifters. The shifters that attacked them were shifters from our Pack. I could tell from this distance that they were possessed. I launched myself in the middle of the fight as I shifted, partially using my claws to take down a shifter that leaped at Malic.

"Thomas! Meesha...Meesha, it's—" We both looked up as a loud screech came from above and dived at us. My mouth fell open at the large owl that swooped down, grabbing one of the possessed shifters and ripping it to shreds. "I told you!" Malic roared just as the ground shook, and a roar sent a blast of energy, knocking us all down to the ground.

"Where...tell me where it is!" A gigantic black wolf with crimson eyes stepped between the possessed shifters that pulled themselves to their feet. "WHERE IS IT," he growled again as a powerful aura expanded out of his being. The mental voice forced its way into every mind that touched our land. I felt some of our weaker Pack members drop to their knees as howls of pain and whimpers surrounded us. Malic came to my side with wide eyes because I knew this thing was Meesha. I was done with this shit, and at least I knew Malic had my back while I dealt with Zammiuntau. With my claws lengthened, I took a step forward, staring evil in the eyes.

"Enough!" I growled and dashed forward, releasing my power. With all the rage inside of me, I ran toward the enemy. I shifted into my wolf, letting my energy fuel the power inside me. My paws hit the ground. Each stroke caused small craters to form. I increased my speed, and Zammiuntau noticed. He lowered his head to look at me, but I was already in his face. I bit his neck and threw him across the field. Blood erupted from Zammiuntau's neck while I stood in front of Malic and the others as they took care of his followers.

"Yesss, yes, Thomas. This is what I like to see from you. Let that evil that lives inside come out to play," Zammiuntau hissed. I stared at him, ensuring he kept his attention on me while Malic got rid of his shifters. I knew things were getting harder because more and more of our own were being infected.

"Don't let them bite you!" Malic shouted. I stared at Zammiuntau as he paced. "You are the Alpha of this pack, aren't you? You should be trying to save your people. Give me what I want, and I will stop this," he growled. Zammiuntau's wounds started to heal before my eyes. I kept staring at him with no reply. What was he looking for, and why hadn't he found it? The main house was untouched, but the bodies of shifters lay scattered across the grounds. "I can sense that you are no ordinary Alpha. Pandora was right about that," he shared.

"You know nothing of what I am. And what the fuck does Pandora have to do with anything? When I drag you out of Meesha, I will deal with Pandora next," I growled. What was I missing? "What are you?" he asked, sighting at him.

"You know my name, and you know what I am. Don't play a stupid, wolf. I will tell you that what I am in reality will be revealed shortly. Just make sure to survive until then," Zammiuntau laughed.

He pushed an intimidating aura from his body, and dark figures came out as his eyes turned to a bright crimson with black-slitted pupils. His fangs were more apparent while his claws manifested instantly as he stood on two legs. I had no clue where Meesha was, but with this much evil coursing through her, how much more would she be able to take? I shifted into the third from Zammiuntau, revealing his true nature. With the wolf-shaped head but the body of a giant beast, he flexed claws sharper than butcher knives. Zammiuntau roared, but I held my composure. I focused on how to deal with such a Being and tried working out what he needed so badly. Zammiuntau helped Pandora create a vessel, but to do what? Attack the Pack, but to what end? I roared my challenge at him, and we rushed toward each other. At the speeds we were moving, I knew it was as if we had disappeared for a second until our claws collided. A barrage of slashes sounded like thunder as our attacks met. Swiftly, we both moved across the rough ground as I tried pushing him further away from the Pack. With each step, a loud bang would follow. My mind ran scenarios of what brought him here and why he was just pacing in front of the house. It held the same wards as the property but more substantial. Still, it wouldn't matter because he wore my child like a bodysuit. He would have access to everything, everything except—

My mind went blank as I started feeling numbing throughout my body.

"You are getting sloppy, Thomas!" Zammiuntau hissed. "You will tell me what I need to know," Zammiuntau growled. I didn't reply, but I knew he was right. Zammiuntau's attacks were getting stronger and stronger, while I felt weakened with each attack.

I had to do something, and fast. The more I thought about the tattoos and his words, the more I realized where I had seen the picture before. That night, when I read the book to find the ritual to call a Necromancer, I saw it. It was written in a language I didn't know, but I knew anything in that book was to bring something to you or to open something. Sweat came down his forehead as we fought.

"Now watch you, wolf!" Zammiuntau shouted. I froze when I heard the last word. Multiple arms emerged from Zammiuntau's back, and his mouth opened wide. The dark void of his gapping mouth made his name make sense. *Devour*. The arms caught my limbs before slashing me across the chest. A loud howl dispersed across the grounds. I collapsed on the ground while Zammiuntau stood above me. He reached down, and I felt the tip of a claw press into my temple. I screamed at the pain as he ripped through my mind, looking for what he sought. He sucked in my memories and knowledge, taking everything I was and devouring it all.

I knew what he sought. "Now, do you see what's standing before you, Alpha?" Zammiuntau closed his massive jaws as a sinister smile spread across his face. My body shook as I tried holding onto myself. What had been done, and how had he managed to do it? I felt the blue light pulse inside of me. That part of me was hidden deep, and I didn't think even he could touch it. The energy began to spread throughout my body. I could feel something moving in my veins like it tried eating away at my soul. "I see that I overestimated you, wolf. You are as worthless as all the others. You couldn't even save your child when you had her this entire time," he added. I could feel the dark energy inside me demanding more pain, more blood. The energy seemed to burst through my system, pushing out whatever Zammiuntau had tried to do to me. I moved suddenly and twisted backward. I landed on my feet. I had one fist on the ground to stop myself from sliding. I didn't stop there and launched myself into the air. I crashed into Zammiuntau, but I didn't give him time to think before I bit down into his neck. A moment of silence went by as I let the dark energy given to me by Shannara feed.

"You never learn, do you?" Zammiuntau roared. The arms on his back caught me by the neck and crushed me to the ground. I slashed out with my claws, catching him across the face. The injury instantly started to heal again. "You are done, wolf. Now that I know where the book is, I will need to find someone to help me get past the barrier. Little Meesha should have been able to, but I see things have changed," Zammiuntau said before tossing me. I flew over the rough ground until I reached the woods again. I slammed into a tree and heard the snap of the trunk.

"There is always a way to get things done. The hard part was getting here," Zammiuntau said as he turned away. I stared at the house and saw the doors open, and Leodora was thrown out. She was shifted into her lion form as she slammed into the crowd of possessed wolves.

"Leodora!" Malic roared. I slammed my clawed hand to the ground when I saw Lena step out of the house. She leaned down and rubbed away the ward symbol on the door.

"It is open, my Lord," Lena shouted. I growled and pushed myself to my feet.

"You still keep coming when you are clearly outmatched in every way. You will lose your Pack, your brothers, your children, and your Mate," Zammiuntau gritted. He turned his head one hundred and eighty degrees to stare at me, letting the wolf's face slip. Meesha's large brown eyes stared at me, "You're too late, Thomas."

Zammiuntau sent a crimson and black energy blast toward me before he flashed and was gone. I was already moving when he appeared in front of Lena.

I moved and was at the doors in just seconds, but seconds too late. Lena growled, raising a hand that was rimmed in crackling white energy.

"You all will bow down," Lena screamed. I backhanded her off the stone steps and moved inside. Screams filled the house, but I knew where he was going. He saw it in my thoughts, and now that he was inside, nothing would keep him out of Dimitri's office.

"Get into the basement! Now!" I roared. I crashed through the already broken door to see Zammiuntau standing, holding open the book.

"Why won't you just fucking die—"

The arms that came out of his back began to disappear. His eyes widened when he dropped the book from his hand. Damn, he just noticed what I had done. I smiled as my canines grew while I cracked my neck. "What did you do to me? What did Pandora do to you?" I smiled without response as I moved closer to pick up the book. "You stole my ability, didn't you," Zammiuntau snarled.

"I did. I also took a good portion of your energy as well," I replied. The dark part of me wanted more. It commanded more blood, pain, and energy.

"I see. I wouldn't smile too long because you are getting some company," he hissed.

"Thomas! I put Lena down. Where is Meesha?" I spun around at Lika's voice.

"Lika! No!" Her hands were covered in blood, and the glow of her eyes burned with hate when she saw Zammiuntau. Lika's mouth was open, but she was frozen in place.

"How about I show you something amusing, Alpha, something...that would probably torture you from the inside out," Zammiuntau sneered.

"Do you think I will let you stop my Master? You think this child could touch me, and I do nothing about it? All of you will bow or burn once they are free," Lena grunted. Her clawed hand wrapped around Lika's throat.

"D...don't—" I growled. I saw Lika's eyes flash as she gritted her teeth. The ring in her eyes grew as her hands shifted. She reached backward with blinding speed and ripped Lena's arm off. That was when other shifters came rushing into the room. "No!" I roared. I pushed the command to stop, but it was too late to stop them. Intense pain rushed through my body, and I saw some of my Pack freeze in place before I heard hissing laughter.

"I shall enjoy this," Zammiuntau said, dashing toward us. I felt his claws across my back and saw when he cut down the three Pack members, Kyle, Jayden, and Keishawn. They came to assist me, and this was what they got for it. Zammiuntau disappeared. I looked back, seeing the book was gone. The two other shifters, Neka, and Cory, broke through the frozen state as Lika limped back into the room with wide eyes. She had a cut along her face, and her right arm looked broken. Zammiuntau showed behind Neka.

"No, no!" I roared just as Zammiuntau pierced her heart with one of his claws. Cory took a step back, watching as Neka fell to the ground. I felt my power rise as the feeding was complete. I slammed my hands together and sent a blast at Zammiuntau. He went flying, and I followed as he slammed into the wall. The blast shook the foundation, so the wall had no chance. Zammiuntau went straight through it, and I was right behind him. He twisted in the air and mumbled some words before bringing a fist to the ground and opening a colossal carter, causing a dust cloud to blur my vision for a moment. I couldn't let him recite anything from that book. We fell into the black hole, and I knew this was where it all would end.

"Alpha, this is just the start of your nightmare," Zammiuntau snarled. "Nothing will stop the Cadejo! We will reign! We are all one," Zammiuntau hissed in distorted voices.

"I said, enough!"

We slammed to the bottom, but I didn't pause. I could still feel the pain from his mental attack, but none of that mattered. I rushed toward Zammiuntau, swinging my claws widely, but he blocked the attack quickly. We pushed each other back and forth, standing on equal ground, until out of nowhere, demonic energy rose around us. Zammiuntau looked up and smiled widely before trying to bite my head off. His wolves dropped into the hole and roared. Zammiuntau jumped back, holding the book out as he signed out symbols.

"I say when it is enough, wolf. I am a demon while you are just an Alpha! Nothing special. Kill him!" Zammiuntau commanded suddenly. The possessed wolves jumped on me, and I noticed that some of them were from my Pack. They began to shift, their fur turned pitch black, and their eyes changed to vermilion red. Their fangs dug deep into my flesh. Their dull eyes held no recognition, and when I reached for their wolves, I found nothing.

"How can this happen?" I roared. I slammed a wolf into the dirt and kicked another into the rock wall. My hand came out, ripping out the throat of another. I saw Zammiuntau shift back into the body of Meesha as he began reading the ritual.

I fought and fought. I opened my emotions and slammed fear and submission into them, but nothing. They felt nothing and knew nothing but the hunger to fight and kill.

"I can't win," I grunted. Zammiuntau was going to complete the ritual, and I couldn't get close enough to stop him. I stopped attacking. Their fangs were still sinking into my skin. I felt the blood pouring out from the injuries, and my vision blurred.

"Thomas!" I felt the sea crash into my mind and smelled Remi's sweet scent before the wolves' bodies were blown away. Remi slammed onto the ground, but she didn't stop moving. I pulled myself to my feet. Her presence seemed to clear my mind as the blue energy inside me intensified. That's when I felt it. I used the energy to rid the poison inside of me from Zammiuntau's blood. It was almost the same as what affected Remi, but it was different. Once I managed to remove it, turned to help Remi. We had to get these wolves down and stop Zammiuntau before shit got more real than it already was.

"Remi, we need to stop him. I need a way through to him," I growled. I felt her in my soul, and the knowledge that she was alive lifted a heavy weight I didn't know I was carrying. Doubts began to assault me as I fought the wolves who blocked me from Zammiuntau.

What if I fall here and now? My family, Pack, and children will suffer. I would fail just as my parents did, knowing all of them counted on me.

I felt the power of Remi's sonar blast slam into the shifters and aimed at Zammiuntau.

"Do not let it use your emotions against you! You control them. They do not control you! Remember where your power comes from," Remi exclaimed.

Kannuck told me I alone had the power to save them. I knew what needed to be done, and I needed to get close enough to do it. I roared while twisting around to slash out at any remaining possessed shifters in my path. I could feel Remi like she stood next to me, but I knew she was fighting to keep them off my back. I stumped on the ground with all my power, making it crack violently in different directions. The hole became wider as debris fell. I sent out the blue energy and used the falling rocks like missiles sending them directly at Zammiuntau. A large rock knocked the book from its hand, but his energy knocked the other off course. His crimson eyes burned as the Black Dog showed himself again.

Zammiuntau leaped at me, and I jumped, unsheathing my claws again. I hit the floating boulders furiously, shattering them into flying projectiles that flew directly toward Zammiuntau. With each hit, I jumped from side-to-side, trying to reach the book, him. Zammiuntau reached out for the book, but I slammed into him while cutting the head off a shifter who tried to get in my way. We both slammed hard to the ground, but I managed to kick the book away. I didn't know how much of the spell he had done, but I knew I couldn't let him complete it. Zammiuntau stood on all fours and howled up to the sky. We were so far down that I could barely see the blue or feel the sun on my skin. He shifted once more as he stood on both his back paws. His fur became longer, and his tail split into two, the dark aura that surrounded him before completely covered his body. Dark flames engulfed him, but when he opened his mouth, the words that spilled from his lips were guttural.

"Show me! Show me your true form, wolf," Zammiuntau growled.

"I will show you exactly what I am," I growled. The Alpha power inside of me demanded that I take him down by any means necessary. I could feel everyone now. They all were tired because the enemy kept raising or creating more. All of this had to stop even if I died in the process. I moved and stood in front of Zammiuntau before he noticed me. My claws slammed into his chest, and I gripped his cold heart.

"If you kill me now, you will only kill this pathetic host I am in. You would kill your own child?" Zammiuntau grunted in pain. "If you let me finish what I have started in that book, then I will exchange Meesha's life," he sneered.

"No."

"Then kill your child and lose her soul forever. Either way, it is a win/win," Zammiuntau grinned.

"I have another proposition for you," I said. I could feel the blue energy build wanting to feed, and my wolf peeking through as I squeezed the un-beating heart. The energy craved something more, and it only enforced the knowledge that I was right about what I had to do. I knew that if I destroyed the heart, Zammiuntau would fall, but he would not die. It would be Meesha who died in the end. There was another way, and it was the only way to do what had to be done. Kannuck was right because only I had that gift to get it done.

"Speak!"

"How about me? My body in exchange for my child. Would you pass up the opportunity to inhabit a Rayne Alpha?" Thomas asked.

"Fascinating!" Zammiuntau growled, but I could see the greed in his eyes. "You would do that to save this weak child? Not long ago, you didn't think you had children. Now you risk your soul for something created out of evil?" he snarled.

"Absolutely," I growled.

"Thomas! No, what—" I could hear Remi screaming as she began to fight harder to get to us.

"It is done! I accept," Zammiuntau roared.

I released his heart and broke free of him. He clapped his clawed hands, making the dark aura pour from its body. Zammiuntau's body shifted back to the tiny form of Meesha. The dark energy streamed out of her nose and eyes until it all left her body. Meesha fell to the ground, unconscious but alive. The entity manifested into a thick cloud and crimson and black dust spreading widely over me. I stood still as it entered my body, completing the deal that was made.

"Now, you shall be mine. You allll will be oursss," the demon hissed in a horrific voice. It engulfed me and covered me in shadows. I felt the evil and darkness of it and the intentions it had for us all. It wanted the world, but their part in this game was to take out the wolf shifters nation. For any of that to happen, they needed the bloodline of the Dire Wolves to submit. That's where they had it fucked up because we were Alphas. We made others submit.

Dark fur and black flames began to cover my body as the demon's essence dug its way into my soul. I had to hold on until he was trapped inside my body and keep my sanity from the evil consuming me. I put my hands over my head and struggled to keep control of my mind.

"We had a deal, Alpha. Your body is mine now!" Zammiuntau's voice resonated through my thoughts as the black flames turned more aggressive.

"Thomas!" Remi screamed.

"You aren't the only devour of souls," I growled. "Your soul belongs to me," I shouted. I released the blue energy, and in the back of my mind, I felt a presence and saw laser blue eyes staring back at me. The face in my thoughts opened its mouth and inhaled.

"Impossible! This is impossible! What are you?" Zammiuntau roared. I gathered all the dark energy into myself before forming a sphere of blue light with my hands. I placed my palm to my chest and pushed it inside, imprisoning the demon while I absorbed its soul.

I fell to the ground while the black flames turned blue before disappearing into thin air. The howls and screams of the possessed shifters came to a sudden silence. They all ceased to exist, burned up by the blue flame that lived inside me. I felt the souls the demon collected begging for release, and I had no problem giving them peace. The scent of the ocean covered me before Remi placed a hand on my face.

"Are you crazy?!" she cried. I opened my eyes to stare into a teal gaze. She held Meesha to her chest as she looked me over. Remi sucked in a breath as she caressed my face.

"What?"

"One of your eyes is crimson...wait, wait, the indigo is absorbing it," Remi whispered. "What happened? Is he—is Meesha—"

"He is no more, Princess. He will never come for our family again, but he will not be the last. The prophecy is real, and they will come. I stopped him from completing the ritual, but I know something slipped through. He had too long with the book," I said. I pushed to my feet and looked around. I picked up the book, but its pages were now blank.

"Whatever comes *AETERNUM,* we will stop it together," Remi promised. I looked down at Meesha and smiled as she opened her large brown eyes.

"Thomas, did you save mommy and daddy?"

I knew exactly what she meant because I felt their souls pass through me as they moved on to where they needed to go.

"Yes, baby."

"Good. Can I go see Lika and Oceayn now," she yawned before falling back to sleep.

"At least the threat to our children is dead now. All we need to do is figure out how to be parents. That might be harder than all this shit," Remi smirked.

I looked up, but I knew some of that was wrong. They would never be safe until all the Cadejo were destroyed because now they had the Dire Wolf bloodline inside them. But that wasn't my main concern. There was another out there who was still a threat.

"We still have one more, Princess. We can't forget about the bitch Pandora. She is the one who set this all in motion," I stated.

"And we will deal with her and that fucking box as well. But first, we need to heal our Packs."

THOMAS

We climbed out of the hole, and the first person we saw was Malic. He ran over to us while looking up at the sky. I knew what he was looking for this time around. I wouldn't allow him to think he was tripping.

"Thomas! What the fuck happened? Is Meesha okay?" he panted. I saw Max coming over, but he took it slowly so he could help Lika. Meesha shifted in my arms, blinked up at Malic, and then looked at me before she smiled.

"I can call you Uncle Malic now!"

Malic reached out, took Meesha from me, and hugged her tightly.

"You always have silly," he said. His brown eyes stared a hole in the side of my face, but I couldn't keep my eyes off Lika. She was hurt, but I could see that she was already healing. Remi sucked in a breath before running over to Lika. I turned back to Malic, who had his brows raised.

"So you are going to stand here like I didn't tell you from the jump that you had a thing for Remi? I mean, I knew you got down, but two kids in a matter of days is wild," he smirked.

I knew his joking was him trying to reign in his emotions, so I could feel how he was feeling about this owl. We had to sit down and tell him what had happened. I didn't know how this shit was possible when all the Owl shifters died out over one hundred years ago. If that owl was who I believed it was, this entire situation would blow up in our faces, and I wasn't sure if Malic would forgive us for doing what we thought was best.

"You did, brother. I won't argue with you in front of my kid, though," I laughed.

"We all need to get cleaned up, and then we will need to assess the damage and figure out who we lost. Can you stay for a few days until we figure this out?" Malic asked. Meesha had already fallen back to sleep. Remi returned to us with Lika by her side and smiled at Malic.

"This is your other niece. Talika, this is your uncle Malic, and yes, they are twins," Remi stated.

"You're another Alpha?" Lika frowned.

"You do know about the Rayne family, right?"

"We can tell her all about it later. She needs rest, and I need to see if Alex is good in Florida for a few days," I said. I pulled Lika to me and hugged her, breathing in her scent. She wrapped her good arm around my waist. I looked at Remi and felt my entire being settle.

"Let's get cleaned up, and these two settled to get some rest. I will call Alex and Quinn to report what went down," Max said. I nodded, and we all turned as one and went back inside the house.

After we got Meesha settled and she told us everything the demon was saying to her, it made me want to kill that bastard again. I could see the rage in Remi's eyes, but she held it together enough to kiss Meesha before we left the room. Remi already had enough on her mind, and I knew she would need to find the outpost here to take back her kingdom. After speaking to Dax and Devana, we did get the confirmation that Atlantis was real, but it was lost long ago, and no one knew where it was any longer. Not even the Sirenian people and Remi could sense that this species was created by one of her people. I knew what she was thinking, but she better get ahold of it really fast if she thought I would let her search on her own.

We barely made it to our room when my Mate completely lost it, tearing through the room and throwing a bedside table. Everything clattered onto the floor with a loud bang. Instantly, my wolf was pacing, wanting to come out and settle his Mate but knowing that wouldn't help.

Especially when his Mate—my Mate— was a Royal Alpha Orcinus shifter from another realm.

I'd researched before that when an Orca was showing aggressive behavior to let them cool down. I just hoped that it was the same for an Orcinus Livyatan shifter. But Remi had another thing coming if she presumed I wouldn't be her constant to calm her down, especially when she let anger show over shit she could not control. She might have relied on herself in the past, but not anymore.

Remi had *me*.

From our time together at this point, I knew that she needed to take her anger out on something. Naw, my little princess needed them walls hit good by her Alpha until she couldn't even remember her own name.

"Remi, you need to calm the fuck down," I snarled, reaching over to snatch her wrist as her teal-blue eyes pierced mine. Her Orcinus rode on the surface, baring her teeth that were probably enough to make others submit, but she had another thing coming if she thought I would this time.

My wolf instantly surfaced, snarling right in return for *my* stubborn Mate.

"Make me," she challenged, and that was all it took for me to snap completely. I crashed our mouths together, more irate than I was turned on. She threw an arm around my shoulder and, rather than pulling me away, dropped the other one down, groping me and causing me to become half-hard through the fabric of my jeans.

"How can I calm down, Thomas, when I need to leave my children and you behind? I have to find my brother and his people. I need to see about my kingdom. It has been far too long."

"I get it," I growled.

"Do you? Do you really, because they are not safe? They weren't even safe with us, so I know coming along on this mission is a no-go. Hell, Pandora is still out there, and who knows what she wants? I don't know what to do. You need to stay—"

"I wish you would say that shit out loud. Don't you think I've thought about this already? They will be as safe as we can make them safe. Alex and Oceayn will protect Lika with their lives. She is going into training, Remi. She is not a child, even though we see her that way. Talika is an Alpha, and we can't put her in a box. She needs to learn, and we will ensure she has all the resources needed to accomplish that."

"And Meesha? She's a child, and Meesha needs one of us to be present," Remi sighed.

"She needs to know that we will be there for her and love her. I want her safe, and I know you do as well. I know one place to keep her safe, and nothing will get in to touch her. I spoke to Quinn, and the Cross Academy will take Meesha when we are ready. Quinn has offered to let her stay with him and his Mate. We can see her anytime we please and know that she will be safe," I asserted. Remi stared into my eyes, and I leaned down, taking her lips.

Even with my mouth entirely occupied by the kiss, it only took her a few tries before she got my jeans undone, and her hand was in my boxers. I thickened instantly, hardening in her hand, my lips and teeth finding the side of her neck as I inhaled her scent.

"Yes, Alpha," she panted.

Before long, we had stripped bare in the moment's heat. I ignored her movement as she tried to capture my lips again. I wanted to leave marks so everyone knew she was my Mate. So she knew that she was mine. Then, once she looked at herself, she would understand I wasn't going anywhere. I knew what her body needed and what she craved, so I suckled hard against the sensitive spot beneath her ear until she hissed out a groan.

The way she cried out in pain and pleasure overrode my every sense.

Fuck her.

Breed her.

Mate her.

Once again, my wolf was riding the surface. More so now than ever before because I knew only she could quiet the darkness inside of me. However, we weren't there yet, and the last thing I wanted was her thinking she was running shit this time.

When the time came, it would happen again.

Her hand slid over my leaking tip, her soft thumb pad brushing the mushroom head. I was panting against the side of her throat for a moment before batting her hand away. "You need to understand something, little princess."

"What's that?" she whispered, her eyes low and hazy, but anger swirled in them as well.

"That you're mine," I growled lowly into her ears. I knew she was fighting between her building lust and her anger. I'd do anything to settle her because seeing her upset drove me and my wolf wild. "You got that anger, take it to your Alpha and let me handle it."

"I don't need you to handle it," she snarled as I gripped a handful of her hair, tugging harshly.

"I don't fucking care. You're my Mate, and I am your *Aeternum*, which means I will *fucking* handle it, because it's my job," I seethed, probably making it worse. My nose flared, and without a doubt, I knew my words aroused her.

Despite being an Alpha, I knew she struggled with craving my dominance.

Smelling the air, I let out a low rumble, my eyes gleaming when she bit her lips, knowing precisely what I was smelling. I suppose that was one of the perks of having a keen sense of smell, using her arousal and manipulating to benefit me. "Thomas—"

"Did you want me to fuck you that badly?" I questioned, my tongue gliding over the skin of her throat. "Are you that wet for me? You've been driving me crazy since we first met, but I didn't know exactly why. Did you know? Did you have this feeling," I continued to ask as I sucked her skin. My hand slowly disappeared down the front of her so I could feel every inch. Her smooth brown skin felt like silk, and I couldn't help squeezing her thick ass. I released her cheek and let my hand drift back to the front so I could feel between her thighs. Remi's swollen folds were slick with her juices, answering my question for me. "You are. Were you waiting for me to fuck that anger out of you?"

"No."

While her mouth said one thing, her scent told me another thing entirely.

"Liar," I mused, nipping her ear. "You need your Alpha to fuck that anger out of you, huh? A little pain and pleasure to make you cum, right?"

"So what are you going to do about it?" she hummed, tilting her head to the side almost curiously. I smiled, and her eyes lingered on me while I brought my wet hand to my mouth and sucked my fingers. I knew her anger was slowly subsiding at that moment, letting wonder win over. Her mouth opened, and her teal eyes grew brighter.

"Simple," I replied, reaching out to caress her cheek. "I'm going to fuck you into proper submission, so you'll come to your Mate next time you need to blow through your anger. First, I'll break you down until you beg and whimper like the good princess I know you are, and then I'll pump you so full of my fucking cum that you won't be able to think of anything else except how full of me you are and my name."

Her breath hitched, and I knew I had her.

Though getting her to submit would be another issue, I would have no problem getting either.

After all, the reward was much more addicting once I successfully got it.

"Thomas, stop messing with me," she panted.

"You remember that safe word you joked about?"

"Seahorse? You're tripping Thomas! I know you're not—"

"Use it if you can handle it, but it shouldn't be a problem for an Alpha like you, right?"

"I—"

In a flash of movement, I picked Remi up and created the portal room with the fairy dust. I stepped through and into our private space. I dumped Remi onto our bed face first, then hoisted her ass into the air. Her arousal filled my nose, causing me to growl. I went to nudge her legs apart so I could look at her drip for me.

If given a chance, I would have locked her away for good for my eyes only. Just so I could see her like this any time I wanted.

I used one hand to cup her soaked folds while the other tightly held onto her hips, piercing just a bit of her flesh. She gasped, digging her fingers into the silken sheet when I probed her wet entrance with my thick fingers. Remi was shivering, and I watched as her skin seemed to shimmer like it was covered in baby blue dust. I knew she was biting her lip, but she outright moaned when I replaced my fingers with my length. I pushed the head in and gave her just a few inches.

I teased her.

I wanted to show her who was in control.

I wanted to show her that when she was angry, she came to me, and I'd take care of it. Whatever the problem, we would figure it out.

I'll always take care of Remi—whether or not she asks me to. I knew she would do the same for me.

Period.

"You like that, little princess," I snarled as I continued to rub the tip along her dripping slit in a shallow, teasing stroke. I brought a hand down, making her jolt in surprise. "I bet you've been waiting all night for this, haven't you? You've been waiting for me to fuck what belongs to me?"

"I'm not something...you can own," she gritted out. "I...can do what I want."

There she went again, trying to prove me otherwise, but I loved the challenge even more.

"You are. Remember you said the words first? You told me that you owned me. If we are being honest, you told anyone who looked at me that you owned me, so don't play innocent." I growled. "Maybe I need to teach your body again, huh?"

Remi turned her head so that her cheek was lying on the bedsheet. I kept dragging my head, slick with her arousal, over her wet core. Every time she would buck her hips upward, I would hold her down, making sure I wouldn't spear her just yet.

"Thomas," she panted. I mockingly laughed at her before grabbing her hand, securing them tightly against her back. I pulled her up onto her feet. "What are you doing," she gasped.

I wanted to keep Remi on her toes. So I fastened a belt to her wrists and ensured her binds were on securely. Then I shoved her sexy ass against the wall, making her teal-tipped curls fall into her eyes. I brushed them back as she glared at me. There was just enough room so I could reach her ass when I needed it. The 24-Point Bondage Wood Frame stuck out some so I could get to every part of her body. "Now stay like that, and I'll consider going a bit easier on you when I come back. You are not to move, do you understand me, little princess? You want to be a good girl, right?"

She didn't say anything or nod in agreement, pressing her lips together and lowering her eyes in submission. That was probably the best I would get right now, and it was good enough for me. Satisfied with her answer, I went to the wall and long trunk on the opposite side of the space. I rummaged through it and found what I was looking for quickly. I returned to see Remi still pressed against the wall, with all her curves exposed. I licked my lips, knowing what was about to come.

Slowly, she lifted her head, and I could see her trying to peer over her shoulder to see what I had in my hand. However, she didn't get a glimpse before I slapped her thigh with the firm, curved brown wooden paddle.

"Oh," she cried out, though it seemed more out of surprise than pain. She wriggled gently, and a smile made its way to my face, seeing how her teal eyes glowed before they went slack as I punished her. Slowly, I began to find a rhythm as I repeatedly laid the back of the paddle on her thighs, ass, and clit. I loved how her breathing sped up and how she strained at the bindings. Here in this place, her powers were dampened to the point she could not break free if she were the one in submission.

Mine.

Mine.

Fucking *mine*.

"Does this feel good?" I questioned. "Or is it not enough?"

"T-Thomas," she continued to cry out without answering my question. Instead, she started to pant and moaned while I rhythmically spanked her ass with the paddle. I knew this high and how it calmed your thoughts, giving you something else to focus on. I know she can probably feel the stinging at this point, yet she didn't give me her safe word or beg for mercy. Even when the belt around her wrists started to loosen, she never once wanted to fight me off. I dropped the paddle and stepped forward, breathing in the scent of the ocean and what was just Remi. I grabbed one breast and pinched her nipple.

"Oh, God. Thomas," she moaned. I leaned down and bit her neck hard, causing her to arch toward me, craving my bite. I knew she wanted to be claimed again by the throbbing of her skin, the beating of her pulse as she tried to grind herself against me. "Do it! Please, just do it," she cried. I let my tongue snake out and licked it instead while I pinched her nipples once more. I stepped back, and she growled, making me chuckle. I slapped her clit with the palm of my hand and wrapped my other hand around her neck. I slapped her clit again and then began rubbing her swollen clit in circular motions while I squeezed her throat. I sped up the movement as I licked over her lips while she made a keening noise as her body began to shudder.

"You want to cum, don't you?" I grunted. I let her go and stepped back as she groaned.

At this point, I was throbbing as pre-cum continued to leak. Hell, watching her had me wanting to beg for release. I took a step and was in front of her again, releasing her from the binds. She got up to her tippy toes and turned around, wiggling her paddled ass like some sort of offering. I slowly went to palm at her ass cheeks that were heated from the spanking. I rubbed it slowly she ground herself against me, thinking I was just going to give it to her.

Naw. Not until she begged.

"Beg for it," I demanded, rubbing myself between her creases. I spun her around to face me and then walked her backward to the bed. She was in a daze and looked drugged as she ran her fingers along my skin and scratched at my back. Remi's legs hit the mattress, making her fall backward. I climbed over her as she let her thighs fall apart so I could settle between them. It only allowed me to nudge her swollen clit, making her body jump underneath my touch. "Come and tell me who's going to fuck you good right now."

"You, Thomas," she whispered. "My *Aeternum*, my forever, my eternal."

"Good girl."

I grabbed her wrists and pinned them over her head as I shoved the entire length inside her tight core in one single perfect motion. Thanks to how wet she was already, I slid in deep. Remi's back hollowed out while fighting against my hold on her wrists.

I wasted no time setting a ruthless, savage pace with long, deep strokes into her tight channel. I could feel her wet heat gripping me as her walls fluttered around me, trying to adjust to my size. I knew I wouldn't savor this, needing to punish and remind her who she submitted to.

"Thomas..." she cried out. I didn't give her any time to adjust, setting the fastest, most driving pace I could manage while making sure she couldn't move. I maneuvered her wrists to hold them in one hand and kept them pinned over her head. I settled my other hand at the base of her neck while I drove deeper inside. I felt my wolf at the surface as nothing but animalistic urges to mark her washed over me.

Punish her.

Love her.

Keep her.

I slammed in and out of her as she rolled her hips, trying to fuck me from the bottom. I let my hand slide up her neck and felt her pulse go wild at my touch. And based on the noises tumbling out of her mouth, it was a no-brainer what she wanted. Not wasting another minute, I let her go, sat back on my heels, and pushed her legs up, pulling them toward me. I slammed back into her opening while holding her hips off the bed, ensuring she took every inch.

"Please, please, Thomas, let me cum, please," she moaned.

"You know what you need to do," I growled while she squeezed her core around me harder. I squeezed her ass and smacked it hard. I loved to hear her moan and scream when she felt the sting. I leaned down, letting her legs fall to the side to hold myself over her while nipping hard on her earlobes. "You wanted me to fuck you this whole night, huh? You're always so mouthy and talkative, making me think you just want me to put something inside it. Or did you just need your Alpha?"

Remi's eyes squeezed shut as she seemed to lose herself in the feeling of me working in and out of her—reminding her that I owned her. Remi gripped back onto my hands to the best of her abilities while little moans tumbled out of her mouth. I titled her hips and sank deeper as I ground into her tight core.

"Oh...God," she sobbed.

"I'm your fucking God," I growled darkly, biting particularly hard on her collar to show her who was in charge.

"T-Thomas, *Aeternum*... Alpha...please. Fuck...fuck me, make me come."

"See, that wasn't so hard, was it?" I murmured. I leaned back once more and pulled her with me. I rolled her to her hands and knees and spread her ass cheeks apart. I ran the pad of my thumb over her tight hole, making her shiver. "Next time," I said as I slammed into her tight opening again. Finally, she cried out, and I wanted her to know that I was the one that's giving her all the pleasure tonight.

Her Mate.

I wrapped my arm around her waist, pulling her harder on me as her ass smacked against my pelvis. She whimpered when I dragged her up, so her back was against my chest. Remi bounced on me and began grinding against me while moaning my name repeatedly. She was on the verge of cumming, but I wasn't ready for that yet. I wanted more from her. I wanted everything she was willing to give. It wasn't just for me, but it was for her as well. I could feel her soul as it sang with calmness, lust, love, and peace as I pushed deeper inside her. I let go of her waist, and she fell back to the bed, still throwing it back, but I stilled her with a touch and pulled out.

"No, no, no, no!"

I smirked as I got off the bed and moved to the black chair in the corner of the room.

"Come here," I growled. Remi stumbled from the bed without protest. She stood between my legs while I looked at her naked, sweat-soaked body. "Turn around," I grunted. Remi did what she was told, and I guided her to sit that tight, wet glove down, taking every single inch. Just across was a small mirror, and I knew she could see everything as I shoved two fingers into her mouth, which she suckled on right away, while the other went to caress and pinch her nipples.

"Th-Thomas," she slurred, her tongue lapping my fingers.

"Dance for me," I growled, spanking her ass and letting it crackle in the air. "If you want my cum filling you up to the brim, you gotta work for it, little princess. I'm not letting you out of here until your tight little sheath is filled and you understand that you are mine and I am yours. Do you want to throw a tantrum? Then take it out on me. I can fucking handle it but know for damn sure you will not leave without me. Where my Mate goes, I go."

"Yes," she whined, sucking harder on my fingers in her mouth as she began to rise and then drop down hard. Every time she sank onto me, and I filled her up and stretched her out, a shudder would wrack down her spine while I pumped my fingers in the same rhythm.

"I'm going to cum deep inside of you, Rehema," I gritted my teeth, becoming drunk off her. "'I'm going to fill you with all my thick, white essence. I know that's what you want, and you'll get off on it, won't you?"

Remi nodded firmly as she whimpered, squeezing her walls around me the next time she dropped down, taking me deeper. I didn't know how long she continued to bounce on my thick shaft until her thighs shook and were about to give up.

I began to kiss, bite and then suck hard on her neck. I know she would have demanded that I bite her on any other occasion, but she's too much into working herself up so she could cum all over me to care at this point. It felt so good to stretch and fill her while playing with her breasts, and she whimpered and whined, waiting for the words she needed.

"Thomas," she gasped out. "I...I'm...oh, please."

I removed my fingers from her mouth and placed them on her hips as I pushed up, taking her harder and deeper. I pulled away from where I had been sucking on her delicate throat with a loud, audible pop. The spot where I marked her seemed to call to me, and I felt my teeth lengthen and my claws grip her skin. I let my other hand wrap around her throat again and raised her head. I was panting as she moaned. "Tighter, tighter. Please, Alpha," she groaned.

"Cum for me, Mate," I growled and squeezed her neck tightly with clawed hands. I didn't even realize I had moved until I felt her skin in my mouth and my teeth sinking deep, marking her all over again.

It triggered her orgasm because she clamped down hard on me as she milked me for everything I had. I needed her to remember the feelings she was getting for handing over her submission.

I grabbed her hard until she was crushed against my chest. I turned her head, crashing my lips hard into hers as we swallowed one another's moans. She cried out as my balls tightened up, cum erupting to pulsate inside her, shooting right into her womb. I had to mark and coat her insides, ensuring she was filled. She ground on me, riding me to draw out every last remnant of my thick cum as our tongues battled.

Pulling away from our heated kiss, I wasn't finished as I buried my face into the crook of her shoulder and bit down, hitting bone, then sucking to make sure my mark would be seen. She gasped, and I could feel her core beginning to leak as her juices slid down her thighs onto mine, and I knew she knew now.

Remi was fucking mine.

She may be angry about things she can't control, but I knew what she needed to get her mind right. If finding her brother is what we had to do, then we would do it together.

Only I'm able to settle that fire inside of her soul. I licked her neck and saw the spots that didn't fully heal. My wolf settled seeing the mark because it told him that her *Livyatan* had submitted. Now all we had to do was figure out how to find a place no one thought existed. Remi already knew but didn't know where to begin to look for it. Now we needed to find someone as old as the stories, and I knew only one *Being* that might know where Atlantis could be. If Remi could not contact her brother, I just hoped Shannara will do me one more favor.

Malic

I stood outside while we rebuilt the damaged or destroyed homes from the fight last week. I was glad Thomas could stay and keep the remaining Pack members calm until things had been explained. These past few years have been hell on this Pack, but we all knew its reason. I turned to sense Thomas and Remi walking toward me, with Lika beside them. I still could not believe Thomas had two kids or believe the story of how it happened. When Dax and Dimitri found out what happened, my little brother would be in a world of hurt if he was still here. Now it seemed like we had to find a place that none of us thought existed, but apparently did or still did.

"Alex should be here any minute now," Remi stated. She stared up the long driveway with sadness in her eyes.

"She will be fine, your Majesty. Alex will take care of her and teach her the ins and outs. It's best when it's coming from someone else, trust me," I said. Remi's teal gaze turned on me, and I could feel the crushing weight of her age.

"Don't start that mess, Malic. I am not messing with you," she laughed. Lika moved to wrap her arms around Remi.

"It's all good. You know I need this, and I am turning twenty-one very soon," Lika smiled.

"What! Oh my gosh, Lika. Why didn't you say anything? Thomas, she can't—"

"Mom, it's fine. For real, it's all good. I won't have time because I will be training while you're taking care of the Pack until I'm finished with Uncle Alex."

"Remi, she's right. We'll celebrate once she's finished her training. It's all good, Princess. We won't miss it and will leave once it is over. It will work out," Thomas laughed. Max came jogging over with a look of fear on his face.

"What? What else happened? I don't know how Dax deals with this shit," I grunted.

"There is a truck coming down the road," Max said.

"Ahh yeah, Alex is on the way. It's probably him," Thomas said. I looked around at all the commotion and was proud that everything was just about right. We still had to hold a judgment meeting and dig into the women from the rogue wolf's Pack. After the shit with Lena, everyone was suspected. Maeze felt horrible that she didn't pick up on it and offered to return here to deal with the girl, but it fell to me. Lika ripped her up pretty well, but we managed to save her life. I wanted answers from the girl before she was sentenced. She knew more about what the demon was trying to accomplish. Nothing had popped up on that right now, but I knew it wouldn't be long before another enemy showed itself.

"Naw, this is not Alex. It's—"

I turned around when I heard the truck coming down the road. I sucked in a breath and heard Thomas groan as if in pain.

"Fuck!"

"That's what I been saying! It's Tripp!"

"Tripp?" Remi frowned. Sometimes I forget Remi hasn't been around all our lives.

"Yeah, Tripp Grady. Chief of Police across state lines, but don't get it twisted because his territory bumps right against ours," I grunted. The truck pulled to a stop, and I saw some shifters notice it and start moving further away.

"He's a wolf?" Lika asked.

"No, naw, he's something...something else," I said. Thomas moved to stand in front of Remi and Lika. Another car pulled behind the large navy and green SUV. I could smell the smokey scent of Alex in the other car. He hopped out of the white car, and I could tell he knew who was in the truck. Alex moved with speed over to where we stood.

"Why the fuck is he here? It couldn't have been that bad," Alex asked.

The door to the SUV opened, and a tall, dark-skinned man stepped out. His skin was a midnight black, and his eyes were the same shade. The man was as tall as Dax, or maybe a few inches taller. By looking at him, you wouldn't think he was the chief of anything. He wore all black, from his shirt to his jeans and boots. No one missed the two Glocks in his holster. I closed my eyes because why in the hell would Jamel and Ezra pick a time to show up over here now?

"Who the hell called twelve?" Jamel asked.

"Just keep your mouth shut, Ja. I am not trying to answer a challenge for your dumb ass," Max growled.

"Damn who is that?" Lika asked stepping forward. I saw the way Jamel looked at her and knew it would be a damn problem. Thomas narrowed his eyes at Lika but I saw Remi looking as well which had Thomas stepping in front of them both.

"Who? I am not scared to fight the Terminator over there. Man, I will—" Jamel grunted.

"Shut up!" I snapped.

I knew he felt the Alpha energy I put out because he never finished his sentence. A few shifters stayed around to see what was happening and who this person was that so easily came onto our land. The ones who left already knew what was up and didn't want to be around if Tripp Grady was in a bad mood. Max and Alex came to flank me on either side. I noticed Leodora from the corner of my eye, but I didn't stop her from coming over. She was one shifter that knew what Grady was, and the more standing with us, the better. You didn't take chances with some 'gods,' and he was one of them.

"Malic, why is he here?" Leodora asked. Alex moved slightly to let her stand beside me. Leodora and her pride had known Grady for some time, and at least he had a good relationship with her people.

"No clue," I said, taking a step forward.

"Malic," Tripp boomed. His voice sounded like the rumbling of thunder.

"Grady, why are you here? Should you be patrolling your little town in Virginia?"

"Where is Daxton? I don't have time to play with you young pups today."

"I am Alpha. My brother is away taking care of Pack business, so whatever you need here, it will have to go through me," I answered. I held eye contact with him and held a measure of respect in my tone. You also had to show some backbone, or he would run all over you, and there wasn't shit you could do.

"Is that right?" he chuckled. His dark gaze traveled over us but lingered on Remi for a second before looking back to me.

"What happened here last week? I was coming this way to ask about another matter, but then I felt—"

"We handled it. It was Pack business, and it is done. It did not spill into your territory, so it isn't your concern," I stated. I didn't say another word as his dark brow raised as he assessed me.

"You dogs always have some shit going on when Daxton is not here to reign the young in, but that is neither here nor there. I want to know why

I am getting owl sightings. Why is there an enormous owl in my town, and what do you have to do with it?"

I swallowed hard at his words, but I didn't want to confirm or deny shit. I didn't have beef with this owl, and it did nothing to really harm me. I honestly was glad I had another *Being* who had seen what I saw.

I knew that I wasn't crazy.

"What makes you believe I would know what you are talking about?"

Grady stared at me for a long moment before reaching into his pocket. I felt my brothers tense, but no one made a move. I watched as he pulled out one of my Endeavor Limited Edition watches. One of my watches had gone missing a few weeks ago.

"This doesn't belong to you? Your name is engraved on the back, and your scent is all over it. So let's try this again. Why is there an owl that was thought to be extinct attacking my town's farm animals?"

I bit down on my tongue because I did not know why the owl was fucking around in Grady's territory. The fact that he kept confirming what I had been saying was fucking with me. Finally!

"I can't answer that. That watch went missing a while back, and I have no clue how it got to your town," I said.

"Well, figure it out, or I will. You all have a connection with those *Beings*. Figure it out and keep that thing off my lands," Grady growled.

"We hear you, Grady. It will be dealt with," I said. I wanted to know what he meant by that and why didn't I know about any connection. Grady tossed my watch at me, and I caught it as he turned and headed back toward his SUV. We watched as he climbed inside before anyone said a word. Leodora turned to me and placed a hand on my cheek.

"Well, he's leaving. That wasn't so bad, right?" She smiled. I blinked and looked down at her before looking at my brothers, who stared at each other. My eyes narrowed, but before I said anything, Leodora was suddenly gone and thrown across the yard. A woman stood in front of me with long, thick black hair. She was short but curvy, and her scent was something I knew all too well. She turned to look up at me. It was like I was looking at stars in the night sky. It was endless, and I swore that I saw stars dying and others being born the longer we stared at each other. She broke contact and turned back to Leodora. The woman turned to the side and pointed at me while staring at a heaving Leodora.

"MINE!"

Leodora was fast as a shifter and was in the woman's face in a second. She drew back her hand, and I saw her nails lengthen. I reached out, catching her hand before she could make contact.

"Malic, she...what are you doing?"

"Aht, no touching," I growled. Leodora stared at me with wide eyes, and I saw their pain. I let her arm go, and she stepped back slightly. I turned back to the woman, and she looked at me as she backed away. "Wait!"

Before the word could leave my tongue, she had shifted, and all I could see were large wings as she disappeared into the sky. I knew I stood there staring for a minute before I looked at everyone who watched me.

"*Kotori*," Max whispered. I didn't think he meant to say the name out loud but he did. I turned to face my twin and waited for his eyes to focus on me.

"I fucking told you I saw a big ass owl! Now, someone tell me what the hell is happening, and no more lies. I want the truth. I think I deserve it."

I gripped my watch tightly as Max swallowed. He looked at Alex and Thomas and I could tell whatever he had to say I was not going to like this shit at all.

Until Next Time...

Giveaway

Do you want a chance to win a *Deadly Secrets BOOK BOX*? If so all you need is proof that you left your review on Amazon and Goodreads to enter into a chance to WIN! Send in your proof to the email listed below and you will be entered into a drawing. The last day to submit your proof will be 9/5/2022 and I will do the drawing inside of the Sinful Secrets Facebook group on 9/9/2022. Thank you all for reading and giving me a reason to keep writing!

Email: authore.bowser@ebowserbooks.com

Shades Of Passion A Deadly Secrets Story Sneak Peek

Chapter One

Shani

I still wasn't sure if I could go through with the training. I didn't want to leave the kids, but I honestly didn't want the constant reminder of my father. It was hard enough not to think about him and what he had to witness the day he was murdered. I felt as if I had lost my entire world in one day until I met my actual family. At first, it seemed like I was just a babysitter for Lily and Garrett, but that was completely wrong. Taria and Toya made me feel as if I had always been a part of their world and family from the jump. They treated me as if I was their children's older sister and their child. All of them spoiled the hell out of me and made sure I never felt anything less than loved. I felt so bad because I honestly never really opened up about my past.

I knew my outburst was mainly because of my body's changes as I came into my power. I also knew my power was trippin because I knew someone was stalking me. It was someone from the Pack I used to belong to, and it scared the fuck out of me. I shook my head, clearing those thoughts from my mind to focus on my meeting with the True Alpha. There was a difference when speaking with just Quinn. Now that I was eighteen, it was time to put my training into overdrive and learn everything I could so I could be the greatest Delta a True Alpha has ever had before. I took a deep breath before walking into Quinn's massive office to run into Maeze.

Maeze sported leather tights with a leather corset that hugged her athletic frame perfectly. Looking at Quinn, I noticed it was only us three in the room, "my bad, am I early?"

Quinn motioned for me to have a seat as Maeze went to stand on the side of him facing me. "No, Shani, you are on time as usual. I will get straight to the point. How you handled those bugs and protected the twins further proved that you are ready for your training to become my Delta. I know your birthday is tonight, and your body will begin to undergo even more changes with you turning eighteen. You have to begin training this week so you can home in on the Kannuck-given gifts you may have already noticed developing over this past year."

"You are special in ways you do not understand just yet, but Remi and I will teach you how to control the rage you harbor for reasons I will not probe. Being a GammaZeta, I know what role every member of the Pack needs to play, and it is my honor to train you to do yours for our True Alpha," Maeze smiled.

Not wanting to seem afraid, I nodded my head, but Quinn must've felt it through our bond, "there's no need to be afraid. Change is good. No matter what, you will always be my little shadow. I remember you used to follow me around trying to stay hidden like I couldn't sense you near," he smiled. "Maeze will be here for two days, then you will leave with her to train on Dax's pack land," the command laced his voice. I'm sure it wasn't intentional, but he had to ensure that I understood he was serious. I am a wolf in the Pack of the True Alpha, so I wouldn't dare disobey a direct order. Quinn stood and held out his arms. I stood and walked into his embrace. This was my father figure since losing mine.

Don't get me wrong, Dax and his family took me in, but Quinn, Michael, Toya, and Taria felt more at home. I always thought I was just a babysitter, but they never asked me to watch the twins. I always offered because I love them like they are my blood siblings. Pulling away from Quinn, I smiled and gave Maeze a warm smile before turning to leave. Before I could make it out the door, Quinn's voice said, "Toya wants to talk to you. She's in Taria's room."

~Deadly Secrets~

Walking down the long hallways, my thoughts drifted to my decision not to attend a traditional university. I want to learn more about my wolf bloodline, my father, and why I am so different from other wolf shifters that attend the school. None of them have unique gifts like I do, but Maeze said it was normal for my lineage to possess extra power throughout the generations. In a split second, I was standing in the room with Taria and Toya, but I hadn't used the door, and nobody seemed to see me. Oh shit, it's happening again. Taria's fangs lengthened, and Toya's flame appeared in the palm of her hand. "Show yourself before I light your ass up," Toya looked in my direction but not in recognition. Her lips were in a tight line.

"It's me! You can't see me?" I yelled, but they didn't seem to hear me. Toya threw the ball of white fire at me as I tumbled out of the way, bumping into an end table and causing a lamp to crash to the ground beside me. Toya lit another flame in her palm and prepared to launch it at me again.

"Stop! My Queen that is Shani," Blossom appeared from the shadow of the fallen lamp and reached down to help me to my feet.

"Oh shit! Sorry, Shani, I couldn't sense that it was you," Toya rushed to my side and hugged me tighter than she had ever hugged me. "I swear I would never hurt you, not unless you think you're grown or some shit, but other than that, you have to know this was unusual."

Taria walked up and hugged both of us with tears in her eyes, "I am so proud of you, Shani. Even though you knew we would not hurt you on purpose, you still dodged her reckless ass fastball."

"Shut the fuck up, Taria. Somebody had to protect us with your slow-ass reaction time," Toya laughed as she guided me to a lounge chair to have a seat as she and Taria sat at my sides. "Did you know you were in the shadows?"

"Not until I tried speaking to you both and didn't get the response I was hoping for. I don't know what's happening to me. Wolves should not be able to do this," I covered my face with my hands.

"Explain the Rayne brothers...okay then. Just accept that you're a boss-ass shifter. That's why you have boss-ass god moms and dads. We'll figure this shit out," Toya moved my hands away from my face as Taria wiped the tears that had slipped from my eyes.

"I don't understand why you're so upset. The shadows are a privilege that you should be proud of," Blossom shrugged as she picked up the lamp to set it back on the end table.

"That is not why we asked you here, tonight you turn eighteen, so we want to take you out to celebrate," Toya stood and started twerking, singing, "one time for the birthday girl, two times for chick, three times for the birthday chick, Fuck it up if it's your birthday chick!"

I covered my eyes again, seeing someone who was like a mom to me twerk better than Shannara's sister, Lireil, who had become my best friend. Slowly lifting one eyelid, I peeked to see Taria twerking with her, making me laugh as I got up to dance with them. "Damn, Shani, you're gonna be breaking these boy's hearts out here! Who taught you how to dance?" Toya praised.

"You forget I have lived with you two long enough to watch how ya'll dance while you cook and clean. As for breaking hearts, I'm not even thinking about a boyfriend right now. My hormones are all over the place."

"Maybe you should think about boys. Damon told me getting under a guy is the best way to tame raging hormones. That's why I seek him out when I am upset. It seems to be true," Blossom smiled proudly. All of us looked at each other before howling in laughter. Blossom is so powerful, but she believes whatever Damon and Toya say. The two worst people to take advice from. "What?" She looked at us, waiting for a response. I decided to let Taria fill her in since that was her Queen and Damon's sister-in-law.

"Blossom, if that works for you, then I guess it is true. Shani better not be getting under any boys just yet. She should save herself for marriage," Taria pointed. I know she had good intentions, but at that moment, all I wanted to do was sink to the floor. My heart sank from my chest into my stomach as fear and shame washed over me. Even trying to keep my past at bay, it still crept up when I least expected it. Like now, my eighteenth birthday should be a celebration, but all I could remember was my twelfth birthday six years ago when I lost my mother and father. Sweat beads formed on my forehead as my palms grew clammy. "Shani, are you okay?"

Taria snapped me out of my trance when she touched my arm, forcing me to look into her eyes filled with love and concern. "Yes, I will get going to start preparing for tonight. Where are we going? How should I dress?" I hurriedly changed the subject as I stood and tiptoed backward towards the door.

"Don't worry about where we're going. Dress like a grown woman because that's what you'll be when the clock strikes twelve."

Cam burst through the door just as I moved to open it, saying, "tell Mike ya'll need me to be the bodyguard for tonight!"

"Only if you promise to be on your worst behavior," Toya smirked.

Both sets of Cam's fangs appeared as he smiled wickedly, "you know I will, lil-bit."

~Deadly Secrets~

I rushed out and headed to my room to find Lireil standing by the door, waiting for me. Unlocking my door, I let her in and followed her. "What's up? Is everything okay?"

"Yes, I'm just checking on you, I know tomorrow will be rough, so I wanted to come to spend the night with you," Lireil finished, and that's when I noticed the duffel bag she held and a grocery bag full of snacks. How had I missed that before? My senses were all over the place, and I was about sick of it. I reached out and hugged Lireil, causing her to drop the bags. "Damn girl, I can't breathe."

I let her go, "you know, despite what others think about you, you're a really good person. I'm glad I opened up to you, but I can't hang out with you tonight."

"Sha, stop tripping. I will not let you have a pity party in your room alone. Jian will be stopping by later to watch movies with us too. Maybe we can sneak off to that club agai—"

"Bitch, I told you we can't go to the math club meetings anymore," I winked and pointed to my phone as I typed, 'shut up. They have super hearing around here' "Toya and Taria are taking me somewhere tonight. I'm glad you and Jian thought of me, though. We can hang out tomorrow while I pack to leave for training."

"Technically, Jian is the one who remembered your birthday, so you can thank him for that because his memory is impeccable. I did remember what happened to you, so I wanted to do something special for you," she paused. "Wait! Did you just say packing to leave? Again?! Damn, what are you, these people maid or something?" Lireil scrunched her face.

This is the shit I am talking about with her. She can be so sweet yet so insensitive in the next moment. "Lu, you gotta chill with the 'these people's comments because 'these people are my family, and I will kill anyone who comes against them. You're starting to sound like the ops for real. I am the Delta for the True Alpha's Pack, that may not mean anything to you, but this is like becoming the vice president of the United States to me, so all I need you to do is be happy for me as my friend." Lireil rolled her eyes before smiling and walking over to my closet.

"What are you wearing?"

"I was hoping you could help me with that. They said to dress like an adult," sighing. I sat on my bed Indian style.

"I have just the thing. I bought it for you as a gift," she ran over to the duffel bag she had dropped to the floor and pulled out a gift bag from a popular lingerie shop in the mall. What the hell? Lireil had to have lost her mind if she thought I would wear lingerie out with Taria and Toya! She pulled a nude lace one-piece thing that buttoned in the private area, a black leather skirt, some nude strappy sandals with rhinestones on the straps, and a leather dog collar.

"I didn't know the lingerie shop sold all of that," my mouth hung open. "And I know you don't think I'm finna walk around with a damn dog collar on. You think you're so fucking funny."

Lireil fell on the floor laughing as I had just told the most comical joke in the world. Catching her breath, she said, "First of all, I got the skirt and shoes from somewhere else in the mall, but I put them all in the same bag to save space. Second, it's called a choker and is popular amongst humans to give us an edgy look. Third, before you even say anything, keep the white bra on. It will be perfect with the nude top. You'll be the baddest bitch wherever you're going," Lireil finished handing me the clothes.

I didn't even comment on the fact that she still believed she was human because she would argue me down. I was thankful for her because I would probably wear a regular t-shirt and some shorts. I could walk in high heels because Toya's ass stayed buying them for me, saying I gotta keep her legacy alive, but I hated wearing them because guys always tried to shoot their shot thinking I was assessable. I sucked my teeth as I stood to get changed. Lireil and I changed in front of each other all the time hell. We had the same thing. Plus, as a wolf, I am accustomed to being naked around others. Once I was fully dressed, Luriel whistled. "Yassss bestest, you're about to give some fine man a heart attack tonight, Or should I say some fine thing? Or dog? Or—"

"Lu, stop while you're ahead before your brain explodes." We both laughed because her ass would be naming all the damn species in the school if I let her. There was a knock on the door, and I knew it was Jian by his scent. He smelled of a fresh breeze. Walking over, I opened the door smiling when he stood staring at me. "Ji, you just gonna stand there looking stupid?"

"She looks fine, huh Ji? I told her the guys would be tripping over their feet tonight behind her. We both know she only has eyes for that one shade, though," Lireil egged.

"Damn...I mean, uh yeah, you look beautiful, Shani. Where are you going?" Jian scurried in, and I closed the door behind him. He held a bag that I presume held movies we were supposed to be watching. "I didn't get a text about our math work tonight," he sat on my bed. See, that's why I fucks with Jian. He knew how to be discreet with our club-hopping adventures. Lireil is acting slow as hell about her new way of life.

"We aren't going, Ji. Shani got invited to go somewhere with the adult women tonight."

Jian's head bobbed up and down in understanding, "oh. Please try to enjoy yourself, for all of us."

"I will. We all can catch up tomorrow before I leave for training on Rayne Pack land," I walked over and hugged Lireil as Jian stood to squeeze us both tight. "I love you so much, and I can't wait until you turn eighteen, so we can party together."

"We already—" I bumped Lireil with my hip just as another knock sounded on the door, causing a current of panic to crash into my heart. Whew, her ass would get us caught up one day.

"Come in!" I yelled as the Vampire King Michael Vaughn and my True Alpha Quinn Savir stalked into my room. Jian and Lireil's mouths snapped shut as they approached. The kids in the school were all scared of the two most powerful men in the world, but I had been around them and the Rayne pack long enough to be accustomed to their massive presence. They paused, looking at each other, then back at me.

"What the fuck do you have on?" Michael demanded.

"Where the fuck do you think you're going," Quinn followed.

I rolled my eyes as a smile graced my face causing them to crack a smile too. They spoiled me as if I were their child, and I knew Taria and Toya had talked to them about letting me go out with them. "I don't know where I'm going, and I did not pick this outfit out."

"I know it was my wife, her ass knows better than to have my little shadow outside dressed like this," Quinn assumed, and I did not clarify. Hell, I wasn't about to tell them who really picked it out.

"We came to tell you, whatever TNT does tonight, do the complete opposite. They are bad influences," Michael warned.

"Yes, GM, I understand," I called him GM for god-daddy Mike and Quinn GQ for god-daddy Quinn, but the other acronym worked well too because Mike runs shit, and Quinn is smooth as fuck to tame Toya's wild ass. Mike extended his arms, and I gravitated towards his embrace, then went into Quinn's warm hug. They were like day and night, even down to the skin color, but they both kept a level head as leaders of their species. "I can't promise I won't bite a few heads off if trouble finds us."

Quinn smiled down at me, "I would expect nothing less from my Delta. I trust you, Shani. You always do the right thing." He let me go as he turned towards Jian and Lireil, "thank you both for giving Shani some friends closer to her age, her ass used to be surrounded by little kids."

Lireil side-eyed Quinn and Mike as Jian stepped forward, bowing, saying, "it was our pleasure. Shani is easy to get along with, and we are all just cliqued. More or less."

"I see. Enjoy your night out, little shadow. You may not get another in a long time."

"Thanks, GQ and GM. I promise to be on my best behavior," I waved, watching as Mike's gaze lingered on Lireil with a masked look in his eye. I've been around him long enough to know that he saw something beyond what meets the eye. I just hoped her dumb ass didn't get kicked out of the school for having an attitude with them for nothing. I closed the door and turned to Lireil, "what was that?!"

"What do you mean?"

"I mean, you must fix your face and thoughts before you catch one. You feel me," I said, crossing my arms.

"So they would hurt me?"

"No, and you know that. I love you like a sister, but they are my family, and I don't play about my family," I frowned. I heard the slight growl in my words, but I saw the vacant look in her eyes. She blinked, and I saw when she came back to herself. I felt something was off, but I brushed it off, knowing that this life was still new to Lireil. I just hoped all this hostility would pass soon, but I knew Jian and I would do whatever it took to help her get through this mess.

Thanks for reading!

About the Author

E. Bowser is an author of paranormal romance, mystery, and suspense. E. Bowser loves to come home and write whatever stories come to mind. E. Bowser always wanted to write a story that people would like to read and give their feedback to make her next better. She loves to read herself and takes great pleasure in doing so. In middle school, E. Bowser started writing short stories about life, anything horror or paranormal. E. Bowser loves to write whatever her imagination can come up with over a cup of tea.

Thank you for reading. I hope you enjoy the series so far! Please review I love them or feel free to contact me on Facebook, Twitter, Instagram, good reads, book bub, or through my website. Thank you again for reading, and keep looking for more Deadly Secrets series!

Follow or contact me at the links below to see what is coming up next!

www.ebowserbooks.com

www.facebook.com/authorE.Bowser

https://www.bookbub.com/authors/e-bowser

https://www.goodreads.com/ebowser

Twitter: @ebowser0110

IG: @e.bowserbooks

TikTok: @ebowserauthor

Books By This Author

Deadly Secrets Brothers That Bite Books 1-5

The Deadly Secrets is an exciting series focused on Taria, Michael Quinn, and LaToya are friends and lovers fighting against evil forces.

Deadly Secrets Awakening Book 1

Deadly Secrets Revealed Book 2

Deadly Secrets Consequences Book 3

Deadly Secrets Consequences Book 4

Deadly Secrets Royalty Book 5

Deadly Secrets Novellas/Novelettes

This collection of stories will give you a glimpse into the lives of Taria, Michael, LaToya, and Quinn, along with many others. Sit back and fall back into the paranormal world of Deadly Secrets.

Desires of the Harvest Moon

Twice Marked Witches and Wolves

Rise of the Phoenix

A Vampire and His Alpha Mate

A Hunter Touched My Soul

Brothers That Bite Chronicles Volume 1

The Babysitter's From Hell: Halloween Short Story

Rescued By Fire: Gio & Selena's Story

Scorched By Desire: Sire & Lydia's Story

The Crown Series Books 1-3 On-Going series

This series would be best read if you start with Deadly Secrets Series Brothers That Bite books 1-5 and other novellas.

Taria, LaToya, Michael, and Quinn are back together again in Deadly Secrets Hunters Regin: The Crown Series. Taria Cross was turned into a Vampire by Michael Vaughn, and she became his Queen. Not only does she have to figure out this new part of her life, but she is a Hunter as well, and that is a whole other list of duties.

Deadly Secrets Hunters Reign Book 1
Their Sirenian Queen
Deadly Secrets A Vampires Temptation Book 2
Deadly Secrets When Queens Are Crowned Book 3
Twice Marked A True Alpha And His Witch Deadly Secrets Story

The Rayne Pack Series On-Going

Follow the Rayne Brothers as they find their Mates and fight the forces of evil. See how Dax, Max, Malic, Alex, Jarod, and Thomas fight for those they love while being attacked on all sides.

An Alpha's Claim Book 1
Submission To An Alpha Book 2

Dream Walker: Visions of the Dead On-Going Series.

What if you had the ability to see things before, they happened? Saw a zombie outbreak unfold before your very eyes? Could you embrace visions of the dead coming back to life? For Kaylee, who has been chosen to receive this gift, these visions are the beginning of a nightmare.

Dream Walker: Visions of the Dead Book 1
Dream Walker: Visions of the Dead Book 2
Dream Walker: Visions of the Dead Book 3
Dream Walker: Visions of the Dead Novella (Collection of short stories)

www.ingramcontent.com/pod-product-compliance
Lightning Source LLC
Chambersburg PA
CBHW081138300726
48982CB00006B/998

* 9 7 9 8 9 8 5 5 5 2 5 9 1 *